國家圖書館出版品預行編目資料

文法實戰問題集／Peter Dearman・Judd Piggott・Iris Yu 等編著.
--初版. -- 臺北市：日月文化，2008.12
352 面，21*23 公分（易說館）
ISBN：978-986-6542-31-2（平裝）
1. 英語　2. 語法
805.1892　　　　　　　　　　　　　　　　　97019014

文法實戰問題集

編　　　著：Peter Dearman・Judd Piggott・Iris Yu
總　編　輯：陳思容
責　任　編　輯：游明芳
執　行　編　輯：張曉莉
文　法　解　析：林曉芳・陳玉娥・廖冠惠
校　　　對：游明芳・林錦慧・林雅玲
封　面　設　計：唐曉珍
排　版　設　計：健呈電腦排版股份有限公司

董　事　長：洪祺祥
總　經　理：蕭艷秋
行　銷　總　監：張淑貞
法　律　顧　問：張　靜
財　務　顧　問：蕭聰傑

出　　　版：日月文化出版股份有限公司
發　　　行：日月文化出版股份有限公司
地　　　址：台北市信義路三段 151 號 9 樓
電　　　話：(02)2708-5509
傳　　　真：(02)2708-6157
E - m a i l：service@heliopolis.com.tw
日月文化網路書店：www.ezbooks.com.tw
郵　撥　帳　號：19716071 日月文化出版股份有限公司

總　經　銷：大和書報圖書股份有限公司
電　　　話：(02)8990-2588
傳　　　真：(02)2299-7900、2290-1658
印　　　刷：禹利印製企業有限公司
初　　　版：2008 年 12 月
定　　　價：290 元
I　S　B　N：978-986-6542-31-2

雖然在英語環境中學習英語已成趨勢，但如果讀者以為這樣就可以不學文法，那是不可能的。即使是英語母語人士也必須從基本文法開始學起，才能講一口標準的英語。非母語人士更不用說了，沒有文法的基礎，英語學起來將事倍功半，非常困難而且容易出錯。

但是文法向來讓人聞之色變，望之卻步，英語學不好的人常常將原因歸咎於文法太難。其實，真正原因是沒有按部就班打好基礎，這當中，沒選對文法書又是關鍵之一。為使讀者輕鬆學習英語文法，做好基本功，易說館編輯部特別聘請專業英語人士依照文法觀念理解難易度的順序來編撰此本初級文法書。

本書內容包括完整初級文法概念、各類範例，最適合想完整理解整套初級文法及加強某部份文法概念的讀者。每篇文法後面皆附帶 20 道練習題，用字精簡切中要點，出題方向更完全針對本書文法內容，提供讀者立即檢驗學習效果的依據。自我測驗後更可參考由專業教師所做的詳解，立即解決文法學習可能存在的盲點，對相似的文法規則舉一反三，融會貫通。

由於本書共收錄初級程度必備完整文法概念，所以不論是參加初級英檢、升學、就業、各類檢定考試都非常適用。現在，就讓我們來看看學習文法有多輕鬆 easy 了吧！

>>> 目 錄

01 原級、比較級、最高級　　　　007
測驗　　011
解析　　015

02 助動詞 would、should、might、could　　022
測驗　　028
解析　　032

03 spend、take 及 cost 的用法　　039
測驗　　042
解析　　046

04 remember、forget 及 stop 的用法　　053
測驗　　055
解析　　058

05 未來式　　065
測驗　　071
解析　　075

06 感官動詞、連綴動詞與使役動詞　　082
測驗　　087
解析　　091

07 授與動詞　　098
測驗　　101
解析　　105

08 情狀副詞　　112
測驗　　116
解析　　120

09 | 反身代名詞 127
測驗 130
解析 134

10 | 不定代名詞、所有代名詞及雙重所有格 141
測驗 147
解析 151

11 | 現在完成式 158
測驗 163
解析 167

12 | 被動句 174
測驗 180
解析 184

13 | 附加問句 191
測驗 195
解析 199

14 | 動名詞 206
測驗 210
解析 214

15 | 不定詞 221
測驗 226
解析 230

16 | 現在分詞片語、過去分詞片語與介系詞片語 237
測驗 239
解析 243

>>> 目 錄

17 情緒動詞改變而成的現在分詞和過去分詞以及
非情緒性形容詞   250
    測驗   254
    解析   258

18 關係代名詞引導的形容詞子句   265
    測驗   270
    解析   274

19 that 所引導的名詞子句   281
    測驗   282
    解析   287

20 連接詞   294
    測驗   300
    解析   304

21 倒裝句   311
    測驗   314
    解析   318

22 假設語氣   325
    測驗   328
    解析   332

23 直接問句、間接問句與名詞片語   339
    測驗   342
    解析   346

01 原級、比較級、最高級

比較的定義與形式

» 定義：形容詞、副詞會因性質、數量、狀態等程度上的不同，而在語形上起變化。
» 形式：比較的形式因程度上的差異，可分成原級、比較級、最高級三種變化。
» 原級維持形容詞、副詞的原形，不和他物比較。
» 比較級通常為兩者之間的比較，表達其中一者比另一者程度更高之意。
» 最高級用於三者以上的比較，表達眾群體中程度最高者。

三級數的規則變化（I）

» 較短的原級（單音節的字）後面加 er 成為比較級；加 est 成為最高級。
» 較長的原級（雙音節或雙音節以上的字）前面加 more 成為比較級；加 most 成為最高級。
» 比較級之後常接 than；最高級之前常加 the。

▌主詞 1 ＋ be 動詞＋形容詞比較級＋ than ＋主詞 2▐

I am **older than** you.
我年紀比你大。

She is **more** beautiful **than** Mary.
她比瑪莉還美。

▌主詞＋ be 動詞＋ the ＋形容詞最高級▐

I am **the oldest** in my class.
我是班上年紀最大的。

She is **the most** beautiful in the party.
她是派對裡最美的。

主詞 1 ＋一般動詞＋副詞比較級＋ than ＋主詞 2

The old man walks faster **than** the young boy.
這位老先生走得比那年輕男孩還快。

John works **more** diligently **than** his classmates.
約翰工作起來比他的同班同學們還勤奮。

主詞＋一般動詞＋ the ＋副詞最高級

The old man walks **the fastest** among the three.
這位老先生是三個人當中走最快的。

John works **the most** diligently in his class.
約翰是班上工作最勤奮的人。

三級數的規則變化（II）

» 原級若為「單音節字尾原有 e」者，只加 r、st，形成比較級、最高級。

» 原級若為單音節，且其字尾為「短母音＋單子音」者，須重複子音字，再加上 er、est，形成比較級、最高級。

» 原級若為單音節，且其字尾為「子音字＋ y」者，須把 y 改成 i，再加上 er、est，形成比較級、最高級。

nice – nicer – nicest

She is a nice girl.
她是個好女孩。

She is nicer **than** any girl I have ever seen.
她比我看過的任何女孩都還要好。

She is **the nicest** girl I have ever seen.
她是我所看過的女孩當中最好的一個。

hot – hotter – hottest

The weather here is hot.
這裡的天氣很熱。

The weather here is hot**ter than** <u>that</u> in Taipei.

這裡的天氣比台北還熱。

【說明】that 用來代替前述的 the weather，以避免重複。該句可還原成：

The weather here is hot**ter than** <u>the weather</u> in Taipei.

The weather here is **the** hot**test** in Taiwan.

這裡的天氣是全台灣最熱的。

happy – happier – happiest

John is happy in the class.

約翰在班上很快樂。

John is happ**ier than** his neighbor in the class.

約翰在班上比他鄰座的同學還快樂。

John is **the** happ**iest** in the class.

約翰是班上最快樂的學生。

三級數的不規則變化

» 以下形容詞／副詞的比較級、最高級有不規則的變化形。

	原級	比較級	最高級
形容詞	good	better	best
	bad	worse	worst
	many	more	most
	much	more	most
	little	less	least
	far	further	furthest
副　詞	well	better	best
	badly	worse	worst
	far	farther / further	farthest / furthest

good / well – better – best

You look better when you put on this coat.
你穿上這件外套看起來好看多了。

I know her better than anybody else.
我比任何人更了解她。

He is the best student in my class.
他是我班上最優秀的學生。

Which book do you like the best?
你最喜歡哪本書？

bad / badly – worse – worst

My running nose gets worse today.
我流鼻水的症狀今天變得更嚴重了。

He answered the question worse than expected.
他比預期中還答得差。

Of all the articles here, this one is the worst.
這裡所有的文章裡，這篇寫得最糟。

I typed the worst among us.
我們當中，我打字打得最差。

題 目

1. The first band was terrible, but this one is even _____.
   a. as bad as
   b. worst
   c. the least bad
   d. worse

2. Living in the country is _____ than living in the city.
   a. healthier
   b. more quietly
   c. just as good as
   d. more healthier

3. While you were sleeping, they showed _____ movie on TV!
   a. good
   b. the better
   c. the best
   d. worst

4. How could rubies possibly cost _____ diamonds?
   a. as much as
   b. as little as
   c. less than
   d. more expensive than

5. I must say, your English has gotten _____.
   a. more good
   b. well
   c. the best
   d. much better

6. The longer I wait, _____ difficult it becomes.
   a. the more
   b. the most
   c. more and more
   d. more

7. To become a world-class athlete, you must always keep trying _____ harder.
   a. hard and
   b. hard by
   c. hardest and
   d. harder and

8. John is the youngest person in our class, so you must be _____ than him.
   a. younger
   b. much younger
   c. older
   d. more older

9. Your bed looks more _____ mine.
   a. softly than
   b. comfortable than
   c. harder than
   d. or less than

10. Their house is about three times _____ as ours.
    a. as big
    b. more expensive
    c. less expensive
    d. bigger

11. This painting looks almost _____ that one.

    a. worse as

    b. the same as

    c. as different than

    d. simpler as

12. How much _____ do we have to go?

    a. far

    b. more far

    c. farthest

    d. farther

13. We both have dark brown eyes. Your eyes are _____ as mine.

    a. dark

    b. more dark

    c. darker

    d. just as dark

14. You don't know them _____ I do because they are my cousins.

    a. more than

    b. as well as

    c. well than

    d. much as

15. Please write letters to us as _____ as you can.

    a. often

    b. busy

    c. little

    d. frequent

16. You can donate as much or _____ money as you like.
    a. as little
    b. as few
    c. the most
    d. as often

17. Robert didn't spend much money, but Susan spent _____.
    a. more than him
    b. as much as him
    c. the least of all
    d. less than

18. She saves more money than you because she is _____ you.
    a. more thriftily than
    b. thriftier than
    c. less wastefully than
    d. as thrifty as

19. John gets his substantial height from his father, who is much _____ his wife.
    a. higher than
    b. taller
    c. the taller
    d. taller than

20. I've never skied farther than that field. That field is _____ I've ever skied.
    a. further
    b. farther
    c. the farthest
    d. farther than

解 析

1.

解答：**d**

英文 **The first band was terrible, but this one is even <u>worse</u>.**

中譯 第一個樂團很爛，但這個甚至更糟。

解說

題目中的 even 有「更、甚」之意，為比較級用法，表後者比前者更糟，故選 d。

a. as bad as 為「和……一樣差」，應該用原級。

b. worst 為最高級，不合此意。

c. the least 為「最少」之意，無 the least bad 之用法。

2.

解答：**a**

英文 **Living in the country is <u>healthier</u> than living in the city.**

中譯 住在鄉下比住在城市裡更健康。

解說

此句為比較級用法，故選 a。

b. be 動詞後面應加形容詞，不用副詞。

c. as good as 為「和……一樣」之意，應該用原級。

d. more 後面要加形容詞原級，但 healthy 的比較級為 healthier。

3.

解答：**c**

英文 **While you were sleeping, they showed <u>the best</u> movie on TV!**

中譯 你睡覺時，電視上播了一部最棒的電影！

解說

表最高級，最高級形容詞之前加定冠詞 the，選 c。

a. movie 為可數名詞，若用 good，之前得加上冠詞。

b. 比較級前一般不加定冠詞。若改為 a better movie 即可。

d. 最高級之前要加 the。

4.

英文 **How could rubies possibly cost <u>as much as</u> diamonds?**

中譯 紅寶石怎麼可能跟鑽石一樣貴？

解說

　　原句意為「紅寶石怎會和鑽石一樣貴？」，as ... as 表「和……一樣」之意，故選 a。

　　b. 珠寶皆為高價產品，b 為一樣便宜之意，不合語意。

　　c. 此句有驚嘆質疑的語氣，若選 c 則失去此意，畢竟常理中紅寶石本就比鑽石還便宜，故不會問：「紅寶石怎可能會比鑽石便宜」。

　　d. more expensive than 之前應接 be 動詞，非原句中的 cost。

5.

英文 **I must say, your English has gotten <u>much better</u>.**

中譯 我必須承認，你的英文已經比以前好多了。

解說

比較級之前加 much，表強調。much better 有「好多了」之意，選 d。

　　a. 應該為 better

　　b. get well 表身體健康狀態，此不合語意。

　　c. get better 為比以前更進步之意，既然是和以前比，故用比較級，不用最高級。

6.

英文 **The longer I wait, <u>the more difficult it becomes</u>.**

中譯 我等得愈久，情況就變得愈艱難。

解說

　　「the＋比較級 ... the＋比較級」表「愈……，就愈……」，為固定用法，故選 a。

英文　To become a world-class athlete, you must always keep trying <u>harder and harder</u>.

中譯　要變成世界級的運動員，必須持續益加努力嘗試。

解說

「比較級 and 比較級」表「愈來愈……」之意，為比較級的強調用法，選 d。

英文　John is the youngest person in our class, so you must be <u>older</u> than him.

中譯　約翰是我們班上年紀最小的人，所以你的年紀一定比他大。

解說

依照語意，John 已是班上最年輕，故選 c。

a、b 不合語意，d 應改為 much older 才合文法。

英文　Your bed looks <u>more comfortable than</u> mine.

中譯　你的床看起來比我的舒服。

解說

此句中 look 後面應加形容詞，故選 b。

a. 為副詞，應改為 looks softer than mine。

c. harder 已是比較級，不應再加 more。

d. more or less 為「或多或少」之意，在此不合用法。

10.

英文　**Their house is about three times <u>as big as</u> ours.**

中譯　他們的房子大約是我們的三倍大。

解說

　原句意思是「是……的三倍大」，應用 as ... as 之句型，之前再加倍數，選 a。

11.

英文　**This painting looks almost <u>the same as</u> that one.**

中譯　這幅畫看起來幾乎跟那幅一模一樣。

解說

　the same as 表「和……一樣」之意，選 b。

a. worse 為比較級，後面應加 than。

c. different 後頭有 than，可知為比較級，應改為 more different than 方合文法。

d. 應改為 as simple as。

12.

英文　**How much <u>farther</u> do we have to go?**

中譯　我們還得再走多遠啊？

解說

　「much ＋比較級」表「……多了」，此句問還要走多遠，far 的形容詞為 farther 或 furhter，故選 d。

13.

解答：**d**

英文 We both have dark brown eyes. Your eyes are <u>just as dark</u> as mine.

中譯 我們倆都有深棕色的眼睛。你眼睛的顏色就跟我的一樣深。

解說

　　原句中 mine 之前有 as，可知為「as ＋原級＋ as」句型，故選 d。

14.

解答：**b**

英文 You don't know them <u>as well as</u> I do because they are my cousins.

中譯 你沒我那麼了解他們，因為他們是我的表親。

解說

　　原句為「你沒有像我一樣地了解他們」，know 後面接副詞，well 在此當副詞用，「和……一樣」為 as ... as 句型，故選 b。

15.

解答：**a**

英文 Please write letters to us as <u>often</u> as you can.

中譯 請儘量常寫信給我們。

解說

　　as ... as 句型，應用原級，而動詞 write 之後應接副詞，often 在此為頻率副詞，表「常寫信」，故選 a。

　　b. busy 為形容詞，且不合語意。

　　c. little 雖可當副詞，但此不合語意。

　　d. 應改為 frequently。

16.

解答： **ⓐ**

英文　You can donate as much or <u>as little</u> money as you like.

中譯　你的捐款或多或少都隨意。

解說

此為 as ... as 句型，在此應用形容詞原級，但 money 不可數，故用 little，選 a。

b. few 後面加可數名詞。

c. the most 為最高級。

d. often 為副詞，不可修飾名詞 money。

17.

解答： **ⓒ**

英文　Robert didn't spend much money, but Susan spent <u>the least of all</u>.

中譯　羅伯沒花太多錢，但蘇珊是所有人中花得最少的。

解說

　按照語意，原句想表達「Robert 沒花很多錢，但 Susan 是所有人之中花最少錢的人」，故選 c。

18.

解答： **ⓑ**

英文　She saves more money than you because she is <u>thriftier than</u> you.

中譯　她存的錢比你多，因為她比你節省。

解說

thrifty 為形容詞原級，表「節儉的」。此句為形容詞比較級，故選 b。

a. more 之後加原級，應改成 more thrifty than。

c. wastefully 為副詞，在此應該用形容詞，因原句中有 be 動詞 is。

d. as ... as 為「和……一樣」之意，在此不合語意。

英文　John gets his substantial height from his father, who is much <u>taller than</u> his wife.

中譯　約翰驚人的身高遺傳自父親，他父親比太太高多了。

解說

「much ＋比較級」表強調比較之程度，選 d。

a. 形容人的身高多用 tall。

b. 比較級後頭要接 than。

c. 應改為 taller than。

英文　I've never skied farther than that field. That field is <u>the farthest</u> I've ever skied.

中譯　我滑雪從未超出那片滑雪場的範圍。

解說

此句為最高級句型，表「所滑過最遠的」。最高級之前加定冠詞 the，far 的最高級為 farthest 或 furthest，故選 c。

02 助動詞 would、should、might、could

助動詞的定義、形式與用法

» 定義：助動詞為動詞的一部分，之後接原形動詞，可用來表達可能、必然或義務等意思，亦有表達時式、否定、疑問或加強語氣等作用。

» 形式：常見的助動詞有 would、should、might、could，分別為 will、shall、may、can 的變形，前者可視為後者的過去式。

» 用法：

1. 一個句子一般來說只有一個助動詞，因而不與助動詞 do / does / did 連用。

2. 助動詞一般與原形動詞連用，不單獨使用於句子的結構中。

3. 助動詞否定的縮寫：

would not = wouldn't	should not = shouldn't
might not = mightn't	could not = couldn't

助動詞的句型

» 於一般的肯定句中加入助動詞。把助動詞置於主詞之後、一般動詞之前，即成助動詞的肯定句。

» 於助動詞的肯定句中加入 not，即成助動詞的否定句。not 緊連於助動詞之後，或可縮寫成 wouldn't、shouldn't 等形式。

» 把助動詞往前移至句首，句末加上問號，即成助動詞的疑問句。

» 助動詞不須隨主詞的不同而作變化，亦即不用因主詞人稱種類的不同而作改變。

» 助動詞後必須接原形動詞。若句中的一般動詞因主詞為第三人稱加 s，或因過去式而加 ed 等，必須一律改回原形動詞。

主詞＋助動詞（would、should、might、could）＋原形 V

He should finish the work by Friday.
他應該在週五前完成這項工作。

I could handle the situation by myself.
我可以自己掌控情勢。

主詞＋助動詞（would、should、might、could）＋ not ＋原形 V
主詞＋助動詞否定縮寫（wouldn't、shouldn't、mightn't、couldn't）＋原形 V

The train might not arrive on time.
火車可能不會準時到達。

I wouldn't mind if you sit by my side.
我不會介意你坐我旁邊。

助動詞（would、should、might、could）＋主詞＋原形 V？

Should I go there alone?
我該自己前往那裡嗎？

Would you please do me a favor?
能請你幫個忙嗎？

助動詞否定縮寫（wouldn't、shouldn't、mightn't、couldn't）＋主詞＋原形 V？

Shouldn't you do your homework right now?
你現在不是該寫作業嗎？

Couldn't she help you now?
她現在無法幫你嗎？

would 的用法

would 被視為 will 的過去式時，通常用來表達過去的意志或習慣。

He would insist on his own views.
他很堅持己見。

I would sometimes visit my uncle when I lived there.
還住那裡的時候，我有時候會去拜訪我舅舅。

可表示客氣或委婉的語氣。

Would you mind if I sit here?
你介意我坐這嗎？

Would you call me back as soon as possible?
你能儘快回我電話嗎？

可表示推測。

This method would work, I guess.
我想這方法或許管用。

That would be great.
那樣可能會很棒。

可用於假設句法。

If I were you, I would tell the truth.
如果我是你的話，我就會實話實說。

If I have brought the money with me, I would have bought it yesterday.
如果我有帶錢的話，我昨天就會把它買下。

should 的用法

表義務、必要、應該做某事。

You should learn to adapt yourself to the new environment.
你應該學著適應新環境。

We should not chat in class.
我們在上課中不應該交談。

表推測、理所當然之事。

Since she was born in 1950, she should be more than fifty years old now.
因為她生於 1950 年，現在應該超過 50 歲了。

Tom should have arrived now.
湯姆現在該到了才對。

表達驚訝或憐憫，帶有感情意味。

It is surprising that you should arrive so early.
你這麼早就到了，真令人意外。

It is a pity that he should fail the exam.
他考試沒過，真可惜。

用於動詞如 suggest、insist、require 等之後，表示建議、要求、命令等。但 should 亦可省略，直接加原形動詞。

The doctor suggests that I (should) take exercise at least twice a week.
醫生建議我一週至少運動兩次。

The teacher insists that we (should) finish the assignment by Monday.
老師堅持我們週一前得完成作業。

might 的用法

Might I talk to you for just a few minutes?
可以跟您借幾分鐘說個話嗎?

Might I use your computer?
我可以用您的電腦嗎?

You might want to consult Mr. Wang about this issue.
關於這件事,你或許可以去請教王先生。

It might be better to keep alert.
或許你該保持警覺。

You might consider Tom my friend, but I know nothing about him.
你或許以為湯姆是我的朋友,但我對他一無所知。

It might rain in the afternoon.
午後可能會下雨。

You might not say such words if you had been there yesterday.
要是你昨天在場的話,你現在可能就不會說這種話了。

If you were older, you might understand what I say.
如果你年紀再大一點,你可能就會了解我說的是什麼意思。

could 的用法

當作 can 的過去式，表當時情境。

When we entered the building, we could smell burning.
進入大樓的時候，我們可以聞到燒焦的味道。

Even though she spoke very fast, I could understand what she said.
即便她說得很快，我還是可以了解她在說什麼。

表達與事實相反之假設語氣，表假設的能力。

He is so strong that he could lift a car.
他壯到可以舉起一輛車。

I am so hungry that I could swallow a horse.
我餓得可以吞下整匹馬。

表推測，預想可能的結果。

What he said could happen.
他說的有可能會發生。

It could be true.
有可能是真的。

用於疑問句時，表質疑、不可置信之意。

How could you do such a thing?
你怎能做出這種事來？

Who could understand what he is talking about?
有誰能聽懂他到底在講啥？

題 目

1. I would if I could, but I can't, so I _____.
   a. wouldn't
   b. would
   c. couldn't
   d. won't

2. What _____ you say if I told you I had read your diary?
   a. did
   b. will
   c. should
   d. would

3. I _____ gotten into Harvard if I had spoken better during my interview.
   a. might have
   b. maybe
   c. could
   d. will have

4. I _____ want to be in his shoes.
   a. wouldn't
   b. couldn't
   c. hadn't
   d. would've

5. I'm busy right now. _____ you answer the door for me?
   a. Should
   b. Might
   c. Could
   d. May

6. I _____ live there if I had the money, but I don't.
   a. can
   b. will
   c. should
   d. would

7. We looked hard, but _____ find your new apartment.
   a. might not
   b. weren't able to
   c. wouldn't
   d. shouldn't

8. I look tired because I _____ sleep well last night.
   a. can't
   b. couldn't
   c. shouldn't
   d. wouldn't

9. The Joneses said that they _____ come, but not to expect them.
   a. mustn't
   b. must
   c. might
   d. would

10. I forgot to bring my money, so I _____ buy groceries on the way home.
    a. hadn't
    b. wouldn't
    c. couldn't
    d. shouldn't

11. Richard and June _____ come over this afternoon.
    a. may
    b. might
    c. would
    d. Either a or b

12. Be careful, or the dog _____ bite you.
    a. must
    b. would
    c. should
    d. might

13. _____ I borrow your stapler?
    a. Will
    b. Would
    c. Shall
    d. Could

14. That's impossible! Sean _____ have the password to that account.
    a. could
    b. might
    c. couldn't
    d. might not

15. Excuse me, Miss. _____ I trouble you for a glass of water?
    a. Might
    b. May not
    c. Should
    d. Shall

16. We're all packed now. _____ we go then?
    a. Maybe
    b. Shall
    c. Might
    d. Mustn't

17. _____ you be in class right now?
    a. Couldn't
    b. Aren't
    c. Shouldn't
    d. Won't

18. You _____ put on your glasses or you _____ be able to read the fine print.
    a. could ; wouldn't
    b. should ; might not
    c. would ; might
    d. should ; may

19. Her parents don't think _____ get married so young.
    a. she should
    b. she can
    c. she could
    d. she might

20. I never have any money. I knew I _____ bought that car!
    a. shouldn't have
    b. couldn't have
    c. might not have
    d. wouldn't have

解析

1.　　　　　　　　　　　　　　　　　　　　　　解答：**d**

英文　**I would if I could, but I can't, so I won't.**

中譯　如果我能我就會去做，但我不能，所以我不會去做。

解說

　　I would if I could 用過去式，表示與現在事實相反，即實際上是做不到的。but I can't 為「但我做不到」，用現在式，表事實。既然承認自己做不到，未來就不會去做。故選 d。

2.　　　　　　　　　　　　　　　　　　　　　　解答：**d**

英文　**What would you say if I told you I had read your diary?**

中譯　如果我坦承我讀過你的日記，你會怎麼說？

解說

　　由於提問者目前尚未讀，此句為與現在事實相反的假設語氣，故選 d。

3.　　　　　　　　　　　　　　　　　　　　　　解答：**a**

英文　**I might have gotten into Harvard if I had spoken better during my interview.**

中譯　要是我在面試時講得好一點，我可能已經進哈佛了。

解說

　　此句為與過去事實相反的假設語氣，故選 a。

4. 解答：ⓐ

英文 **I wouldn't want to be in his shoes.**

中譯 我不會想要落入他的處境。

解說

　　wouldn't 在此表意願，意為「不想」，選 a。in one's shoes 表示「站在某人的立場，處在某人的狀況」。

5. 解答：ⓒ

英文 **I'm busy right now. Could you answer the door for me?**

中譯 我現在很忙。你可以去幫我開門嗎？

解說

　　could 在此為表示客氣詢問對方意願的用法，選 c。

6. 解答：ⓓ

英文 **I would live there if I had the money, but I don't.**

中譯 如果有錢我就會去住那兒，但我沒錢。

解說

　　此句為與現在事實相反的假設語氣，選 d。

7. 解答：**b**

英文　We looked hard, but <u>weren't able to</u> find your new apartment.

中譯　我們很努力找，但沒辦法幫你找到新公寓。

解說

　　weren't able to 為過去式用法，表示「無法達成某事」，選 b。

8. 解答：**b**

英文　I look tired because I <u>couldn't</u> sleep well last night.

中譯　我看起來很累，因為我昨晚無法好好睡。

解說

　　本題時間明確指出為昨天晚上，而 couldn't 在此為 can't 的過去式，表示「無法達成某事」，選 b。

9. 解答：**c**

英文　The Joneses said that they <u>might</u> come, but not to expect them.

中譯　瓊斯一家人說他們可能會來，但不必特意等他們。

解說

　　此句為過去式用法，might 表「可能」，選 c。

解答：**c**

英文 I forgot to bring my money, so I <u>couldn't</u> buy groceries on the way home.

中譯 我忘了帶錢，所以沒辦法在回家路上順道去買菜。

解說

此句為過去式用法，couldn't 為 can't 的過去式，表「無法做某事」，選 c。

11. 解答：**d**

英文 Richard and June <u>may</u> come over this afternoon.
Richard and June <u>might</u> come over this afternoon.

中譯 理查和君今天下午可能會來。

解說

此句表「推測」，a 或 b 皆有此意，但通常 might 較 may 更不確定。

12. 解答：**d**

英文 Be careful, or the dog <u>might</u> bite you.

中譯 請小心，不然那條狗可能會咬你。

解說

此句為含蓄的推測用法，might 表「可能」，選 d。

13.

英文　<u>Could</u> I borrow your stapler?

中譯　我可以跟你借釘書機嗎？

解說

　　could 為禮貌且含蓄的詢問用語，表「是否可以」，選 d。

14.

英文　That's impossible! Sean <u>couldn't</u> have the password to that account.

中譯　不可能！西恩不可能會有那個帳戶的密碼。

解說

　　本題前句已說明 impossible，表「不可能」，故後者必須用否定句。couldn't 有「不可能做到」之意，選 c。

15.

英文　Excuse me, Miss. <u>Might</u> I trouble you for a glass of water?

中譯　小姐，不好意思。能麻煩妳給我一杯水嗎？

解說

　　此句題意為說話者想麻煩別人做某事，故用肯定疑問句。might 用以客氣詢問「是否可以」，選 a。

解答：**b**

英文 **We're all packed now. <u>Shall</u> we go then?**

中譯 我們現在都打包好了。可以出發了嗎？

解說

依題意須用肯定疑問句，shall 為客氣語氣，表「建議做某事」，選 b。

17. 解答：**c**

英文 **<u>Shouldn't</u> you be in class right now?**

中譯 你現在不是應該在上課嗎？

解說

shouldn't 表「應該做某事」，為否定式反問法，選 c。

18. 解答：**b**

英文 **You <u>should</u> put on your glasses or you <u>might not</u> be able to read the fine print.**

中譯 你該戴上眼鏡，不然可能會看不見印得很小的字。

解說

should 為表「建議做某事」；might not 為含蓄推測「無法達成某事」。此句型有「你應該……；否則你可能無法……」之意，選 b。

英文　Her parents don't think <u>she should</u> get married so young.

中譯　她的父母認為她不該這麼年輕就結婚。

解說

　　should 表「應該做某事」之意，選 a。

英文　I never have any money. I knew I <u>shouldn't have</u> bought that car!

中譯　我一直沒什麼錢。我就知道我當初不該買那輛車！

解說

　　shouldn't 表「不應該做某事」之意，後面加上完成式用法，表「不該做某事但已經做了」，選 a。

03 spend、take 及 cost 的用法

spend、take 及 cost 的意義與區分

» spend、take 及 cost 三者均有「花費」的意思，以表示花費時間或金錢等。

» spend 的主詞通常為人；take、cost 的主詞通常為事物；take 亦常見以虛主詞 It 開頭的句型。

» spend 後面可加時間長度或金錢多寡來表示「某人花費多少時間或金錢做某事」；take 後面常加時間，表示做某事「需要、花費或佔用」多少時間；cost 之後則多加金錢，有「某事物花費多少錢」之意。

spend 的用法

» spend 後面若接動詞，動詞必須以 V-ing 方式呈現，表示某人花費多少時間做某事。

» 句型通常為：人＋ spend(s) / spent ＋時間／金錢＋動名詞。

某人花多少錢

I spent one thousand dollars on the bike.
我花一千元買這部腳踏車。

How much (money) do you spend on this new computer?
你花多少錢買下這台新電腦？

某人花多少時間（做某事）

She spends a lot of time doing her homework.
她花很多時間寫她的作業。

How many hours do they spend fixing this machine?
他們花了幾個鐘頭修理這部機器？

take 的用法

» 形容某事物花費、需要或佔用多少時間時，通常有兩種表達方式。

» 其一為事物直接當主詞，後接 take 與時間，表達「某事花費多少時間」。亦可在 take 之後加上主詞的受格，之後再加時間，表達「某事花費某人多少時間」。

» 另一則用虛主詞 It 開頭。以 It 為句首的表達方式也分兩種：分別為 It + takes / took +時間，表達「做某事須花費多少時間」；或是 It + takes / took +某人+時間，表達「做某事須花費某人多少時間」。

主詞（事物）+ take / took +時間
主詞（事物）+ take / took +人+時間

The train will take four hours.
這趟火車旅程得花上四個鐘頭。

The explanation took us more than half an hour.
該解說耗了我們半小時以上。

It + takes / took +時間
It + takes / took +人+時間

It takes around 25 minutes to finish the tape.
聽完這捲帶子大約要花 25 分鐘。

It took him one hour to cook the fish.
料理那條魚足足花了他一個鐘頭。

cost 的用法

» 以 cost 來表達「花費多少金錢」時，主詞通常為某物，其後接 cost，再加金錢。亦可在 cost 之後接某人，後頭再加金錢，表達「某物花費某人多少金錢」。

» cost 亦有「付出代價」或「使喪失某物」之意。之後常接受詞（即某人），再加所付出的代價或所喪失的東西。

某物花多少錢→主詞（事物）＋ cost(s) ＋金錢；主詞（事物）＋ cost(s) ＋受詞（人）＋金錢

The book costs 200 dollars.

這本書要價兩百元。

The car cost her around ten thousand US dollars.

這車花了她大約一萬美元。

使付出代價、使喪失→主詞（事物）＋ cost(s) ＋受詞（人）＋名詞（加所付出的代價／所喪失之物）

His business success eventually cost him his marriage.

他的事業成就最終還是讓他賠上了婚姻。

The surgery costs the boy his sight.

外科手術讓這男孩喪失了他的視力。

題 目

1. Where would you most like to _____ your vacation, and when would you like to _____ the time off?
   a. take ; spend
   b. spend ; take
   c. take off ; take
   d. spending ; be taking

2. Everyone please rise now and _____ a minute to pray for those who lost their lives in the earthquake.
   a. have
   b. have taken
   c. take
   d. spending

3. This is going to take _____ time.
   a. a long
   b. some
   c. 15 minutes of your
   d. All of the above

4. You really should _____ more time with your girlfriend.
   a. spend
   b. take
   c. be spending
   d. Either a or c

5. It only _____ a few people to change the world.
   a. takes
   b. is taking
   c. spends
   d. costs

6. A minute of your time is all that it _____.
   a. takes
   b. costs
   c. spends
   d. spent

7. Ralph _____ some time in Korea, so he can speak the language a bit.
   a. used
   b. spent
   c. took
   d. All of the above

8. Sally told her colleagues that she really needed _____ a vacation.
   a. to cost
   b. to take
   c. to spend
   d. None of the above

9. Don't _____ more than ten minutes on each question or you'll run out of time.
   a. spend
   b. have
   c. to spend
   d. be taking

10. I might buy this souvenir. How much _____ it _____?
    a. does ; spend
    b. will ; take
    c. does ; cost
    d. cost ; is

11. I can't believe you _____ all your money so fast. Now I'll have to lend you some.

    a. spend

    b. spent

    c. cost

    d. took

12. You can buy one toy as long as it _____ too much.

    a. doesn't spend

    b. didn't spend

    c. doesn't cost

    d. costs

13. Thank you! I hope it didn't _____ a lot. You always _____ too much on me.

    a. spend ; cost

    b. cost ; pay

    c. cost ; spend

    d. None of the above

14. I'm ready _____ any amount of money. The _____ doesn't matter to me.

    a. to spend ; cost

    b. to cost ; spending

    c. to spend ; price

    d. Either a or c

15. A flat tire _____ him the victory in the biggest car race of the year.

    a. cost

    b. costed

    c. spent

    d. took

16. Mr. Johnson says we need to reduce _____ or the company will go out of business.

    a. cost

    b. costs

    c. the cost

    d. costing

17. How much time does it _____ to get to the train station?

    a. cost

    b. spend

    c. have

    d. take

18. How _____ does it _____?

    a. much ; cost

    b. many ; cost

    c. much ; costs

    d. many money ; cost

19. The accident _____ the driver a broken leg.

    a. spent

    b. took

    c. cost

    d. made

20. You need to pay whatever the price tag says it _____.

    a. can cost

    b. costs

    c. takes

    d. spends

解析

1.　　　　　　　　　　　　　　　　　　　　　　　解答：**b**

英文　**Where would you most like to spend your vacation, and when would you like to take the time off?**

中譯　你最想去哪裡度假，還有你想要何時休假？

解說

　　spend 表「度過」之意，take... off 表「休假」之意。此句為詢問某人想在哪裡度過假期，及何時休假，選 b。

2.　　　　　　　　　　　　　　　　　　　　　　　解答：**c**

英文　**Everyone please rise now and take a minute to pray for those who lost their lives in the earthquake.**

中譯　現在請大家起立，花一分鐘為地震的罹難者禱告。

解說

　　take 後面加時間，表「花費多少時間」之意，選 c。

3.　　　　　　　　　　　　　　　　　　　　　　　解答：**d**

　　　　This is going to take a long time.

英文　**This is going to take some time.**

　　　　This is going to take 15 minutes of your time.

　　　　這得花上一段長時間。

中譯　這得花上一些時間。

　　　　這得花上你十五分鐘時間。

解說

　　take 後面加時間，表「花費多少時間」之意，故以上皆可，選 d。

4.　　　　　　　　　　　　　　　　　　　　　　　　　解答：**d**

英文　You really should <u>spend</u> more time with your girlfriend.
　　　You really should <u>be spending</u> more time with your girlfriend.

中譯　你實在該多花點時間陪女友。

解說

　　spend 的主詞通常為人，spend 加時間，表「某人花費多少時間（做某事）」之意。此句用若簡單現在式，表事實；若用現在進行式，強調現在應該做某事，故 a、c 皆可。

5.　　　　　　　　　　　　　　　　　　　　　　　　　解答：**a**

英文　It only <u>takes</u> a few people to change the world.

中譯　只需要少數幾個人就能改變世界。

解說

　　虛主詞 It 之後加 take，表「耗費、需要或佔用」之意，故選 a。

6.　　　　　　　　　　　　　　　　　　　　　　　　　解答：**a**

英文　A minute of your time is all that it <u>takes</u>.

中譯　只需要你一分鐘的時間。

解說

　　虛主詞 it 之後加 take，表「耗費、需要或佔用」之意，故選 a。

7.

英文 **Ralph spent some time in Korea, so he can speak the language a bit.**

中譯 勞夫在韓國待了一段時間，因此他會說一點韓語。

解說

　　spend 的主詞通常為人，spend 加時間，表「某人花費多少時間（做某事）」之意。此句為過去式，故選 b。

8.

英文 **Sally told her colleagues that she really needed to take a vacation.**

中譯 莎莉跟同事說她實在很需要度個假。

解說

　　take 在此有「需要」之意。題意為「Sally 的確需要一個假期」，故選 b。

9.

英文 **Don't spend more than ten minutes on each question or you'll run out of time.**

中譯 別在一個題目上花超過十分鐘，否則你的時間會用光。

解說

　　don't 之後須加原形動詞，spend 加時間，表「某人花費多少時間（做某事）」之意。選 a。

解答：**c**

英文 I might buy this souvenir. How much <u>does</u> it <u>cost</u>?

中譯 我可能要買這件紀念品。它要賣多少錢？

解說

　　詢問某物值多少錢，用cost。此句為簡單現在式疑問句，表詢問事實，故選c。

11. 解答：**b**

英文 I can't believe you <u>spent</u> all your money so fast. Now I'll have to lend you some.

中譯 真不敢相信你這麼快就把錢全花光了。現在我還得借你一點。

解說

　　spend 的主詞通常為人，spend 加金錢，表「某人花費多少錢」之意。此句為已花完的狀態，故用過去式，選 b。

12. 解答：**c**

英文 You can buy one toy as long as it <u>doesn't cost</u> too much.

中譯 只要不是太貴，你可以買一樣玩具。

解說

　　it 在此表某物，某物值多少錢要用動詞 cost。此句為簡單現在式，且依題意為否定式，故選 c。

13.

解答：**c**

英文 Thank you! I hope it didn't <u>cost</u> a lot. You always <u>spend</u> too much on me.

中譯 感謝你！我希望這沒有花你太多錢。你老是為我破費太多。

解說

cost 之前的主詞通常為「物」，表某物值多少錢；spend 則以「人」當主詞，此句表某人花多少金錢在某人身上，故選 c。

14.

解答：**d**

英文 I'm ready <u>to spend</u> any amount of money. The <u>cost</u> doesn't matter to me.
I'm ready <u>to spend</u> any amount of money. The <u>price</u> doesn't matter to me.

中譯 我準備好不計代價了。價格多少我都不在乎。

解說

spend 的主詞通常為人，cost 當名詞時近似 price 之意，表價格。選項 a 或 c 皆可，故答案為 d。

15.

解答：**a**

英文 A flat tire <u>cost</u> him the victory in the biggest car race of the year.

中譯 爆胎讓他與年度最大型賽車的冠軍擦身而過。

解說

cost 意為「付出時間、勞力、代價」或「使喪失某物」，過去式亦為 cost。選 a。

英文　**Mr. Johnson says we need to reduce <u>costs</u> or the company will go out of business.**

中譯　強森先生說我們需要減少公司成本，不然公司會倒閉。

解說

　　cost 當名詞時，有「費用、成本」之意，為可數名詞，須加 s，故選 b。

英文　**How much time does it <u>take</u> to get to the train station?**

中譯　到火車站需要多少時間？

解說

　　take 有「需要、花費、佔用」之意，句型「it ＋ take ＋時間＋ to」表「做某事需花費多少時間」之意，故選 d。

英文　**How <u>much</u> does it cost?**

中譯　這要賣多少錢？

解說

　　問某物值多少錢，用 how much 問，後頭省略了不可數的 money。花多少錢用 cost 問，助動詞 does 後面須加原形動詞，故選 a。

19.

英文　**The accident <u>cost</u> the driver a broken leg.**

中譯　這起意外讓駕駛斷了一條腿。

解說

　　cost在此為「喪失某物」或「使付出什麼代價」之意，為過去式用法，故選c。

20.

英文　**You need to pay whatever the price tag says it <u>costs</u>.**

中譯　標價多少你就得付多少。

解說

　　cost 在此表「花費多少金錢」之意，此為簡單現在式，故選 b。

04 remember、forget 及 stop 的用法

remember、forget 及 stop 的用法

» remember、forget 及 stop 之後通常有兩種表達形式，即不定詞與動名詞。

» remember、forget 及 stop 之後若接不定詞，即「to ＋原形 V」，有記得、忘記「去做某事」及「停止原先動作，去做某事」之意。

» remember、forget 及 stop 之後若接動名詞，即 V-ing，有記得、忘記「做過某事」及「停止做原先在做的某事」之意。

主詞＋ remember / forget / stop ＋ to ＋原形 V.

Remember to call me when you arrive.
到的時候記得打電話給我。

He forgot to post the letter on his way home.
他忘記回家途中要順道去寄信。

They stopped to watch the show.
他們停下來看表演。

主詞＋ remember / forget / stop ＋ V-ing.

I remember mentioning the story to you.
我記得曾對你提過這個故事。

She forgot posting the letter.
她忘了信已寄出。

The speaker suddenly stops talking and leaves the conference.
演說者突然停止說話並離開會場。

題 目

1. You must remember _____ the door properly when you leave the house.
   a. shutting
   b. to close
   c. close
   d. closing

2. I don't remember _____ her at the banquet that night.
   a. to see
   b. met
   c. meeting
   d. introduced to

3. Did you _____ to pick up a quart of milk on the way home from the mall?
   a. remember
   b. forgot
   c. remembering
   d. remembered

4. I must have forgotten _____ that question.
   a. answer
   b. the answer
   c. answered
   d. to answer

5. Kyle _____ to take out the trash this morning.
   a. forgets
   b. is forgetting
   c. forgot
   d. forgotten

6. If you don't stop _____ your mosquito bites like that, they'll start bleeding.
   a. to scratch
   b. scratch
   c. scratching
   d. and scratch

7. We didn't start _____ the turkey until 4:00, so dinner will be a little late.
   a. cooking
   b. to cook
   c. cook
   d. Either a or b

8. They stopped a few times _____ the roses as they were _____ through the field.
   a. to smell ; walking
   b. smelling ; walking
   c. smell ; walked
   d. to have smelled ; walking

9. Those strange letters finally _____ appearing in our mailbox.
   a. stop
   b. stopped
   c. to stop
   d. stopping

10. If you see Jonas at the club, remember _____ hello for me.
   a. you said
   b. I said
   c. saying
   d. to say

11. _____ to go to that café I told you about when you visit Barcelona.

    a. Don't forget

    b. Remember

    c. We remembered

    d. Either a or b

12. I _____ to lock the door when I left the house, but I don't remember _____ the windows first.

    a. remember ; to close

    b. remembered ; closing

    c. remember ; closing

    d. remembered ; to close

13. As Alzheimer's disease progresses, its victims lose the ability _____ the immediate and recent past.

    a. remembering

    b. remember

    c. to remember

    d. Either a or b

14. Kevin stopped _____ years ago.

    a. smoking

    b. to smoke

    c. smoke

    d. None of the above

15. You ask me how I can _____; I ask you how I could _____.

    a. remembering ; forget

    b. remember ; forgetting

    c. remember ; forget

    d. remembering ; forgetting

16. Wang Chien-ming _____ for the Yankees in 2005.

    a. began pitching

    b. started pitching

    c. started to pitch

    d. All of the above

17. Vladimír Vidim set a world record by biking 702 km in 24 hours without

    _____.

    a. stopped

    b. stopping

    c. to stop

    d. have stopped

18. This group was formed for one purpose: to stop the law from _____.

    a. passed

    b. being passed

    c. be passing

    d. All of the above

19. This train makes several _____ in small country towns, so it takes

    a while to get to Taidong.

    a. stops

    b. stopping

    c. stoppings

    d. stop

20. Jane _____ her backpack at the bus stop.

    a. couldn't remember

    b. didn't remember

    c. forgot

    d. Either b or c

解析

1.
解答：b

英文　You must remember <u>to close</u> the door properly when you leave the house.

中譯　離開屋子時，你一定要記得把門關好。

解說

remember 後加「to ＋原形動詞」表「記得去做某事」，選 b。

2.
解答：c

英文　I don't remember <u>meeting</u> her at the banquet that night.

中譯　我不記得吃喜酒那天有見過她。

解說

remember 後加動名詞，表「記得曾經做過某事」，選 c。

3.
解答：a

英文　Did you <u>remember</u> to pick up a quart of milk on the way home from the mall?

中譯　你從購物中心回家路上，有記得去買一夸脫的牛奶嗎？

解說

remember 後加「to ＋原形動詞」表「記得去做某事」，選 a。quart 是（液體）容量單位。

4. 解答：**d**

英文　I must have forgotten <u>to answer</u> that question.

中譯　我一定是忘記回答那個問題了。

解說

　　forget 後加「to ＋原形動詞」表「忘記去做某事」，選 d。

5. 解答：**c**

英文　Kyle <u>forgot</u> to take out the trash this morning.

中譯　凱爾今天早上忘記把垃圾拿出去。

解說

　　forget 後加「to ＋原形動詞」表「忘記去做某事」，且此句時間副詞為 this morning，為過去式，故選 c。

6. 解答：**c**

英文　If you don't stop <u>scratching</u> your mosquito bites like that, they'll start bleeding.

中譯　如果你再不停止那樣猛抓蚊子叮咬的地方，那裡就要開始流血了。

解說

　　stop 後加動名詞，表「停止持續做某事」，選 c。

7. 解答：**d**

英文 We didn't start <u>cooking</u> the turkey until 4:00, so dinner will be a little late.
We didn't start <u>to cook</u> the turkey until 4:00, so dinner will be a little late.

中譯 我們四點鐘才開始烤火雞，所以晚餐會晚一些。

解說

　　start 後加動名詞，表「開始持續做某事」；start 後加不定詞，表「開始去做某事」。此句 a、b 均符合題意，故選 d。

8. 解答：**a**

英文 They stopped a few times <u>to smell</u> the roses as they were <u>walking through</u> the field.

中譯 他們走過原野時，幾次停下來聞玫瑰花香。

解說

　　stop 後加原形動詞，表「停止（原先做的事）去做某事」。在此為「他們停下來幾次去聞玫瑰花香」，選 a。

9. 解答：**b**

英文 Those strange letters finally <u>stopped</u> appearing in our mailbox.

中譯 那些奇怪的信終於停止出現在我們的信箱裡了。

解說

　　stop 後加動名詞，表「停止持續做某事」。在此為陳述過去之事實，故選 b。

10. 解答：**d**

英文 If you see Jonas at the club, remember <u>to say</u> hello for me.

中譯 如果你在俱樂部看見約拿，記得幫我問候他一聲。

解說

remember 後加「to ＋原形動詞」表「記得去做某事」，選 d。

11. 解答：**d**

英文 **Don't forget to go to that café I told you about when you visit Barcelona.**
Remember to go to that café I told you about when you visit Barcelona.

中譯 去巴塞隆納玩的時候，別忘了記得到我跟你提過的那間咖啡店。

解說

題意為「別忘記或記得去做某事」，為祈使句，a 或 b 均可，故選 d。

12. 解答：**b**

英文 **I <u>remembered</u> to lock the door when I left the house, but I don't remember <u>closing</u> the windows first.**

中譯 我離開家時有記得鎖門，卻忘了先關窗。

解說

remember 後加動名詞，表記得曾經做過某事。此題譯為「離開房子前我記得去鎖門，但我不記得我已先把窗戶關上」。前句表過去，後句則陳述現在事實。選 b。

13.

解答：**c**

英文　As Alzheimer's disease progresses, its victims lose the ability <u>to remember</u> the immediate and recent past.

中譯　隨著阿茲海默症惡化，患者會喪失當下及近期的記憶力。

解說

　此題意為「失去記憶的能力」，ability to 加原形動詞，表「……的能力」，選 c。

14.

解答：**a**

英文　Kevin stopped <u>smoking</u> years ago.

中譯　凱文幾年前就不抽菸了。

解說

　stop 後加動名詞，表「停止持續做某事」。選 a。

15.

解答：**c**

英文　You ask me how I can <u>remember</u>; I ask you how I could <u>forget</u>.

中譯　你問我怎麼會記得，我才要問你我怎麼可能會忘哩。

解說

　can 和 could 為助動詞，後面必須加原形動詞。選 c。

16.

英文
Wang Chien-ming <u>began pitching</u> for the Yankees in 2005.
Wang Chien-ming <u>started pitching</u> for the Yankees in 2005.
Wang Chien-ming <u>started to pitch</u> for the Yankees in 2005.

中譯　王建民 2005 年開始在洋基隊投球。

解說

　　began 意同 started，表「開始」之意，此為過去式。began 或 started 之後若接動名詞，表「開始持續做某事」之意；若接原形動詞，則表「開始去做某事」。此題 a、b、c 均符合題意，故選 d。

17.

英文　**Vladimír Vidim set a world record by biking 702 km in 24 hours without stopping.**

中譯　Vladimír Vidim 創下連續二十四小時不停騎自行車 702 公里的世界紀錄。

解說

　　without 為介系詞，其後若接動詞須為動名詞，故選 b。

18.

英文　**This group was formed for one purpose: to stop the law from <u>being passed</u>.**

中譯　這個團體是為了一個目的而成立：阻止該法案通過。

解說

　　from 為介系詞，其後若接動詞須為動名詞，此處又必須用被動，所以變成 being passed，故選 b。

19.

解答：a

英文　This train makes several <u>stops</u> in small country towns, so it takes a while to get to Taidong.

中譯　這輛火車在幾個鄉鎮都有停，所以花了一段時間才抵達台東。

解說

　　stop 在此當名詞用，表「火車停靠站」，為可數名詞，加 s，故選 a。

20.

解答：c

英文　Jane <u>forgot</u> her backpack at the bus stop.

中譯　珍把她的背包掉在公車站忘了拿。

解說

　　此題意為「珍忘了她的背包」，即把背包遺留在公車站，表過去式，故選 c。

05 未來式

未來式的用法和句型

» 未來式泛指未來將發生的動作。

» 助動詞 will 為未來式常用的表達方式。will 不隨主詞人稱作變化,即第一、第二、第三人稱單數與複數主詞,之後都直接加 will。

» will 之後必須接原形動詞。

» 未來式直述句為簡單現在式的變形。將簡單現在式的一般動詞改為原形動詞,主詞之後加上助動詞 will,即形成未來式直述句。

» 未來式疑問句:將未來式直述句的助動詞往前提到句首,句末加上問號,即形成未來式疑問句。

» 未來式的句尾常有未來時間副詞作修飾。未來時間副詞為表示未來的時間,如 tomorrow(明天)、tomorrow morning / afternoon / evening(明天上午/中午/傍晚)、next +時間(下一段時間)、the day after tomorrow(後天)、in +一段時間(一段時間後)、in the future(未來)等。

» 未來式的縮寫:

1. 人稱代名詞的主格可以和 will 縮寫成「主詞 'll」。如:I will = I'll、you will = you'll、he will = he'll。

2. 未來式助動詞的否定 will not 可縮寫成 won't。

主詞+ will +原形 V +未來時間副詞.

I will talk to him later.
我晚一點會跟他談。

He'll (=He will) come to see me next week.
他下週將會來看我。

主詞＋ will not / won't ＋原形 V ＋未來時間副詞.

They won't (＝will not) come to the party next week.
他們下週將不會參加派對。

They will not visit us tomorrow morning.
他們明天早上將不會拜訪我們。

Will ＋主詞＋原形 V ＋未來時間副詞？

Will you tell him the truth tonight?
今晚你會告訴他實情嗎？

Will John go to Taipei with me the day after tomorrow?
約翰後天會和我一起去台北嗎？

be going to、be about to

» be going to、be about to 也可用來代替助動詞 will，表達未來式。

» 之後必須接原形動詞，表示「接近未來」之意。

» 相較於助動詞 will 不隨主詞人稱作變化（即單複數均用 will, will 本身字尾不加 s），be going to、be about to 適用於任何人稱，但 be 動詞必須隨主詞人稱、單複數作變化。如 I am going to、you are about to、she is going to、they are about to 等。

主詞＋ am / are / is ＋ going to / about to ＋原形 V（～未來時間）.

He is going to cook this evening.
他今晚將下廚。

She is about to leave.
她即將離開。

> 主詞＋ am / are / is ＋ not going to / about to ＋原形 V（～未來時間）.

I am not going to see a doctor next Friday.
我下週五不會去看醫生。

He is not about to tell the truth.
他不會說出實情。

> Am / Are / Is ＋主詞＋ going to / about to ＋原形 V（～未來時間）？

Are you about to take a trip?
你即將去旅行嗎？

Is she going to marry John next month?
她下個月將和約翰結婚嗎？

未來式疑問句的答法

» 以 Will 開頭的未來式疑問句，其答法可分為詳答與簡答，兩者的答句中除了 Yes / No 之外，均必須有 will 或 will not（won't）。

» 詳答為包含疑問句中動詞的完整答法；簡答則省略原句中的動詞與後頭的修飾語，只保留主詞加助動詞。

> Will ＋主詞＋（not）＋原形 V ～？

Will you lend me your car?
你將把車借給我嗎？

Will he come tomorrow?
他明天會來嗎？

> Yes, 主詞＋ will.

Yes, I will.
是的，我將會借給你。

Yes, he will.
是的，他會來。

Yes, 主詞＋ will ＋原形 V ～ .

Yes, I will lend you my car.
是的，我會把我的車借給你。

Yes, he will come tomorrow.
是的，他明天會出席。

No, 主詞＋ won't.

No, I won't.
不，我不會借你。

No, he won't.
不，他不會來。

NO, 主詞＋ won't ＋原形 V ～ .

No, I won't lend you my car.
不，我不會把我的車借給你。

No, he won't come tomorrow.
不，他明天不會來。

用 be going to 開頭疑問句的回答

» 用 be going to 開頭的疑問句，其回答要有 be 動詞。

» 答句用 Yes 或 No 回答，且 be 動詞要根據答句的主詞作變化。

Am / Are / Is ＋主詞＋（not）＋ going to ＋原形 V ?

Are you going to rent the room?
你將租下那房間嗎？

Is he going to take charge of the next meeting?
他將主持下一次會議嗎？

▌Yes, 主詞＋ Am / Are / Is.

Yes, I am.
是的，我將會租。

Yes, he is.
是的，他將主持。

▌Yes, 主詞＋ Am / Are / Is ＋ going to ＋原形 V.

Yes, I am going to rent the room.
是的，我將租下那間房。

Yes, he is going to take charge of the next meeting.
是的，他將主持下一次的會議。

▌No, 主詞＋ Am / Are / Is ＋ not.

No, I am not.
不，我將不會租。

No, he isn't.
不，他將不會主持。

▌NO, 主詞＋ Am / Are / Is ＋ not ＋ going to ＋原形 V ～.

No, I am not going to rent the room.
不，我將不會租那間房。

No, he isn't going to take charge of the next meeting.
不，他將不會主持下一次的會議。

來去動詞可以用現在進行式代替未來式

» 來去動詞為 go, come, leave, arrive 等有動作往返意味的動詞。

» 來去動詞通常用現在進行式來表示即將發生的動作。

> **主詞＋ am / are / is ＋來去動詞＋ ing ～未來時間.**

I am leaving for London this evening.
我今晚將動身前往倫敦。

She is arriving tomorrow afternoon.
她明天下午會到。

有疑問詞的未來式疑問句

» 所謂疑問詞，為用來詢問「如何／怎樣」、「什麼」、「誰」、「哪裡」、「哪個」、「何時」、「為什麼」等，英文除了 how 之外，泛指「wh- 疑問詞」，分別為 what、who、where、which、when、why 等。

» 有疑問詞的未來式疑問句，通常為疑問詞置句首，後接未來式問句。

» 答句不以 Yes 或 No 回答，而是根據疑問詞所問的內容作答覆。以未來式問，就以未來式答。

> **疑問詞（what, who, where, which, when, why, how）＋ will ＋主詞＋原形 V？**

A: What will you do this weekend?
B: I will visit my cousin in Kaohsiung.
A：你這週末要做什麼？
B：我將拜訪我住高雄的表親。

A: When will she finish her homework?
B: She will finish it by six o'clock.
A：她何時會完成她的作業？
B：她將在六點前完成。

題 目

1. I _____ give my mother flowers for her birthday. She _____ be so surprised.
   a. will ; will
   b. will ; is going to
   c. am going to ; will
   d. am going to ; is going

2. It's all _____ ; we _____ hold the wedding on the 27th of June.
   a. going to be planned ; will
   b. planned ; will to
   c. planned ; are going to
   d. planned ; will plan to

3. A: Have you decided what to tell them?
   B: Yes. I _____ them the truth.
   a. will tell
   b. am going to tell
   c. plan to tell
   d. Either b or c

4. You forgot to submit the form, so you _____ to fax it to us immediately.
   a. will have
   b. are going
   c. will
   d. None of the above

5. When _____ your bedroom? I'm tired of seeing this mess every day!
   a. are you cleaning
   b. are you going to clean
   c. will you clean
   d. will you have cleaned

6. Why _____ try harder in school? We know you're not stupid.

   a. will you to

   b. won't you

   c. aren't you going to

   d. aren't you going

7. I'm driving in that direction now, so I _____ drop you off on the way.

   a. will

   b. am going to

   c. was going to

   d. None of the above

8. Who do you think _____ be the next president?

   a. will

   b. is going to

   c. going to

   d. Either a or b

9. If we use this strategy, the project _____ very successful.

   a. will be

   b. will being

   c. was

   d. is

10. Look out! _____ your head on the corner!

    a. You

    b. You're hitting

    c. You're going to hit

    d. Either a or c

11. _____ over to see you right now.
    a. I'll come
    b. I'm coming
    c. I'm going to come
    d. All of the above

12. Do you promise you _____ tell a single soul?
    a. will not
    b. won't
    c. are not going to
    d. Either a or b

13. Mom, I've told you a million times, _____ careful during the trip.
    a. I'm
    b. I'll be
    c. I'm being
    d. Either b or c

14. Why _____ to the beach party next week?
    a. aren't you coming
    b. won't you come
    c. aren't you going to come
    d. All of the above

15. We're selling our house because _____ to Philadelphia.
    a. we're moving
    b. we're going to move
    c. we'll move
    d. Either a or b

16. Don't lose this ticket; _____ need it to pick up your laundry.
    a. you'd
    b. you've
    c. you'll
    d. you would

17. A new hairstyle _____ make you feel much better.
    a. will
    b. will always
    c. will have
    d. Either a or b

18. The company _____ an outing the Saturday after next.
    a. is going to go on
    b. is going on
    c. will be going on
    d. All of the above

19. I knew you _____ go to the party.
    a. will
    b. won't
    c. would
    d. Either a or b

20. By this time next year, we _____ have started the experiment.
    a. will
    b. are going to
    c. will be going to
    d. Either a or b

解析

1.

英文 **I am going to give my mother flowers for her birthday. She will be so surprised.**

中譯 我要送花給我媽當生日禮物。她會嚇一大跳。

解說

　　be going to 和 will 均可表未來式，但前者有表示近期、眼前即將發生的事情之意味；後者則表示未來較遠的時間。選 c。

2.

英文 **It's all planned; we are going to hold the wedding on the 27th of June.**

中譯 全部都計畫好了，我們要在 6 月 27 日舉行婚禮。

解說

　　It 代稱所計畫之事。前句用簡單現在式表事實，後句表示發生在即之事，故用 be going to，選 c。

3.

英文
A: **Have you decided what to tell them?**
B: **Yes. I am going to tell them the truth.**
B: **Yes. I plan to tell them the truth.**

中譯
A：你決定好要跟他們說什麼了嗎？
B：決定了。我要跟他們說實話。
B：決定了。我打算跟他們說實話。

解說

　　此句題意表述「未來計畫去做某事」，being going to 有此意思，will 則帶有承諾意味。由於未來計畫去做某事只是一種計畫，並非帶有承諾意涵，故本題 b 或 c 均可，選 d。

4. 解答：**a**

英文 You forgot to submit the form, so you <u>will have to</u> fax it to us immediately.

中譯 你忘了交那份表格，所以你必須立刻傳真給我們。

解說

此題表示說話者提出「未來必須做某事」之意，選 a。

b. 陳述事實，無建議意味。

c. will 之後不可直接加 to，須加原形動詞。

5. 解答：**b**

英文 When <u>are you going to clean</u> your bedroom? I'm tired of seeing this mess every day!

中譯 你何時要整理臥室？我受夠了每天看這一團亂！

解說

be going to 有「未來計劃做某事」之意，本題說話者問對方何時計劃清理房間，選 b。

6. 解答：**b**

英文 Why <u>won't you</u> try harder in school? We know you're not stupid.

中譯 你在學校為何不用功一點？我們知道你不笨。

解說

此題說話者帶有建議對方承諾做某事之意，為否定反問用法，選 b。

c. be going to 則為計劃做某事，由於 try harder（更努力試）為一種決心，非計畫，故本題用 will，而不用 be going to。

7.

英文　I'm driving in that direction now, so I <u>will</u> drop you off on the way.

中譯　我現在要開往那個方向，所以會在途中放你下車。

解說

　　will 表非眼前急迫將發生之事，而是表示較遠一點的將來時間。will 同時也帶有承諾意味。選 will 是因此題說話者並非立即要讓對方下車，也可看成說話者承諾待車子開到一定地方後會讓對方下車，故選 a。

8.

英文　Who do you think <u>will</u> be the next president?
　　　Who do you think <u>is going to</u> be the next president?

中譯　你覺得誰會是下一屆總統？

解說

　　此題可用 will 表示詢問將來的下任總統，或是用 be going to 表示詢問即將產生的下任總統，故 a 或 b 均可，選 d。

9.

英文　If we use this strategy, the project <u>will</u> be very successful.

中譯　如果我們採用這個策略，這個計畫將會非常成功。

解說

　　此為條件句，表「如果我們……，就會……」，通常用 will 表示。這裡的 will 亦帶有承諾意涵，承諾或預期如果做了什麼事就會得到如何的結果，故選 a。

10.
解答：**c**

英文 Look out! You're going to hit your head on the corner!

中譯 小心！你的頭要撞到桌角了！

解說

　　此題意為「小心！你的頭快撞到了！」，用 be going to 表「眼下即將發生之事」，故選 c。

11.
解答：**d**

英文
I'll come over to see you right now.
I'm coming over to see you right now.
I'm going to come over to see you right now.

中譯 我現在馬上要去看你了。

解說

　　a. 表示一種承諾。

　　b. come 是來去動詞，可用進行式來表示即將發生之事，相當於 be going to。

　　c. 表示即將發生之事或是一種計畫。

　　　以上情形均可，故選 d。

12.
解答：**d**

英文
Do you promise you <u>will not</u> tell a single soul?
Do you promise you <u>won't</u> tell a single soul?

中譯 你答應不會跟任何人說這件事嗎？

解說

　　用 will 表示一種承諾，此為否定式，will not 等同 won't。選 a 或 b 均可，故選 d。

英文　Mom, I've told you a million times, I'll be careful during the trip.

中譯　媽，我已經跟妳說好幾百遍了，我旅行途中會小心的。

解說

　　用 will 表示一種對未來的承諾，選 b。

英文
Why aren't you coming to the beach party next week?
Why won't you come to the beach party next week?
Why aren't you going to come to the beach party next week?

中譯　你下週為何不來參加海灘派對？

解說

　　用法同 11 題，此題為否定式疑問句，選 d。

英文
We're selling our house because we're moving to Philadelphia.
We're selling our house because we're going to move to Philadelphia.

中譯　我們正在賣房子，因為我們要搬到費城去了。

解說

　　此有表未來計畫的意味，用現在進行式或 be going to 均可表達此意，故 a 或 b 均可，選 d。

16.

英文　Don't lose this ticket; <u>you'll</u> need it to pick up your laundry.

中譯　這張票別搞丟了，你需要用它來領洗好的衣物。

解說

　　用 will 表未來須做之事，選 c。

17.

英文　A new hairstyle <u>will</u> make you feel much better.
　　　A new hairstyle <u>will always</u> make you feel much better.

中譯　新髮型總能讓你心情大好。

解說

　　此題 will 帶有承諾或建議之意涵，加 always 表強調，語氣更重。a 或 b 均可，故選 d。

18.

英文　The company <u>is going to go on</u> an outing the Saturday after next.
　　　The company <u>is going on</u> an outing the Saturday after next.
　　　The company <u>will be going on</u> an outing the Saturday after next.

中譯　公司下下星期六要舉辦員工旅遊。

解說

　　用法同 11 題，will 後又接進行式強調未來即將發生之意味更濃厚。a、b、c 均可，故選 d。

19.　　　　　　　　　　　　　　　　　　　　　　　　　解答：**c**

英文　I knew you <u>would</u> go to the party.

中譯　我就知道你會去參加派對。

解說

　此題為過去式用法，用 would 表示，故選 c。

20.　　　　　　　　　　　　　　　　　　　　　　　　　解答：**d**

英文　By this time next year, we <u>will</u> have started the experiment.
　　　By this time next year, we <u>are going to</u> have started the experiment.

中譯　明年此時，我們就已經展開實驗了。

解說

　此題用 will 表示一種對未來的承諾；用 be going to 表示對未來的計畫。a 或 b 情況均可，故選 d。c 則表預期或承諾未來即將發生，但題意表明未來時間為明年的事，非眼下即將發生之事，故不選 c。

06 感官動詞、連綴動詞與使役動詞

感官動詞

» 感官動詞，指的是與五官知覺有關的動詞，又稱作知覺動詞。常見的感官動詞包括：look、see、watch、sound、smell、taste、hear、listen to 等等。

» 感官動詞後面接形容詞時，形容詞作補語，用來說明主詞的特質、狀態。

感官動詞＋形容詞

• 感官動詞強調個人的知覺與感受，例如：look（看起來）、sound（聽起來）、smell（聞起來）、taste（嚐起來）、feel（感覺上；摸起來）等。此時的感官動詞是不及物動詞，換言之，就是動詞後面不需要受詞。

The food tasted sour.
這道菜吃起來酸酸的。

The flower smells sweet.
這朵花聞起來香香的。

Your job sounds very interesting.
你的工作聽起來很有趣。

You looked tired.
你看起來很累。

感官動詞＋ like ＋名詞「……像……」

• 感官動詞後面如果要接名詞，必須先接上介系詞 like，再接名詞。

The man looks like a thief.
那個人看起來像小偷。

The milk smells like rotten fish.
這牛奶聞起來像臭掉的魚。

The coffee **tastes like** dishwater.
這杯咖啡喝起來像洗碗水。

I **felt like** an idiot when I made that stupid mistake.
犯了那樣愚蠢的錯誤，我覺得自己像個白痴。

感官動詞＋受詞＋原形動詞

- 感官動詞當及物動詞時，後面需要受詞。受詞後面再接原形動詞，強調事實。

I **saw** the boy **enter** the building.
我看到那個小男孩進了那棟建築物。

He **heard** someone **break** the window of Mrs. Wang's house last night.
他昨晚聽到有人打破王太太家的窗戶。

I **felt** someone **touch** my arm.
我覺得有人碰到我的手臂。

感官動詞＋受詞＋現在分詞（V-ing）

- 感官動詞當及物動詞，受詞後面接現在分詞，強調動作正在進行，表主動。

He **watched** people **passing** by.
他看著人們走過。

We **felt** the house **shaking**.
我們覺得房子在震動。

I **saw** a cow **crossing** the street.
我看到一頭牛正在過馬路。

感官動詞＋受詞＋過去分詞（V-ed）

- 感官動詞當及物動詞，受詞後面接過去分詞，強調受詞的被動地位。

I **heard** my name **called**.
我聽到有人叫我的名字。

I **saw** a butterfly **caught** by a boy.
我看到一隻蝴蝶被一個男孩抓到了。

連綴動詞

» 連綴動詞後面接名詞或形容詞作補語（主詞補語），用來說明主詞的特質、狀態等。

» 連綴動詞的功用：連接主詞與補語。

» 連綴動詞是不及物動詞，所以後面不需要受詞，只需要主詞補語。因為連綴動詞不需要受詞，所以沒有被動語態。

» 連綴動詞皆以下列方式表現：主詞＋連綴動詞＋形容詞／名詞。

» 常見的連綴動詞共有下列幾種：

S ＋ be 動詞（is / am / are; was / were）＋形容詞／名詞

I **was** late for work yesterday.
我昨天上班遲到了。

Don't worry. These problems **are** very easy.
別擔心。這些問題很簡單。

Jay **is** a singer.
杰是一名歌手。

S ＋ become / get / turn / grow / fall ＋形容詞／名詞

• become、get、turn、grow、fall 屬於表示「變成」的連綴動詞。

• 這類動詞強調變化的過程，或狀態的轉變，所以經常用進行式表現。

The days **are becoming** shorter.
白天變得愈來愈短。

He **gets** really angry if you talk about his baldness.
如果你提到他的禿頭，他會變得很生氣。

The weather **has** suddenly **turned** cold.
天氣突然變冷了。

Everyone **is growing** older every day.
每個人都在一天天的逐漸老去。（形容詞比較級當補語）

Tim often **falls** asleep in class.
提姆在課堂上常常睡著。

表示「持續；維持」的連綴動詞：keep

• 後面通常接形容詞。

Please **keep** <u>quiet</u> because the baby is sleeping.
小嬰兒在睡覺，請保持安靜。

I like to **keep** <u>busy</u>.
我喜歡保持忙碌。

表示「似乎；看起來好像」的連綴動詞：seem / appear

• 注意，其他的連綴動詞都可以用進行式表現，只有 seem 和 appear 不可以。

He **seems** <u>happy</u>.
他看起來很開心。（形容詞當補語）

He **seems** <u>a nice man</u>.
他看起來像個好人。（名詞當補語）

He **appears** <u>younger</u> than he really is.
他看起來比實際年紀還小。（形容詞比較級當補語）

使役動詞

» 使役動詞表示「命令、允許、要求、交代」某人做某事。

» 使役動詞是及物動詞，後面需要受詞，作為下令或要求的對象。

» 依照受詞後面接的是「原形動詞」還是「不定詞」，使役動詞可歸類為下列幾
類：

make / have / let ＋受詞＋原形動詞

Our teacher **had** us <u>clean</u> the classroom.
我們老師叫我們打掃教室。

I **made** him <u>tell</u> the truth.
我要他說出實話。

His parents **let** Tom <u>take the day off</u> from school.
湯姆的父母允許他請假一天不用上學。

ask / tell / get / want / need ＋受詞＋ to V（不定詞）

Our teacher asked / told us to clean the classroom.
我們的老師交代我們要打掃教室。

He wanted us to leave the room.
他希望我們離開這個房間。

Carl needs me to help him.
卡爾需要我幫他忙。

I got Tom to repair my bicycle.
我要湯姆修理我的腳踏車。

help ＋受詞＋（to）V（原形動詞）表示「幫忙某人做某事」，to 通常省略。

The man helped me (to) carry the luggage.
那位先生幫我提行李。

I helped him (to) find the watch.
我幫他找到了手錶。

題 目

1. Be quiet and _____ the orchestra! The music _____ beautiful.
   a. hear ; sounds
   b. listen ; hears
   c. listen to ; sounds
   d. notice ; seems

2. What _____ so good? It's making me _____ terribly hungry.
   a. tastes ; feel
   b. smells ; feel
   c. smelled ; feel like
   d. smells ; have

3. If you take the pants over to that counter, you can _____ the girl adjust them for you.
   a. have
   b. let
   c. make
   d. Either a or b

4. In case you hadn't _____, Paul and I have been together for several months.
   a. looked
   b. seemed
   c. noticed
   d. watched

5. It is important _____ students _____ comfortable making mistakes when speaking English.
   a. to let ; feel
   b. to have ; to feel
   c. to make ; feel
   d. Either a or c

6. Absence _____ the heart grow fonder.
   a. makes
   b. seems
   c. feels
   d. causes

7. This cake _____ delicious.
   a. looks
   b. smells
   c. tastes
   d. All of the above

8. The Corpse Flower—the stinkiest plant on earth—_____ rotted flesh.
   a. smells
   b. smells like
   c. stinks
   d. tastes

9. Why don't you _____ TV or _____ a book?
   a. see ; read
   b. look ; watch
   c. watch ; read
   d. watch ; see

10. He _____ his little sister _____ him her lunch money.
    a. asked ; give
    b. made ; give
    c. made ; to give
    d. made ; gave

11. Teresa enjoyed going up to the roof at night to _____ the starry sky.

    a. watch

    b. look

    c. look at

    d. Either a or c

12. Honey, you _____ great in that dress!

    a. look

    b. see

    c. are looking

    d. seem

13. You've been drinking. Why don't you _____ me drive tonight?

    a. make

    b. have

    c. let

    d. All of the above

14. _____! You can _____ the ocean from here.

    a. Watch ; look at

    b. Listen ; hear

    c. Look ; see

    d. Either b or c

15. Do you _____ that book on the shelf? Could you hand it to me?

    a. watch

    b. see

    c. have

    d. read

16. Edward's eyes widened when he _____ Olivia's new miniskirt.
    a. noticed
    b. watched
    c. looked
    d. had seen

17. Why don't you _____ the kids have some ice cream?
    a. have
    b. make
    c. let
    d. allow

18. The teacher asked the class _____ down immediately.
    a. sit
    b. sits
    c. to sit
    d. to sat

19. The soldiers _____ the driver get out of the vehicle.
    a. asked
    b. made
    c. told
    d. All of the above

20. Her parents never _____ her go out on dates.
    a. make
    b. allow
    c. have
    d. let

解 析

1.

英文　Be quiet and listen to the orchestra! The music <u>sounds</u> beautiful.

中譯　安靜聽交響樂團演奏！這音樂聽起來很優美。

解說

　　「聽音樂」的動詞要用「listen to ＋ 聽的對象」。hear 作「聽見，聽到」解釋，指的是聽到某聲音但不刻意留意聲音的內容。listen to 則表示非常「用心、專注」地聆聽。聽音樂或聲音，用的器官是耳朵，所以連綴動詞用 sound。故答案選 c。

2.

英文　What <u>smells</u> so good? It's making me <u>feel</u> terribly hungry.

中譯　什麼東西聞起來這麼香？這味道讓我覺得肚子快餓扁了。

解說

　　從第二句的 hungry「飢餓的」可推斷說話者還沒吃東西，所以第一空格應該選的感官動詞是 smell「聞起來」；因為還沒吃過東西，所以用現在式。從第二空格後面的 hungry 可知應填入的動詞是 feels。feel 作為連綴動詞，後面必須接形容詞（hungry）。terribly 是副詞，修飾形容詞 hungry。句中的 make 是使役動詞，作「令人……，使得……」，後面必須接原形動詞（feel）。

3.

英文　If you take the pants over to that counter, you can <u>have</u> the girl adjust them for you.

中譯　如果你把這件褲子拿到櫃檯那邊，可以請那裡的女生幫你修改。

解說

　　助動詞 can 後面必須接原形動詞。前三個選項都是使役動詞，但只有選項 a 的 have 有「請託」的意思。選項 b 的 let 表示「允許、准許」。選項 c 有「逼迫」的意思。故選 a。

4. 解答：**c**

英文　**In case you hadn't <u>noticed</u>, Paul and I have been together for several months.**

中譯　假使你還沒注意到，保羅和我已經交往幾個月了。

解說

　in case 是連接詞，表示「如果；假設」。在這個由 in case 引導的從屬子句中，使用的時態是過去完成式。四個選項的動詞都與眼睛感官有關，但是選項 d 的 watched 後面通常需要受詞。選項 a 和 b 作為連綴動詞，後面要接形容詞或名詞當補語，故答案選 c。

5. 解答：**d**

英文　**It is important <u>to let</u> students <u>feel</u> comfortable making mistakes when speaking English.**

　　　It is important <u>to make</u> students <u>feel</u> comfortable making mistakes when speaking English.

中譯　讓學生講英語犯錯時不會覺得不自在，這是很重要的。

解說

　答案選 a 或 c 皆可。由虛主詞（本身沒有意義，只有主詞的功能）引導的句型「It is ＋形容詞＋ to V」中，意義上真正的主詞，是不定詞這個部分。選項 b 的第二個答案，如果改成原形動詞 feel 就可以選。let / have / make 三者皆用來表示「使人……；令人……」，後面必須接原形動詞。

6. 解答：**a**

英文　**Absence <u>makes</u> the heart grow fonder.**

中譯　離別增情意。

解說

　空格後有受詞 the heart，所以只有選項 a 和 d 可以考慮，因為選項 b 和 c 後面都要接形容詞或名詞。動詞 cause 後面的受詞必須接不定詞（to V）作為受詞補語，但這裡的 grow「變得」是原形動詞，故 a 才是正確答案：使役動詞 make 後面接原形動詞作受詞補語。

7.

解答： d

英文　This cake <u>looks</u> delicious.
　　　This cake <u>smells</u> delicious.
　　　This cake <u>tastes</u> delicious.

中譯　這塊蛋糕看起來／聞起來／嚐起來很好吃。

解說

　　空格後面是形容詞 delicious，前三個選項都是感官連綴動詞，後面可接形容詞，且文意皆合，故三個都對。

8.

解答： b

英文　The Corpse Flower—the stinkiest plant on earth—<u>smells like</u> rotted flesh.

中譯　「屍花」是地球上最臭的植物，聞起來像腐臭的肉。

解說

　　空格後面是名詞，所以答案只能選 b，因為只有介系詞 like 後面可以接名詞。句型：感官動詞（smell, look, taste, sound）＋ like ＋ N。這是一種類似比喻的用法。

9.

解答： c

英文　Why don't you <u>watch</u> TV or <u>read</u> a book?

中譯　你為什麼不看看電視或看看書呢？

解說

　　感官動詞中與眼睛有關的字，中文統稱為「看」，但在英文上是有差別的。see 指的是「看得到」，眼睛功能沒問題。read 指的是「閱讀書面文字」。watch 指的是「觀看動態表演」，例如球賽、節目等等。look 當「看」解釋時，後面必須接介系詞 at，再接「被看的物體」。look at 指的是「盯著某物或某人看」。第一空格後面的受詞是 TV，第二個是 a book，所以答案選 c。

10.

英文　**He made his little sister give him her lunch money.**

中譯　他逼他妹妹把她午餐的錢給他。

解說

　　第一空格用 asked 或 made 皆可，後面再接受詞（被逼迫或要求的對象）。如果用 asked，受詞後面要用不定詞 to give。如果用 made，受詞後面要用原形動詞。所以答案選 b。

11.

英文　**Teresa enjoyed going up to the roof at night to watch the starry sky.**
　　　Teresa enjoyed going up to the roof at night to look at the starry sky.

中譯　泰瑞莎喜歡晚上爬上屋頂去欣賞滿天空。

解說

　　動詞 enjoy 後面必須接 V-ing（going up）。空格前面有 to，表示有待填入動詞以形成不定詞，答案應選 a。watch 的「看」，表示「觀賞、觀看」；look at 表示「注視某物或人」，有「檢視」的意思。例：He looked at the picture and laughed. 「他望著照片，笑了起來。」，故答案選 d。

12.

英文　**Honey, you look great in that dress!**

中譯　親愛的，妳穿這件衣服看起來真漂亮！

解說

　　空格後面有形容詞 great「出色的」，所以只有選項 a 和 d 可以考慮。選 d 與句意不合，因為 seem「看起來」表示推測與不肯定，所以中文也作「似乎」解釋。選 a 才符合句意，look「看起來」指的是外表看起來如何，這是一種觀察。

13.

英文 You've been drinking. Why don't you <u>let</u> me drive tonight?

中譯 你喝了酒,今天晚上讓我開車,如何?

解說

「Why don't you(Why not)＋原形動詞?」這個句型表示「提議、勸誘」,作「為什麼不……?」。空格應填入原形動詞,依照句意,應選 c。因為 make 和 have 都有「命令」的意味在裡面,只有 let 表「允許;准許」之意。let 的受詞 me 後面要接原形動詞 drive。

14.

英文 <u>Listen!</u> You can <u>hear</u> the ocean from here.
<u>Look!</u> You can <u>see</u> the ocean from here.

中譯 你聽!從這裡可以聽到海的聲音。
你看!從這裡可以看到海洋。

解說

注意第一空格後面有驚嘆號。以動詞或動詞片語起首的驚嘆用語,目的在吸引對方的注意力。例如:Look!「你看!」/ Listen!「你聽!」/ Watch out!「當心!」/ Be careful!「小心!」等。按照句意,選項 b 或 c 皆可。

15.

英文 Do you <u>see</u> that book on the shelf? Could you hand it to me?

中譯 你看到架上那本書嗎?可以麻煩你把那本書遞給我嗎?

解說

空格後面的受詞是 that book,所以選項 b 與 d 都是可能答案,必須參看第二句,才能確定空格應填入哪個動詞。hand 在這裡當動詞,作「把……遞給」解。如果選 d,與句意不合,因為 read 表示「閱讀」。答案選 b。see 指的是視覺能力,表示「看得見」。

16.
解答：**a**

英文 Edward's eyes widened when he <u>noticed</u> Olivia's new miniskirt.

中譯 當愛德華看到奧莉薇亞新的迷你裙時，他眼睛睜得好大。

解說

空格後面的受詞是 miniskirt「迷你裙」，動詞應搭配選項 a；notice 表示「發覺、留意」的意思。如果要選 c，還要加介系詞 at，形成 look at＋N（被看的對象）。

17.
解答：**c**

英文 Why don't you <u>let</u> the kids have some ice cream?

中譯 你為什麼不讓孩子們吃一點冰淇淋呢？

解說

選項 a 和 b 皆表示命令，與句意不合。選項 d 的 allow 雖然也可以作「讓……」解釋，但受詞之後必須用不定詞，換言之，have some ice cream 的 have「吃」要改成 to have 才行。所以答案選 c：let＋受詞＋原形動詞。

18.
解答：**c**

英文 The teacher asked the class <u>to sit</u> down immediately.

中譯 老師要求全班立刻坐下。

解說

本題中，使役動詞 ask 表示「要求；命令」，後面接被要求的對象，也就是 the class，之後必須接不定詞，故選 c。

19.

英文　The soldiers <u>made</u> the driver get out of the vehicle.

中譯　這些軍人逼司機下車。

解說

　　從受詞 the driver 後面使用原形動詞（片語）go out of「從……離開」可知，答案應該選 b。如果選 a 或 c，後面必須改成不定詞 to go out of 才行。

20.

英文　Her parents never <u>let</u> her go out on dates.

中譯　她的父母從不讓她出去約會。

解說

　　空格之後的動詞片語 go out 是原形，且根據句意判斷，答案應選 d，表示「准許」某人做某事。如果要選 b，後面要改成不定詞 to go out 才行。

07 授與動詞

授與動詞

» 如果要表示「把某物給某人」，或者「為了某人做某事」，就會使用授與動詞。

» 常見的授與動詞：give（給予）、send（寄送）、bring（帶給）、tell（告訴）、sell（賣給）、write（寫給）、teach（教給）、ask（詢問）等等。

» 因為要把「把某物給某人」，所以授與動詞的受詞有兩個：直接受詞（物）與間接受詞（人）。

» 如何判斷受詞是直接還是間接？從受詞距離主詞的遠近來判斷。東西離手前還在主詞手上，此時東西距離主詞最近，是直接受詞。東西離手後，轉手給另一人，這個「另一人」成了間接受詞。

主詞＋授與動詞＋間接受詞（人）＋直接受詞（物）

My father **bought** me a watch.
我父親買了一只手錶給我。

Maggie **showed** me her picture.
瑪姬拿她的照片給我看。

He **gave** me some books.
他給了我幾本書。

I **lent** him a novel.
我借他一本小說。

She **told** the boy a story.
她告訴這個男孩一個故事。

主詞＋授與動詞＋直接受詞（物）＋介系詞（to / for）＋間接受詞（人）

- 會用介系詞 to 的動詞包括：give（給予）、send（寄送）、bring（帶給）、show（展現給）、tell（告訴）、sell（賣給）、lend（借給）、write（寫給）、teach（教給）等等。

- 會用介系詞 for 的動詞包括：buy（為⋯⋯買）、bring（為⋯⋯帶）、choose（為⋯⋯選擇）、do（為⋯⋯做）、leave（為⋯⋯保留）、make（為⋯⋯做）等等。

- 會用 of 的動詞更少，這類動詞包括：ask（問）、demand（要求）、expect（預期）等等。

- 何時該用 to，何時該用 for，涉及搭配的問題，要視動詞而定。會用 to 的動詞佔大多數。建議讀者，看到一個動詞，記一個。

Part A 五個句子全都可以改寫如下：

My father **bought** a watch for me.
我父親買了一只手錶給我。

Maggie **showed** her picture to me.
瑪姬拿她的照片給我看。

He gave some books to me.
他拿了幾本書給我。

I **lent** a novel to him.
我借了一本小說給他。

She **told** a story to the boy.
她告訴這個男孩一個故事。

其他會用 for 或 of 的例子：

Get a copy of the evening paper for me.
＝Get me a copy of the evening paper.
拿一份晚報給我。

My mother **made** a cake <u>for</u> my sister.
＝My mother made my sister a cake.
我的母親為我妹做了一個蛋糕。

I **ask** a question <u>of</u> him.
＝I asked him a question.
我問了他一個問題。

主詞＋授與動詞＋直接受詞（代名詞 it / them）＋ to / for ＋ 間接受詞（人）

- 如果直接受詞是代名詞 it / them，這時候直接受詞的位置只有一個：授與動詞的後面。

My friends **sent** <u>the flowers</u> to me.
＝My friends **sent** me <u>the flowers</u>.
我朋友送花給我。

【說明】如果一般名詞 flowers 用代名詞 them 代替，句子可改寫如下：

My friends sent <u>them</u> to me.

不可以說：My friends sent me <u>them</u>.（×）

The dog **took** <u>the newspaper</u> to Tim.
＝The dog **took** Tim <u>the newspaper</u>.
那隻狗拿報紙給提姆。

【說明】如果一般名詞 the newspaper 用代名詞 it 代替，句子可改寫如下：

The dog took <u>it</u> to Tim.

不可以說：The dog took Tim <u>it</u>.（×）

題 目

1. My aunt _____ a wedding cake _____ my sister for her wedding.
   a. made ; to
   b. makes ; to
   c. made ; for
   d. makes ; for

2. Please _____ this check _____ the director for me.
   a. give ; to
   b. give ; for
   c. giving ; to
   d. Either a or b

3. Could you _____ how _____ this printer?
   a. tell ; to use
   b. teach me ; I use
   c. show me ; to use
   d. tell me ; use

4. Jack's Japanese wife _____ write _____ the Ambassador for them.
   a. offered ; a letter
   b. offered to ; a letter to
   c. offered to ; to
   d. Either b or c

5. You didn't understand. She was _____ you _____.
   a. offering ; to a job
   b. offering ; a job
   c. offering to ; a job
   d. offering a job for ; doing

6. If you _____ the secret code word, I'll _____ the treasure map.
   a. tell ; show
   b. tell me ; show you
   c. tell to me ; show to you
   d. Either a or b

7. Can you _____ some money right now?
   a. lent us
   b. lend me
   c. borrow me
   d. Either a or b

8. I _____ a letter a month ago, but I haven't heard back from her yet.
   a. wrote Mom
   b. wrote to Mom
   c. sent to Mom
   d. All of the above

9. I _____ a suit _____ you to wear at the ceremony.
   a. chose ; to
   b. chose ; for
   c. have chosen ; of
   d. None of the above

10. Your duty is to do what your country asks _____ you.
    a. to
    b. for
    c. of
    d. on

11. May I _____ a favor _____ you?
   a. borrow ; from
   b. lend ; to
   c. request ; for
   d. ask ; of

12. Can you _____ a glass of water?
   a. get to
   b. get me
   c. get myself
   d. get you

13. A: Is this your ball?
   B: Yes! Give _____!
   a. it to me
   b. me it
   c. to me it
   d. Either a or b

14. Did you send _____ flowers _____ Mother's Day?
   a. some ; to your mom
   b. your mom ; for
   c. our mother ; on
   d. Either b or c

15. Please _____ this letter to the director.
   a. take
   b. deliver
   c. give
   d. All of the above

16. I _____ you a gift _____ Hawaii.
    a. brought ; from
    b. took ; to
    c. gave ; to
    d. brought ; for

17. Her father didn't give _____ to her.
    a. them
    b. it
    c. the money
    d. All of the above

18. Please show _____ to your teacher.
    a. me
    b. my note
    c. they
    d. Either a or c

19. Mrs. Baxter _____ a story _____.
    a. read the children ; for Christmas
    b. read ; to the children
    c. read to ; for the children
    d. Either a or b

20. Can you _____ me _____ money?
    a. borrow ; from
    b. lend ; some
    c. lend to you ; the
    d. None of the above

解析

1.

解答： **c**

英文　My aunt <u>made</u> a wedding cake <u>for</u> my sister for her wedding.

中譯　我阿姨為我姐的婚禮做了一個結婚蛋糕。

解說

　　先判斷時態。婚禮和做蛋糕理當是發生過的事情，動詞宜用過去式。從本題動詞用的是 make 來看，介系詞應搭配 for，for 表示「為了（某人）。介系詞 to 表示「給予（某人）」，有些授與動詞經常與 to 連用。要特別注意哪些動詞經常和哪些介系詞搭配運用。另外，許多食物或飲料的製作，常常會用到 make 這個動詞，例如：make tea／coffee／sandwiches「煮咖啡／泡茶／做三明治」等等。

2.

解答： **a**

英文　Please <u>give</u> this check <u>to</u> the director for me.

中譯　請幫我把這張支票交給主管。

解說

　　本句使用祈使句：句子以原形動詞起首。祈使句語帶請求或命令，前面經常加上 please 表示禮貌。所以空格要填入動詞，而介系詞應該要用 to，表示「給予（某人）」，故答案選 a。

3.

解答： **c**

英文　Could you <u>show</u> me how <u>to use</u> this printer?

中譯　可以請你教我如何使用這台印表機嗎？

解說

　　動詞如果用 tell「告訴」，後面需要受詞，受詞之後再接不定詞。選項 a 的 tell 後面缺少受詞，所以不能選。選項 b 的第一個答案 teach me 是正確的，但是第二個答案要改成 to use 才可以。故答案選 c，show 作「指示；指引」解釋，帶有教導的意思。

4.　　　　　　　　　　　　　　　　　　　　　　　　　　　　解答：**d**

英文　Jack's Japanese wife <u>offered to</u> write <u>a letter to</u> the Ambassador for them.
　　　Jack's Japanese wife <u>offered to</u> write <u>to</u> the Ambassador for them.

中譯　傑克的日籍妻子提議要替他們寫信給大使。

解說

　　動詞offered後面要接不定詞to V，表示「主動提議作某事」。動詞write作「寫信」解釋時，後面不見得一定要受詞the letter，因為光是write一個字，也可以表示寫信。所以選項b或c皆是正確答案。

5.　　　　　　　　　　　　　　　　　　　　　　　　　　　　解答：**b**

英文　You didn't understand. She was <u>offering you a job</u>.

中譯　你沒搞懂。她是要給你一份工作。

解說

　　本題offer作授與動詞，後面先接間接受詞you，再接直接受詞a job，故答案選b。

6.　　　　　　　　　　　　　　　　　　　　　　　　　　　　解答：**b**

英文　If you <u>tell me</u> the secret code word, I'll <u>show you</u> the treasure map.

中譯　如果你告訴我密碼，我會把藏寶圖拿給你看。

解說

　　授與動詞tell和show，後面必須有表人的間接受詞，後面表物的直接受詞才能存在。故答案選b。以tell而言，間接受詞是me，直接受詞是the secret code word。以show而言，間接受詞是you，直接受詞是the treasure map。

英文 **Can you <u>lend me</u> some money right now?**

中譯 你現在能借點錢給我嗎？

解說

　　lend 和 borrow 中文都翻譯成「借」，但 lend 指的是「借出」，表示把東西出借給他人，而 borrow 指的是「借入」，向他人借東西。所以答案選 b。如果把「借」的方向掉換一下，用 borrow，則句子可改寫如下：Can I borrow some money from you?「我可以跟你借點錢嗎？」使用 borrow，後面必須搭配介系詞 from，之後再接「借錢的對象」。

英文 **I wrote Mom a letter a month ago, but I haven't heard back from her yet.**

中譯 我一個月前寫了封信給媽媽，但我還沒有收到她的回信。

解說

　　授與動詞 write 後面如果直接加間接受詞（人），之後再接直接受詞（物）a letter，中間是不需要介系詞的，故答案選 a。如果 write 後面先接直接受詞，才需要在間接受詞（人）前面放介系詞 to：I wrote a letter to Mom。此外，「hear from ＋某人」作「得知、聽到（消息）」解釋。

英文 **I chose a suit <u>for</u> you to wear at the ceremony.**

中譯 我幫你選了一套衣服，讓你在典禮上穿。

解說

　　動詞 chose 通常與介系詞 for「為了……」搭配。某些動詞經常與某些介系詞一起使用，這是習慣用法，必須看一個記一個。答案應該選 b。選項 c 的問題就出在介系詞不能用 of，不然動詞使用現在完成式也是正確的。

英文　**Your duty is to do what your country asks <u>of</u> you.**

中譯　你的責任就是完成國家交代給你的任務。

解說

　　當動詞 ask 作「期望；要求（某人）」時，被要求的對象，前面要接介系詞 of。例：You're asking too much of her.「你對她要求太高了。」注意，介系詞後面接的是受格，不是主格。答案選 c。

英文　**May I <u>ask</u> a favor <u>of</u> you?**

中譯　我可以請你幫個忙嗎？

解說

　　「ask a favor of ＋某人」表示「請（某人）幫忙……」，介系詞只能用 of。選項 c 的動詞 request 的意思和 ask 近似，搭配的介系詞也一樣，所以 for 如果改成 of，就是正確答案。另外，ask 如果作「向（某人）提出問題」解釋時，習慣上也是與 of 搭配：「ask ＋直接受詞＋ of ＋間接受詞」。例：He asked a question of me. ＝ He asked me a question.「他問我一個問題。」

英文　**Can you <u>get me</u> a glass of water?**

中譯　你可以拿杯水給我嗎？

解說

　　動詞 get 作「拿來；取來」解釋，如果後面是間接受詞（人），中間就不需要介系詞，故答案選 b。如果本句 get 後面是直接受詞（物），就要用到介系詞，再接表人的間接受詞：Can you get a glass of water for me? 注意介系詞用 for，表示「為了……」。

英文　A: Is this your ball?
　　　B: Yes! Give it to me!

中譯　A：這是你的球嗎？
　　　B：沒錯！把它給我！

解說

　　在授與動詞的句型中，如果直接受詞（物）用代名詞（it 或 them）表示，此時，動詞後面一定要先接直接受詞，之後再接介系詞 to ＋人。

英文　Did you send <u>your mom</u> flowers <u>for</u> Mother's Day?
　　　Did you send <u>our mother</u> flowers <u>on</u> Mother's Day?

中譯　你母親節那天有沒有送花給你媽？
　　　你母親節那天有沒有送花送給我們的母親？

解說

　　句型：send ＋間接受詞（your mom / our mother）＋直接受詞（flowers）。第一空格後面的 flowers，是表示「物」的直接受詞，空格內應填入間接受詞（人）。第二空格要填入表示時間的介系詞。無論是選項 b 的 your mom 或者選項 c 的 our mother，作受詞都沒問題，只是意思不同。至於 Mother's Day 前面的介系詞，on 或 for 皆可，for 也可以用來表示「在……時間」。所以選 b 或 c 皆可。選項 a 的問題在於 Mother's Day 前面缺少介系詞 on / for。

英文　Please <u>take</u> this letter to the director.
　　　Please <u>deliver</u> this letter to the director.
　　　Please <u>give</u> this letter to the director.

中譯　請把這封信交給主管。

解說

　　動詞 take / deliver / give 都可以表示把「東西」轉交給「他人」。這裡的直接受詞是 this letter，間接受詞是 the director。注意 the director 前面的介系詞是 to，to 習慣和表示「交付東西給他人」的動詞連用。

16. 解答：**a**

英文 **I brought you a gift from Hawaii.**

中譯 我從夏威夷帶了一份禮物要給你。

解說

　　本題的兩個受詞已經出現：間接受詞 you 和直接受詞 a gift。動詞 brought 是 bring「帶來」的過去式。句型：bring ＋人＋物＝ bring ＋物＋ for ＋人。答案是 a 不是 d，因為第二空格後面的名詞是 Hawaii，這是地點不是受詞，所以前面用介系詞 from，表示「來自……（某地）」。如果動詞後面先提到「物」的受詞，就會用到介系詞：I brought a gift for you from Hawaii.。習慣上，動詞 bring 與介系詞 for 搭配。

17. 解答：**d**

英文 Her father didn't give **them** to her.
　　 Her father didn't give **it** to her.
　　 Her father didn't give **the money** to her.

中譯 她的父親不把它們給她。
　　 她的父親不把它給她。
　　 她的父親不把錢給她。

解說

　　a、b、c 三個選項都對，都是表示「物」的直接受詞。特別注意：直接受詞如果是代名詞，必須直接跟在動詞後面，這是唯一的位置。如果直接受詞是一般名詞，例如 money，位置可前可後，所以句子可改寫如下：Her father didn't give her the money.。但是 it 和 them 就無法這樣改寫。另外，習慣上，動詞 give 與介系詞 to 搭配。

18. 解答：**a**

英文 **Please show me to your teacher.**

中譯 請帶我去找你的老師。

解說

　　在「show ＋人＋ to / into 地點」的句型中，動詞 show 作「指引、帶領（某人到……）」解釋，空格內應填入受詞，所以答案選 a。選項 d 的 they 如果改成受格的 them，就可以選。注意，「to your teacher」指的是「到你的老師所在位置」，所以 your teacher 不是受詞，因為這裡的 to 引導出來的是「方向、方位」。例：The waiter showed me to the door.「服務人員送我到門口。」

英文　**Mrs. Baxter <u>read the children</u> a story <u>for Christmas</u>.**
　　　Mrs. Baxter <u>read</u> a story <u>to the children</u>.

中譯　貝克斯特太太在耶誕節唸故事給小朋友聽。
　　　貝克斯特太太唸故事給小朋友聽。

解說

　　第一空格後面的 a story 是表示「物」的直接受詞，選項中應該包含動詞與間接受詞（人）。本題選 a 或 b 都是正確答案。先看選項 a，第一空格填入動詞 read 與間接受詞 the children；第二空格填入 for Christmas，這是點出時間。再看選項 b，第一空格填入動詞 read，間接受詞（人）the children 放在第二空格，前面有介系詞 to。

英文　**Can you <u>lend</u> me <u>some</u> money?**

中譯　你可以借我一點錢嗎？

解說

　　空格前後的 you / me / money 點出了本句的主詞（you）與兩個受詞。第一空格後面是 me，因為動詞 lend 後面就是間接受詞，不需要介系詞，故答案選 b。如果 lend 後面先提表「事物」的間接受詞，句子可改寫如下：Can you lend some money to me?。注意介系詞要用 to。

08 情狀副詞

情狀副詞的定義

» 情狀副詞是副詞的一種，主要用來說明動作是如何進行或動作進行的狀態。

» 總的來說，副詞的主要功用是修飾動詞、副詞、形容詞或整個句子。但是，情狀副詞修飾的對象以動詞為主。

» 情狀副詞多半與形容做事方式、形容做事者心情的用字有關。例如：slowly（慢慢地）、proudly（驕傲地）、fast（迅速地）、carefully（謹慎地）、loudly（大聲地）等等。

情狀副詞的形成

» 情狀副詞的形成，是在形容詞的字尾加 ly。字尾變化有原則可循：

1. 直接在形容詞字尾加上 ly：

   quick → quickly（快速地）　　　　　sad → sadly（哀傷地）

   beautiful → beautifully（美麗地）　bad → badly（不好地）

2. 形容詞字尾是「子音＋ y」者，先去掉字尾 y，之後再加 ily：

   happy → happily（快樂地）　　　　easy → easily（輕易地）

   angry → angrily（憤怒地）　　　　lucky → luckily（幸運地）

3. 形容詞字尾是 -able 的，先去掉字尾 e，再加 y：

   comfortable → comfortably（舒適地）

   possible → possibly（可能地）

4. 形容詞和副詞同形：

   early（早）、fast（快速地）、late（晚；遲）、little（很少）等等。

5. 形容詞和副詞完全不同：

   good → well（良好地）

情狀副詞的用法

» 因為動詞是情狀副詞最主要的修飾對象，所以情狀副詞的位置最常放在動詞或動詞片語後面。
» 如果動詞後面沒有受詞（不需要受詞的動詞，稱作「不及物」動詞），情狀副詞就直接放在動詞後面。
» 如果動詞後面有受詞（需要受詞的動詞，稱作「及物」動詞），情狀副詞會出現在三個位置：動詞後面、動詞的受詞後面、動詞前面。

動詞不需要接受詞：情狀副詞直接放在動詞後面。

She sings beautifully.
她歌唱得很好聽。

Tim walks slowly.
提姆慢慢地走。

動詞需要接受詞：情狀副詞放在動詞的受詞後面或動詞前面。

She carried the box carefully.
＝She carefully carried the box.
她小心搬動箱子。
【說明】句中動詞 carried「搬動」的受詞是 the box。

Carl solved the problem easily.
＝Carl easily solved the problem.
卡爾輕易地解決了這個問題。
【說明】句中動詞 solved「解決」的受詞是 the problem。

如果動詞需要先接介系詞，再接受詞，情狀副詞可以放在受詞後面，或者動詞後面。

He looked **at** the boy angrily.
＝He looked angrily **at** the boy.
他很生氣地看著那個小男生。
【說明】angrily 形容看著他人的表情。動詞 looked 後面要接介系詞 at。

The man <u>shouted</u> at me <u>excitedly</u>.
＝The man <u>shouted</u> <u>excitedly</u> at me.

那名男子激動地對著我大叫。

【說明】動詞 shouted 後面要接介系詞 at，再接受詞 me。

遇到助動詞時，情狀副詞放在助動詞之後。

He can <u>hardly</u> walk.

他快要走不動了。

You should <u>honestly</u> answer my question.

你應該老實回答我的問題。

情狀副詞與形容詞

» 有些動詞本身既可當一般動詞，又可當連綴動詞，所以在使用上容易造成混淆，不知何時該用情狀副詞，何時該用形容詞。

情狀副詞和形容詞的判斷方式：從動詞的意義下手。

• 下列這些動詞最容易造成判斷上的困擾，因為它們本身有兩種身份：連綴動詞和一般動詞，但在意義上是有差別的。

	連綴動詞	一般動詞
look	看起來	看；注視
sound	聽起來；似乎	發出聲音
taste	嚐起來	品嚐
smell	聞起來	聞

• 判斷時，把握一個大原則：

1. 情狀副詞修飾一般動詞，說明的對象是動詞，重點放在形容動作是如何進行的。

2. 連綴動詞（例如：taste、smell、sound、look 等）需要有形容詞或名詞當補語，補語說明的對象是主詞，重點放在形容主詞的特質。

Karen looks happy.

凱倫<u>看起來</u>很高興。

【說明】形容詞 happy 修飾的對象是主詞 Karen，重點放在形容人的外在表情。

Karen <u>looks</u> <u>happily</u> at the dog.

凱倫很高興地<u>看著</u>這隻狗。

【說明】情狀副詞 happily 修飾的對象是動詞 looks，重點放在說明「看」這個動作是如何進行的。

I <u>tasted</u> the soup <u>carefully</u> because it was hot.

因為湯很燙，所以我<u>小心地品嚐</u>。

【說明】情狀副詞 carefully 修飾的對象是動詞 tasted，重點放在說明「嚐」這個動作如何進行—「很小心地」。

The soup <u>tasted</u> delicious.

這碗湯<u>嚐起來</u>很可口。

【說明】形容詞 delicious「美味的」，修飾的對象是主詞 the soup，形容湯的滋味。

The girl <u>smelled</u> the flower <u>excitedly</u>.

那個女孩興奮地<u>聞</u>著那朵花。

【說明】情狀副詞 excitedly 修飾的對象是動詞 smelled，重點放在「聞」這個動作如何進行。

The flower <u>smells</u> sweet.

這朵花<u>聞起來</u>很香。

【說明】形容詞 sweet「芳香的」修飾的對象是 the flower，重點在於說明花的特質。

題 目

1. Laurence walked too _____ for the others to keep up.
   a. quickly
   b. slow
   c. late
   d. slowly

2. If you would get up _____ you wouldn't always be _____ for work.
   a. early ; later
   b. earlier ; late
   c. early ; late
   d. Either b or c

3. _____, the exam wasn't _____ difficult.
   a. Luckily ; terrible
   b. Luckily ; very
   c. Fortunate ; terribly
   d. Lucky ; too

4. Look how _____ that dog sits and waits for its owner to return.
   a. nice
   b. nicely
   c. proper
   d. Either a or b

5. Alice sang so _____ that the others could barely hear her.
   a. softly
   b. quiet
   c. well
   d. little

6. The students _____ finished the test within the three-hour time limit.
   a. easy
   b. most easy
   c. easier
   d. easily

7. Doug carried the _____ boxes up the stairs one by one.
   a. heavy
   b. heavily
   c. softly
   d. largely

8. _____, the bus was a few minutes late, so we were able to catch it.
   a. Lucky
   b. Luckily
   c. Unlucky
   d. Likely

9. The exam looks very _____, so we should think _____ while doing it.
   a. easily ; carefully
   b. difficultly ; well
   c. difficult ; carefully
   d. hard ; careful

10. You must pet this dog very _____, or it may bite you.
    a. seriously
    b. gently
    c. early
    d. nervously

11. I was very _____ for school because I woke up _____ .
   a. lately ; late
   b. late ; lately
   c. early ; late
   d. late ; late

12. The elves in Santa's workshop _____ put the toys into the sleigh.
   a. busily
   b. hasty
   c. early
   d. None of the above

13. The dogs barked _____ every night, bothering the whole neighborhood.
   a. patiently
   b. loud
   c. noisily
   d. Either b or c

14. The broken bone felt _____ , but little Johnny never cried at all.
   a. pain
   b. painful
   c. painfully
   d. hurtfully

15. Why did you get here so _____?
   a. early
   b. late
   c. lately
   d. Either a or b

16. I can't play baseball very _____, but I'm good at basketball.
    a. good
    b. better
    c. well
    d. nicely

17. The house is _____ located near the Shilin MRT station.
    a. properly
    b. conveniently
    c. gladly
    d. None of the above

18. Oh my gosh! I'm _____ sorry.
    a. badly
    b. terribly
    c. well
    d. Either b or c

19. The work was done _____.
    a. nicely
    b. well
    c. messily
    d. All of the above

20. The band played _____, and the crowd loved it.
    a. loud
    b. loudly
    c. good
    d. Either a or b

解 析

英文 **Laurence walked too quickly for the others to keep up.**

中譯 勞倫斯走得太快了，其他人趕不上。

解說

　　句型：「too ＋形容詞／副詞＋ to V」作「太……所以無法……」解釋。too 是副詞，意思是「過於……」。至於 too 後面要接形容詞還是副詞，得看句中動詞是 be 動詞還是一般動詞。本題的動詞是 walked，還是一般動詞，所以 too 後面必須接副詞。如果是 be 動詞，too 後面則要接形容詞。例：The man is too old to work.「這位先生年紀太大，無法工作。」依照句意，答案選 a。又，for the others 中的介系詞 for 意為「對……而言」。

英文 **If you would get up earlier you wouldn't always be late for work.**
If you would get up early you wouldn't always be late for work.

中譯 如果你早點起床，就不會上班老是遲到。

解說

　　第一空格前面是動詞 get up，所以答案應該填入副詞。第二空格前面是 be 動詞，所以答案應填入形容詞。從這個方向判斷，選項 b 或 c 都正確。其中，選項 b 的 earlier 是副詞，這是從副詞 early 衍生而來的「副詞的比較級」。be late for 意為「……遲到」，例如：He was late for school this morning.「他今天早上上學遲到」。

英文 **Luckily, the exam wasn't very difficult.**

中譯 幸好，考試不會太難。

解說

　　第一空格應該填入副詞，副詞放在句首，用來修飾整個句子。第二空格應填入副詞，這是因為空格後有形容詞 difficult，修飾形容詞必須用副詞，very 就是表示「程度」的副詞，故答案選 b。

英文　Look how **nicely** that dog sits and waits for its owner to return.

中譯　你看那隻狗坐得好好的，等牠主人回來。

解說

　　空格前面是疑問詞 how，作「多麼的……」解釋，有強調的意味。how 後面可接副詞或形容詞，至於該選哪一個，關鍵在於句中使用的是一般動詞還是 be 動詞。本句使用一般動詞 sits / waits (for)，所以答案選 b，用副詞來修飾動詞，這是副詞的主要功用之一。

英文　Alice sang so **softly** that the others could barely hear her.

中譯　艾莉絲唱得太輕聲了，其他人幾乎聽不到她的歌聲。

解說

　　句型：「S＋V＋so＋形容詞／副詞＋that＋S＋V」作「太……以至於無法……」解釋。so 是副詞，後面要接形容詞還是副詞，要依據 so 前面的動詞判斷。如果是一般動詞，就用副詞。四個選項都是副詞，從後面的文意判斷「the others could barely hear her」，答案應選 a。選項 b 不合句意，因為 quiet 指的是「無聲狀態下」的安靜。

英文　The students **easily** finished the test within the three-hour time limit.

中譯　學生輕鬆地在三小時的時限內寫完了考卷。

解說

　　空格應該填入副詞來修飾後面的動詞 finished 的狀況，選項中只有 d 是副詞。

7. 解答：**a**

英文 Doug carried the <u>heavy</u> boxes up the stairs one by one.

中譯 道格把重重的箱子一個接一個搬到樓上。

解說

　　空格後面是名詞 boxes，所以答案應該是形容詞，故選 a。one by one 是副詞片語，作「逐一；陸續」解釋。

8. 解答：**b**

英文 <u>Luckily</u>, the bus was a few minutes late, so we were able to catch it.

中譯 幸好公車晚到了幾分鐘，我們才能趕上。

解說

　　空格應填入副詞。副詞置於句首用來修飾整個句子。從後面的句意判斷，答案應選 b。「S + be able to +原形 V」表示「能夠（做某事）」，able 是形容詞，作「能夠的」解釋。動詞 catch 是「追趕；趕上」的意思。

9. 解答：**c**

英文 The exam looks very <u>difficult</u>, so we should think <u>carefully</u> while doing it.

中譯 這次考試看起來很難，我們作答時應該要謹慎思考。

解說

　　因為第一空格前面有連綴動詞 looks，所以第一個答案必定是形容詞。very 是「程度副詞」，用來說明 difficult 到達什麼程度。第二空格前面有動詞，所以答案必定是副詞，用副詞來修飾動詞，故答案選 c。

英文　**You must pet this dog very <u>gently</u>, or it may bite you.**

中譯　你必須非常溫柔地撫摸這隻小狗，否則牠可能會咬你。

解說

　　空格必須填入副詞，用來說明動詞 pet 的狀態。四個選項都是副詞，但從句意判斷，答案應選 b。空格後面的 or 是連接詞，作「否則；要不然」解釋。

英文　**I was very <u>late</u> for school because I woke up <u>late</u>.**

中譯　我很晚才到學校上課，因為我很晚才起床。

解說

　　本題測驗重點 S + be late for + N，第一空格應填入形容詞。第二空格前面是動詞 woke up（原形動詞 wake up），所以答案應填入副詞。從詞性來看，選項 c 的兩個答案好像也可以選，但是句意不合。故答案應選 d。另外，because 是連接詞，用來連結兩個句子。

英文　**The elves in Santa's workshop <u>busily</u> put the toys into the sleigh.**

中譯　耶誕老人工作室裡的小精靈忙著把玩具放到雪橇上。

解說

　　空格後面是動詞 put「擺放」，所以答案應填入副詞。雖然選項 c 的 early 可當副詞，但與句意不合，故答案選 a。

13.

解答：**d**

英文　The dogs barked <u>loud</u> every night, bothering the whole neighborhood.
　　　The dogs barked <u>noisily</u> every night, bothering the whole neighborhood.

中譯　這群小狗每晚吠得震天響，打擾到整個社區。

解說

　　因為空格前面是動詞 barked，所以答案要填入副詞。選 a 與句意不合。選項 b 的 loud 既是副詞也是形容詞，當副詞時，意思和另一副詞 loudly 是一樣的，作「大聲地」解釋。故 b 和 c 都是正確答案。

14.

解答：**b**

英文　The broken bone felt <u>painful</u>, but little Johnny never cried at all.

中譯　雖然骨折的地方很痛，但小強尼從不哭。

解說

　　空格前面是與感官有關的連綴動詞，作「給……的感覺」解釋，連綴動詞後面要接形容詞，故選 b。本句的主詞是 the broken bone，而 the broken bone felt painful 指的是「腳傷帶給小強尼的感覺」。此外，at all 是副詞，作「一點也（沒……）」。

15.

解答：**d**

英文　Why did you get here so <u>early</u>?
　　　Why did you get here so <u>late</u>?

中譯　你為什麼這麼早就來了。
　　　你為什麼這麼晚才來？

解說

　　空格應該填入副詞，用來說明動詞 get「到達（某地）」的狀態。so 作「這麼的……」解釋，so 和 very 一樣都屬於「程度副詞」，用來說明形容詞的程度。從文法和句意來看，選項 a 或 b 都成立。注意：lately 和 late 雖然都是副詞，但意思不同，lately 指的是「這一陣子」。例：I haven't seen her lately.「我最近都沒看到她。」

英文　I can't play baseball very <u>well</u>, but I'm good at basketball.

中譯　我棒球打得不太好，但我對籃球很在行。

解說

　　空格應填入副詞，用以說明動詞 play 的狀態。選項 a 和 b 都是形容詞，無法修飾動詞。選 d 不合句意，故選 c。well 可指「表現出色；滿意地」。「S + be good at + N」表示「對……很擅長」。

英文　The house is <u>conveniently</u> located near the Shilin MRT station.

中譯　這棟房子位於士林捷運站附近，很方便。

解說

　　句型：S + be located in / near / on +地點「位在……」。當動詞 locate 作「位於……」解釋時，經常以被動語態表現，且主詞一定是表示地點的名詞。至於地點前面該用什麼介系詞，依照情況而定，原則上：in +大地點；on +小地點。前三個選項都是副詞，但以句意而言，b 才是正確答案。conveniently 用來說明動詞 be located 的狀況。

英文　Oh my gosh! I'm <u>terribly</u> sorry.

中譯　天哪！我非常抱歉。

解說

　　形容詞 sorry 前面需要有程度副詞來強調形容詞的狀況。從文法和句意，選項 c 是不合的。選項 a 的 badly 雖然也有「非常地」的意思，但通常與「需求；慾望」有關。例：He needs the money really badly.「他真的很需要錢。」terribly 在此的意思不是「恐怖地」，而是「非常地」，有加強語氣的意味。

英文
The work was done <u>nicely</u>.
The work was done <u>well</u>.
The work was done <u>messily</u>.

中譯
這工作做得漂亮。
這工作做得漂亮。
這工作做得亂七八糟！

解說

　　空格應該填入副詞，用來說明動詞 was done 的狀態。論文法和句意，前三個
選項都是答案。選項 a 和 b 的意思很接近，選項 c 的意思則完全不同。

英文
The band played <u>loud</u>, and the crowd loved it.
The band played <u>loudly</u>, and the crowd loved it.

中譯　這支樂團彈奏得很大聲，群眾為之瘋狂。

解說

　　空格應該填入副詞，用來說明動詞 played 的狀況。loud 可以當副詞，意思和另
一副詞 loudly 一樣，都作「吵雜地；大聲地」解釋。故選項 a 或 b 皆是正確答案。

09 反身代名詞

反身代名詞的定義與變化

» 反身代名詞強調主詞與受詞是同一人或同一體。

» 反身代名詞不能單獨作主詞。

» 反身代名詞是代名詞的一種，反身代名詞要根據人稱代名詞作變化：

	單	數	複	數
	主格	反身代名詞	主格	反身代名詞
第一人稱	I （我）	myself （我自己）	we （我們）	ourselves （我們自己）
第二人稱	you （你）	yourself （你自己）	you （你們）	yourselves （你們自己）
第三人稱	he（他） she（她） it（它）	himself（他自己） herself（她自己） itself（它自己）	they （他們）	themselves （他們自己）

反身代名詞的使用時機

反身代名詞當動詞或介系詞的受詞：動詞的作用者就是主詞本身，換言之，主詞和受詞是同一人。

I cut **myself** with a knife.

我被刀子割傷了。

【說明】動詞 cut 的受詞是主詞 I。

She fell off her bike but she didn't hurt **herself**.

她從腳踏車摔了下來，但是沒有受傷。

【說明】動詞 hurt 的受詞是主詞 she。

She looked at <u>herself</u> in the mirror.

她望著鏡中的自己。

【說明】動詞 look 作「注視；看」解釋時，後面要加介系詞 at，再加注視的對象，herself 是 at 的受詞。

> 強調用法：反身代名詞要強調主詞時，可以放在主詞後面或句尾。如果要強調受詞，要放在受詞後面。

I have do it <u>myself</u>.

＝I <u>myself</u> have to do it.

這件事我必須自己來。

I want to see the manger <u>himself</u>.

我想見經理本人。

【說明】反身代名詞 himself 強調的對象是 the manager。the manager 是 see 的受詞。

> 其他慣用語：反身代名詞若不限定指某人時，則寫成 oneself。通常，我們必須依據句中主詞，把 oneself 作轉換。

1. enjoy oneself 玩得開心

We went to Japan last week, and we <u>enjoyed ourselves</u> very much.

我們上個禮拜去日本玩，我們玩得非常盡興。

2. help oneself to ＋ N 請自行取用……

<u>Help yourself</u> to the salad.

請自行取用沙拉。

3. make oneself at home 不要拘束

Please <u>make yourself at home</u>.

請不要拘束。

4. talk to oneself 自言自語

She often <u>talks to herself</u> when she is alone.

她獨自一人的時候經常自言自語。

5. introduce oneself 自我介紹

You have to introduce <u>yourselves</u> at the meeting today.

你們今天必須在會議上自我介紹。

【說明】注意這裡的 yourselves 是複數。

題目

1. Jane and I truly enjoyed _____ at the party last week.
   a. themselves
   b. their selves
   c. ourselves
   d. herself and myself

2. I decided to buy _____ a gift for my birthday.
   a. me
   b. ourselves
   c. myself
   d. Either b or c

3. The old woman often talks to _____.
   a. herself
   b. myself
   c. yourself
   d. Either a or b

4. Don't help me! I can do it _____.
   a. myself
   b. by myself
   c. yourself
   d. Either a or b

5. Was it he _____ who painted this beautiful painting?
   a. himself
   b. hisself
   c. by himself
   d. Either a or c

6. I don't think you did this project _____. Did your parents help
   _____?
   a. yourself ; you
   b. myself ; you
   c. self ; yourself
   d. itself ; you

7. Please sit down and help _____ to the snacks on the table.
   a. yourself
   b. yourselves
   c. ourselves
   d. Either a or b

8. The cat was washing _____ carefully.
   a. its self
   b. itself
   c. by itself
   d. themselves

9. Try it _____ and see how easy it is.
   a. for yourself
   b. by yourself
   c. yourself
   d. Either a or c

10. My colleagues and I couldn't finish the task _____ and had to call
    in some help.
    a. myself
    b. themselves
    c. ourselves
    d. All of the above

11. A: I'm not coming out until you apologize!

B: Fine! Suit _____!

a. it yourself

b. me yourself

c. yourself

d. itself

12. The child cried, sulked and sat off by _____ for the rest of the day.

a. himself

b. herself

c. itself

d. Either a or b

13. He could see a little bit of _____ in the way his son bossed the others around.

a. himself

b. herself

c. myself

d. Either a or c

14. The solar heating unit will pay _____ in less than 4 years.

a. for itself

b. itself

c. its self

d. by itself

15. The fourth grade students organized the classroom party _____.

a. theyselves

b. themselves

c. theirselves

d. None of the above

16. If you don't want to pay someone to fix the sink, then fix it _____.
    a. itself
    b. himself
    c. yourself
    d. ourselves

17. Please make _____ at home. Your beds are in separate rooms at the end of the hall.
    a. yourself
    b. yourselves
    c. your self
    d. Either a or b

18. Mr. Jackson _____ to work every day.
    a. drives himself
    b. drives herself
    c. drives
    d. is driven himself

19. Imagine! It was the president _____ who walked into the room.
    a. himself
    b. herself
    c. itself
    d. Either a or b

20. I took a photo _____ using my cell phone camera.
    a. of me
    b. of myself
    c. itself
    d. Either a or b

解析

1.

英文 **Jane and I truly enjoyed <u>ourselves</u> at the party last week.**

中譯 我和珍上禮拜在派對上玩得很開心。

解說

所謂反身代名詞，指的是句中主詞和受詞是同一人或同一體。本句中，主詞是 Jane and I 兩人。只要主詞是包括「我（I）」在內，且人數在二人以上」，指的就是「我們（we）」，反身代名詞就要用 ourselves，故選 c。enjoy oneself 是慣用語，作「玩得很盡興」解釋。

2.

英文 **I decided to buy <u>myself</u> a gift for my birthday.**

中譯 我打算買個生日禮物送給自己。

解說

空格應填入反身代名詞。因為主詞是 I，所以答案選 c。

3.

英文 **The old woman often talks to <u>herself</u>.**

中譯 那位老太太經常自言自語。

解說

本句的主詞是 the old woman，這是第三人稱單數，代名詞用 she，反身代名詞用 herself，所以答案選 a。talk to oneself 是慣用語，意思是「自言自語」。

4. 解答：**d**

英文　Don't help me! I can do it <u>myself</u>.
　　　Don't help me! I can do it <u>by myself</u>.

中譯　不要幫我！這件事我可以自己來。

解說

　　空格應填入反身代名詞。主詞是 I，所以 a 是正確答案。選項 b 也是正確的：by oneself 是慣用語，作「獨自；靠自己」解釋。

5. 解答：**a**

英文　Was it he <u>himself</u> who painted this beautiful painting?

中譯　這一幅美麗畫作的畫家，就是他本人嗎？

解說

　　主詞是 he，所以反身代名詞要用 himself，故選 a。

6. 解答：**a**

英文　I don't think you did this project <u>yourself</u>. Did your parents help <u>you</u>?

中譯　我不認為這份作業是你自己完成的。你的父母親有沒有幫你做？

解說

　　本題第一句是兩個句子的結合，所以有兩個主詞和兩個動詞：「I don't think」＋「(that) you did this project...」，that 扮演連接詞的角色，引導出 I don't think 的內容。第一空格應該填入反身代名詞，但要注意與其對應的主詞不是 I，而是 you，反身代名詞要用 yourself，因為「(that) you did this project yourself」是 I don't think 的內容。第二空格前面有動詞 help，所以要填入受詞，故答案選 a。

英文　**Please sit down and help <u>yourself</u> to the snacks on the table.**
　　　Please sit down and help <u>yourselves</u> to the snacks on the table.

中譯　請坐下並自行取用桌上的點心。

解說

　　「help oneself to + N」是招待用語，表示「請自行（取用食物）；請自便……」。這是個以原形動詞起首（sit down）的祈使句，動詞前面加 please 表示禮貌。在祈使句的結構裡，表面上沒寫出主詞，但其實主詞隱身背後：you（你；你們）。祈使句是一種「一對一」或「一對多」的用語：第一人稱（I）對著第二人稱（you）說話，而且 you 可指「你」或「你們」。所以，反身代名詞用單數的 yourself 或複數的 yourselves 皆可，a 或 b 皆正確。

英文　**The cat was washing <u>itself</u> carefully.**

中譯　貓咪正小心地清潔自己的身體。

解說

　　本句主詞 the cat 屬於第三人稱，代名詞用 it，反身代名詞用 itself，所以答案選 b。

英文　**Try it <u>for yourself</u> and see how easy it is.**
　　　Try it <u>yourself</u> and see how easy it is.

中譯　你自己試試看，你會發現這很容易的。

解說

　　這是動詞起首的祈使句，隱藏的主詞是 you，反身代名詞是 yourself，故 c 是正確答案。a 也是正確答案，因為 for oneself 是一種慣用語，作「自己；親自」解釋。

英文　**My colleagues and I couldn't finish the task <u>ourselves</u> and had to call in some help.**

中譯　我和我同事無法自己完成這個工作，必須請人幫忙。

解說

　本句主詞有兩人以上：my colleagues and I。因為主詞包括 I 在內，所以從代名詞的角度來看，這是 we「我們」，反身代名詞要用 ourselves，故選 c。

英文　**A: I'm not coming out until you apologize!**
　　　B: Fine! Suit <u>yourself</u>!

中譯　A：除非你道歉，否則我不出來。
　　　B：好！隨你便！

解說

　suit oneself 是慣用語，作「隨……的意」，指的是隨某人意思行事。因為這是兩人對話，所以反身代名詞的 oneself 要改成 yourself，故選 c。句中的 until 是連接詞，作「到……為止」解釋，通常和否定句連用，本句即是一例。

英文　**The child cried, sulked and sat off by <u>himself</u> for the rest of the day.**
　　　The child cried, sulked and sat off by <u>herself</u> for the rest of the day.

中譯　那個小朋友哭鬧、生悶氣、一整天獨自坐在一旁。

解說

　主詞是 the child，空格前面有介系詞 by，可知這是個 by oneself 的慣用語，意思是「獨自；靠自己」。itself 通常是無生命事物的反身代名詞，不能選。題目中的 the child 到底是男是女，並不清楚，所以選項 a 或 b 皆可。「the rest of ＋ N」作「其餘的」解釋。

英文　He could see a little bit of <u>himself</u> in the way his son bossed the others around.

中譯　從他兒子對他人擺出一副上司的架子，他看到了些許自己的影子。

解說

　　只要確認句子的主詞，就知道反身代名詞該用哪個。本題的主詞是 he，反身代名詞用 himself，故選 a。himself 是介系詞 of 的受詞。

英文　The solar heating unit will pay <u>for itself</u> in less than 4 years.

中譯　太陽能供熱裝置不到四年將可獲利。

解說

　　for itself 是另一個與反身代名詞相關的慣用語，代替的對象一定是無生命的事物，作「（它）本身」解釋。在本題中，主詞是 the solar heating unit，是第三人稱單數，答案選 a。本題不可選 b，不合邏輯；如果選 b，表示 itself 是 pay 的受詞，但 the solar heating unit 沒有生命，不具備執行動作的能力。

英文　The fourth grade students organized the classroom party <u>themselves</u>.

中譯　四年級的學生自己在教室開了一場派對。

解說

　　從本題主詞 the fourth grade students 可知主詞有很多人，其代名詞用 they 表示，反身代名詞用 themselves，故選 b。

英文 If you don't want to pay someone to fix the sink, then fix it <u>yourself</u>.

中譯 如果你不想花錢找人修理水槽，那就自己修。

解說

　　主詞是 you，所以反身代名詞用 yourself，故選 c。本題使用了一種最常見的假設語氣：「If＋S＋V（現在式），S＋助動詞（will／may／might... etc.）＋原形動詞」。如果 If 子句使用動詞的現在式，表示假設的狀況未來有可能實現。例如：If you tell me the truth, I'll help you.「如果你告訴我實話，我會幫你。」主要子句通常以「助動詞＋原形動詞（例如：I'll help you.）」表現，但這不是絕對，像本題的主要子句用的是祈使句 then fix it，這在假設用法也是很常見的。

英文 Please make <u>yourselves</u> at home. Your beds are in separate rooms at the end of the hall.

中譯 請不要客氣。你們的床位就在走廊盡頭的獨立房間。

解說

　　與反身代名詞相關的片語很多，make oneself at home 是其中之一，意思是「不要拘束」。本句是祈使句，反身代名詞要用單數還是複數，須根據後面的 your beds 判斷：beds 是複數，表示人數不只一人，所以選 b。又，單看 at home 這個片語，它可以作「輕鬆；自在」解釋。

英文 Mr. Jackson <u>drives</u> to work every day.

中譯 傑克森先生每天開車上班。

解說

　　動詞 drive 當「開車」解釋時，不需要受詞（亦即：drive 是不及物動詞），所以後面不可能出現反身代名詞。只有需要受詞的動詞（及物動詞），後面才會出現反身代名詞（反身代名詞是動詞的受詞）。所以答案選 c 的一般動詞，動詞的現在式表示日復一日的習慣。

英文　**Imagine! It was the president <u>himself</u> who walked into the room.**
　　　Imagine! It was the president <u>herself</u> who walked into the room.

中譯　想像一下！走進這個房間的是總統本人。

解說

　　本句主詞是 the president，這是第三人稱單數，因為不知道性別，所以代名詞用 he 或 she 皆可，反身代名詞用 himself 或 herself，都正確。

英文　**I took a photo <u>of myself</u> using my cell phone camera.**

中譯　我用手機的照相功能自拍。

解說

　　「take a picture / photo of + N」表示「幫（某人／某物）拍照」。例：I took a photo of my friend in the park.「我在公園幫我朋友拍了張照。」my friend 是 of 的受詞。如果拍照的對象正是自己（I），那麼介系詞（of）的受詞要用反身代名詞（myself）。故選 b。

10 不定代名詞、所有代名詞及雙重所有格

不定代名詞

» 不定代名詞是代名詞的一種，顧名思義，不定代名詞代替的對象，並不是特定的人或事物。

» 在「不定代名詞 one, both, either, neither, none, all, none... ＋ of N」的句型裡，動詞的單複數由不定代名詞決定。

下列不定代名詞的動詞要用單數

anybody	任何人	everybody	每個人
anyone	任何人	everyone	每個人
anything	任何事	everything	每件事

nobody	沒有人	somebody	某人
no one (none)	沒有人	someone	某人
nothing	沒有什麼事或物	something	某件事

Everyone understands the importance of education.
每個人都知道教育的重要。

Can I do anything for you?
有什麼事情我可以幫你的嗎？

Someone was in this room before we came in.
在我們進來這個房間之前，有人來過。

> one / ones：one 代替前面提過的名詞，可避免相同名詞重複
> 使用。如果代替的對象是單數名詞，就用 one；如果代替的
> 對象是複數名詞，就用 ones。

"This cup is dirty. Can I have a clean <u>one</u>?"
「這只杯子髒了。可以給我乾淨的嗎？」（one 代替 cup）

My gloves are worn out. I need to buy new <u>ones</u>.
我的手套已經磨損了。我得買一雙新的。（ones 代替 gloves）

some / any

- some 當代名詞，泛指「一些；若干」，用於肯定句，代替可數或不可數名詞。
  some 除了當代名詞，還身兼形容詞的功用。
- any 當代名詞，泛指「任一（事物）」，用於疑問句或否定句，代替可數或不可數名詞。和 some 一樣，any 本身也可以當形容詞。

If you need more paper, I will bring you <u>some</u>.
如果你需要更多紙張，我可以拿一些給你。（some 是代名詞）

"Is there <u>any</u> cookies?" "Yes, there are <u>some</u> in the kitchen."
「還有餅乾嗎？」「有，廚房還有一些。」
【說明】這裡的 some 是代名詞，any 是形容詞，修飾後面的 cookies。

I need <u>some</u> folders. Do you have <u>any</u>?
我需要一些文件夾。你還有嗎？
【說明】這裡的 some 是形容詞，修飾後面的 folders。any 是代名詞。

both / either / neither：用於兩者

- 代名詞 both 表示「兩者都……」，當複數，用在肯定句。

I like Karen and Cathy. <u>Both</u> are my good friends.
我喜歡凱倫和凱西。兩個都是我的好朋友。（both 作代名詞）

<u>Both</u> his parents live in Japan. → both 作形容詞
＝<u>Both</u> of his parents live in Japan. → both 作代名詞
他的雙親都住在日本。

- 代名詞 either 表示「兩者任何一個」，當單數用。

"Would you like tea or coffee?" "Either will do."

「你想喝茶還是咖啡？」「哪一種都可以。」（either 作代名詞）

You can sit on either side.

你坐哪一邊都可以。（either 作形容詞）

Either you or Nancy has to do the washes.

你和南西當中有一人必須洗碗。

【說明】either A or B 表示「不是 A 就是 B」，動詞的單複數由最接近的名詞決定。

- 代名詞 neither 表示「兩者皆非……」，neither 本身具否定意味，動詞通常用單數。

I have two computers, but neither works properly.

我有兩部電腦，但是沒有一部運作是正常的。（neither 作代名詞）

I was looking for my Chinese and English dictionaries. But I could find neither book on the self.

我一直找我的中文和英文字典，但是我在架上一本也找不到。（neither 作形容詞）

Neither my mother nor my father is at home in the daytime.

白天的時候，我爸和我媽都不在家。

【說明】neither A nor B 表示「A 也不……B 也不……」，動詞的單複數由最接近的名詞決定。

all / none：用於三者以上

- 代名詞 all 表示「一切；全部」。all 也可以當形容詞。

All the eggs were broken. → all 作形容詞
＝All of the eggs were broken. → all 作代名詞

蛋全都破了。

All of the students have to stay after school. → all 作代名詞
＝All the students have to stay after school. → all 作形容詞

所有的學生放學後都必須留下。

• 代名詞 none 表示「誰也沒有」。動詞用單複數皆可。none 不當形容詞。

None of my friends **are / is** married.
我的朋友沒有人是已婚的。

> **each / every**：都作「每一個；各自」表示，動詞用單數。但是，只有 **each** 身兼代名詞和形容詞的功用。**every** 只能當形容詞。

Each of the books on the self is mine.
架上的每本書都是我的。（each 作代名詞）

Each / Every painting in the store is on sale for 100 dollars.
店裡的每一幅畫都百元特價。（each / every 作形容詞）

所有格代名詞

» 所有格代名詞是代名詞的一種，形式上是「所有格＋名詞」。

» 和代名詞一樣，所有格代名詞用來代替前面已經提過的名詞，只是這個被代替的對象，屬於他人所有，是他人的所有物。

» 所有格代名詞的雙重身份：所有格兼代名詞。注意：所有格代名詞是「代名詞」，所以後面不可接名詞。

	單 數		複 數	
	主格	所有格代名詞	主格	所有格代名詞
第一人稱	I （我）	**mine** **（我的）**	we （我們）	**ours** **（我們的）**
第二人稱	you （你）	**yours** **（你的）**	you （你們）	**yours** **（你們的）**
第三人稱	he（他） she（她） it（它） Jessie（傑西） 或其他人名	**his（他的）** **hers（她的）** **its（它的）** **Jessie's** **（傑西的）**	they （他們）	**theirs** **（他們的）** **Jessie's** **（傑西的）**

» 所有格代名詞 → 所有格＋名詞

It's my book.　　　→　　It's mine.

這是我的書。　　　　　　這是我的。

It's our house.　　→　　It's ours.

這是我們的房子。　　　　這是我們的。

It's her watch.　　→　　It's hers.

這是她的手錶。　　　　　這是她的。

I gave him my address, and he gave me his.

我給了他我的地址，他也給了我他的。

【說明】句中的 his 指的是 his address。特別注意 his 這個字：既可以當所有格，又可以當所有代名詞。

Your room is as large as mine.

你的房間和我的一樣大。

【說明】句中的 mine 指的是 my room。

雙重所有格

» 在「名詞1＋of＋名詞2」結構中，「of＋名詞」本是所有格的一種表示方法，如果第二個名詞是所有格代名詞，這就形成了所謂的「雙重所有格」。

» 第二個名詞在數量上，超過第一個名詞，這種句型是一種「範圍的限定」。

一般名詞＋ of ＋所有格代名詞

Tom and Tim are classmates of mine.

湯姆和提姆是我的同班同學。（我的同學不只這兩人）

Jay and Jason are neighbors of hers.

杰和傑森是她的鄰居。（她的鄰居不只這兩人）

a, some, each, most, neither, several... ＋名詞＋ of ＋所有格代名詞

• 名詞前面可以加上冠詞、形容詞、數量詞等進行範圍限定。

• 動詞的單複數由 of 前面的名詞決定。

A friend of mine has gone to Japan.

我有一個朋友去了日本。（mine 指的是 my friends）

This tool of yours is useful.

你這個工具很實用。（yours 指的是 your tools）

Any friend of hers is welcome at the party

她歡迎任何朋友參加派對。（hers 指的是 her friends）

Several books of Chris's are missing.

克里斯有幾本書弄丟了。（Chris's 指的是 Chris's books）

題 目

1. If you plan to spend the weekend there, you'll need to bring _____ money.
   a. many
   b. some
   c. a
   d. any

2. You can choose _____ seat you like.
   a. a
   b. any
   c. some
   d. Either a or b

3. _____ of the students passed the test, but _____ of them didn't.
   a. Most ; some
   b. Any ; most
   c. Much ; many
   d. Either a or b

4. _____ rain _____ snow will keep the postmen from their appointed rounds.
   a. Either ; or
   b. Neither ; nor
   c. Not ; or
   d. Either a or b

5. Neither the children nor Francis _____ broccoli.
   a. eaten
   b. eats
   c. don't eat
   d. Either a or b

6. Either one bear or several raccoons _____ going to live in this caged enclosure.

    a. are

    b. is

    c. was

    d. Either a or b

7. Neither Vance nor his sister _____ going to the party.

    a. are

    b. is

    c. isn't

    d. Either a or b

8. Both sugar _____ salt _____ bad for you.

    a. and ; is

    b. as well as ; are

    c. or ; are

    d. and ; are

9. I don't know if anybody _____ going.

    a. is

    b. are

    c. were

    d. will

10. _____ of these overdue customers _____ very much from us.

    a. None ; buy

    b. None ; buys

    c. Not one ; buy

    d. Either a or c

11. Some of the money is _____, but the rest _____ theirs.

    a. ours ; is

    b. his ; are

    c. mine ; are

    d. the Joneses ; is

12. Peter's wish may come true, but I doubt _____ will.

    a. Jess'

    b. Jess's

    c. Jesses

    d. Jesses'

13. That dog of _____ nearly bit me yesterday.

    a. hers

    b. your's

    c. Johns

    d. None of the above

14. Any friend of _____ is a friend of _____.

    a. him ; mine

    b. me ; he

    c. his ; mine

    d. None of the above

15. Some friends of my _____ are coming over to play poker.

    a. sister

    b. sister's

    c. sisters

    d. Either a or b

16. An admirer of _____ was caught sneaking into her _____
    wedding.
    a. her ; friend's
    b. she ; friends'
    c. hers ; friend's
    d. hers ; friends

17. A second cousin of _____ works for NASA as an astronaut.
    a. we
    b. ours
    c. us
    d. All of the above

18. The _____ property is one of the largest in the area.
    a. Smith
    b. Smiths'
    c. Smith's
    d. Either a or b

19. We're going over to _____ apartment for dinner. Would you like to
    come?
    a. the Lins'
    b. the Lin's
    c. Mr. Lin
    d. None of the above

20. Almost _____ person in the room had seen one of her movies.
    a. none
    b. every
    c. all
    d. both

解析

1.
解答：**b**

英文 If you plan to spend the weekend there, you'll need to bring <u>some</u> money.

中譯 你如果打算週末待在那裡，你得帶些錢。

解說

　　空格後面是 money，money 是不可數名詞，所以選項 a 與 c 都不能考慮，因為 many 和 a 後面必須接可數名詞。而 any 雖然可以修飾單、複數名詞，但常用在疑問句或否定句，例：Do you have any money?「你手邊有錢嗎？」some 可以修飾單數或複數名詞，用在肯定句，所以答案選 b。

2.
解答：**d**

英文 You can choose <u>a</u> seat you like.
You can choose <u>any</u> seat you like.

中譯 你可以挑個你喜歡的位子。
你可以挑任何你喜歡的位子。

解說

　　空格後面的 seat「座位」是可數名詞，在這裡用單數，前面用 a 或 any 皆可，any 可以修飾單數或複數名詞，選 a 或 b 都對。選項 c 的 some 只能修飾複數名詞，所以不能選。

3.
解答：**a**

英文 <u>Most</u> of the students passed the test, but <u>some</u> of them didn't.

中譯 大多數的學生考試都過了，但是有些人不及格。

解說

　　兩個空格必須填入與數量有關的代名詞。根據文意，答案選 a。選項 c 的問題出在 much 只能修飾不可數名詞。選項 b 與 c 皆不合句意。

4.

英文 **Neither rain <u>nor</u> snow will keep the postmen from their appointed rounds.**

中譯 無論是下雨還是下雪，郵差還是按照既定路線送信。

解說

選項 a 的 either... or 表示兩者之中，有一個是成立的。neither... nor 是兩者全否定，按照題意，答案應選 b，表示風雨無阻，照樣完成工作。動詞 keep... from ＋ N / V-ing 的意思是「阻礙（人）不能（做某事）」。例：The heavy rain kept her from going mountain climbing.「大雨使得她無法爬山。」

5.

英文 **Neither the children nor Francis <u>eats</u> broccoli.**

中譯 孩子和法蘭西絲都不吃花椰菜。

解說

對等連接詞 neither... nor 本身具有否定意味，作「兩者都不……」解釋。如果用來連接主詞，必須根據「就近原則」，換言之，必須由最靠近動詞的主詞來決定單、複數。本題的 neither... nor 連接了兩個主詞 the children 和 Francis，最接近動詞的主詞是 Francis，這是人名，表第三人稱單數，所以動詞用 eats，故答案選 b。值得注意的是，在 neither... nor 非正式用法中，動詞一律使用複數的例子也是有的，但並不常見。

6.

英文 **Either one bear or several raccoons <u>are</u> going to live in this caged enclosure.**

中譯 會被關在這個圍場的，不是一頭熊，就是幾隻浣熊。

解說

連接詞 either... or 用來連接兩個主詞 one bear 和 several raccoons，主詞一個是單數，另一個是複數，此時採「就近原則」：由最接近動詞的主詞來決定動詞該用單數還是複數。本題中，raccoons 距離動詞位置最近，所以動詞用複數，答案選 a。

7.

解答：**b**

英文 **Neither Vance nor his sister <u>is</u> going to the party.**

中譯 凡斯和他的姐姐都不會參加派對。

解說

　　對等連接詞 neither... nor 連接了兩個主詞 Vance 和 his sister，根據「就近原則」，最接近動詞的是 his sister，故答案選 b。此外，本題使用 go 的進行式表未來：go 是「來去動詞」的一種，習慣上，來去動詞以「進行式表未來」。其他常見的來去動詞還包括：come / leave / visit / leave for「前往（某地）」等等。例：I'm leaving for Japan next Friday.「我下星期五將前往日本。」

8.

解答：**d**

英文 **Both sugar <u>and</u> salt <u>are</u> bad for you.**

中譯 糖和鹽對你都沒好處。

解說

　　對等連接詞 both... and 表示「兩者都是」，主詞是複數，所以動詞也用複數，故答案選 d。片語「be bad for ＋某人／某事」，表示「對……有害處」。例：Drinking is bad for your health.「喝酒有害健康。」

9.

解答：**a**

英文 **I don't know if anybody <u>is</u> going.**

中譯 我不知道有誰會去？

解說

　　不定代名詞 anybody 視為單數，動詞也必須用單數，故答案選 a。

10.

解答： **a**

英文 None of these overdue customers <u>buy</u> very much from us.

中譯 那些欠款未還客戶的消費都不是很高。

解說

第一空格要填入 none，作「一個也沒有」解釋，這是表示「全數否定」的不定代名詞，因為全數被否定，所以主詞是複數，動詞也要用複數。故選 a。

11.

解答： **a**

英文 Some of the money is <u>ours</u>, but the rest <u>is</u> theirs.

中譯 這些錢有一部分是我們的，但其他的都是他們的。

解說

第一空格要填入所有格代名詞，第二空格要填入動詞。前面提到了 some of the money「有一些錢」，money 是不可數名詞，動詞必須用單數 is。後面的 the rest「其餘的錢」是 the rest of the money 的簡略說法，動詞要用單數，故答案選 a。選項 b 和 c 前半的答案是正確的，問題出在後半部的動詞用了複數。選項 d 的問題出在 the Joneses 要改成 the Joneses'（所有格代名詞）。

12.

解答： **b**

英文 Peter's wish may come true, but I doubt Jess's will.

中譯 彼得的願望可能會實現，但我不相信潔絲的也會實現。

解說

人名的所有格代名詞的寫法是：先加上所有格符號，再加 s，所以答案選 b。

13.

英文 **That dog of <u>hers</u> nearly bit me yesterday.**

中譯 她養的那隻狗昨天差一點咬了我。

解說

　　本題測驗雙重所有格的用法，空格後面要填入所有格代名詞。只有 a 是正確答案。句子還原：That dog of <u>hers</u>（= her dogs）nearly bit me yesterday.。從句意判斷，那隻狗只是她養的眾多狗兒其中一隻。在雙重所有格的結構裡「N（一般名詞）+ of + N（所有代名詞）」，在數量上，所有格代名詞一定多於 of 前面的名詞，因此，雙重所有格可說是一種「限定範圍」的句型。

14.

英文 **Any friend of <u>his</u> is a friend of <u>mine</u>.**

中譯 他的朋友就是我的朋友。

解說

　　本題測驗雙重所有格的用法。兩空格皆要填入所有格代名詞，故選 c，於是形成了 any friend of <u>his</u>（= his friends）（括弧內的 his 是所有格，括弧外的 his 是所有格代名詞）和 a friend of mine（= my friends）。本句的動詞單複數由 of 前面的 any friend 決定，所以是 is。

15.

英文 **Some friends of my <u>sister's</u> are coming over to play poker.**

中譯 我姐有幾個朋友要來我家玩撲克牌。

解說

　　本題測驗雙重所有格，答案選 b。主詞的部分：some friends of <u>my sister's</u>（= my sister's friends 括弧內的 my sister's 是所有格）。言下之意，姐姐有許多朋友，這些是其中一些。本句的動詞單、複數由 of 前面的 some friends 決定。

16.

英文 **An admirer of <u>hers</u> was caught sneaking into her friend's wedding.**

中譯 她有一個仰慕者偷偷混進她朋友的婚禮被逮了。

解說

　　本題第一空格測驗雙重所有格的用法，第二空格測驗所有格。答案應選 c。於是第一空格形成了 an admirer of <u>hers</u>（＝ her admirers），按語意，這個仰慕者是眾多仰慕者「其中之一」。動詞的單、複數由 of 前面的 an admirer 決定，所以動詞用過去式單數 was，而不是 were。

17.

英文 **A second cousin of <u>ours</u> works for NASA as an astronaut.**

中譯 我們的二表弟是美國太空總署的太空人。

解說

　　本題測驗雙重所有格的用法，答案選 b。本題的主詞是：a second cousin of <u>ours</u>（our cousins），表示我們家的表兄弟不只一個，二表弟只是「其中之一」。動詞的單、複數由介系詞 of 前面的 a second cousin 決定，所以動詞用單數 works。work for ＋（公司、企業）表示「在（公司、企業）上班」。例：Jay works for an oil company.「杰在一家石油公司上班。」

18.

英文 **The <u>Smith</u> property is one of the largest in the area.**
The <u>Smiths'</u> property is one of the largest in the area.

中譯 史密斯家的房地產是這一帶最富有的。

解說

　　本題測驗重點：姓氏的所有格寫法。空格前面有定冠詞 the，Smith「史密斯」是姓氏，the Smiths 指的是「史密斯一家人」；如果 the Smiths 要用所有格表示，在後面加上所有格符號即可：the Smiths'「史密斯一家人的」。選項 b 是正確答案。此外，選項 a 也是正確答案，這裡的 Smith 當一般名詞，如形容詞一般修飾後面的名詞 property。例：The Lin family is moving to Taipei next month.「林家下個月要搬到台北。」

英文　**We're going over to <u>the Lins'</u> apartment for dinner. Would you like to come?**

中譯　我們要去林家用晚餐。你想去嗎？

解說

　　本題測驗重點：姓氏的所有格寫法。空格應填入所有格，正確答案是 a。the Lins 的意思是「林家一家人」，要變成所有格，在後面加上所有格符號即可。選項 c 如果改成 Mr. Lin's，就可以選。

英文　**Almost <u>every</u> person in the room had seen one of her movies.**

中譯　這房裡的每個人幾乎都看過她的電影。

解說

　　空格後面是單數名詞 person「人」，所以答案只能選 b 的 every「每一」。選項 A 的 none 是代名詞，後面不可能接名詞。選項 c 的 all 表示「全體」，只能修飾複數名詞。選項 d 的 both 表示「兩者」，所以也不能選。

11 現在完成式

現在完成式的意義與使用時機

» 從時間的角度來看，現在完成式強調「過去與現在的關係」，表示某一動作或事件「從過去到目前為止」都還是事實、且有效力。

» 現在完成式的使用時機：

1. 表示到目前為止的經驗。

2. 表示到目前為止仍繼續的動作或狀態。

3. 完成式經常和下列副詞連用：already, just, never, yet, before, once, several times ...

現在完成式的結構：S ＋ have / has ＋ Vpp（過去分詞）

I / we / they / you	have	cleaned finished done
she / he / it	has	bought taken...

• 過去分詞的字尾變化：

A. 規則變化：

1. 直接在動詞後面加上 ed。例如：

enjoy → enjoyed（享受）　　　practice → practiced（練習）

clean → cleaned（清理）

2. 字尾是「子音＋y」：去 y 再加 ied。例如：

study → studied（學習）　　　try → tried（嘗試）

cry → cried（哭泣）

3. 字尾是「短母音＋子音」：重複字尾再加 ed。例如：

plan → planned（計畫）　　　drop → dropped（掉落）

stop → stopped（停止）

B. 不規則變化：拼法呈不規則變化的過去分詞，必須特別背下來。例如：

bring → brought（帶來） think → thought（思考）

write → written（書寫）

- 現在完成式經常用縮寫表示：

肯定：I / we / they / you **have Vpp.** → **I've / they've / you've Vpp.**

she / he / it **has Vpp.** → **she's / he's / it's Vpp.**

否定：I / we / they / you **haven't Vpp.**

she / he / it **hasn't Vpp.**

I've lived in this house for ten years.

我在這棟房子已經住了十年了。

She hasn't finished her work yet.

她還沒完成工作。

現在完成式的使用時機

- 表示到目前為止的經驗：

I have never ridden a horse.

我從沒騎過馬。

She has visited Greece twice.

她去過希臘兩次。

- 表示某種狀態的持續：

My family have / has lived in Taipei for ten years.

我家在台北住了十年。（現在還住在那裡）

I've lost my key.

我丟了鑰匙。（到現在還沒找到）

- 表示到目前為止完成的動作：

I have just finished my homework.

我剛剛做完功課了。

He has already come.

他已經來了。

have / has gone 和 have / has been 的不同

- have gone to ＋地點：表示人到了某地，人「現在還在那裡」。
- has been to ＋地點：表示「曾去過某地」，但人現在已經不在那裡，強調目前為止的「經驗」。

He has gone to Swiss.
他已經去瑞士了。（現在人還在瑞士）

He has been to Swiss.
他以前去過瑞士。（現在人不在瑞士）

現在完成式與 since 或 for 的搭配

- 現在完成式經常與 since 和 for 連用，用來表示某事持續的時間或經驗有多久。
- since 表「時間的起點」，作「從……一直；自從……以來」解釋。如果當連接詞，後面接句子；如果當介系詞，後面接表示時間的名詞。
- for 表示「一段時間」。for 是介系詞，後面接的時間通常以複數表示。

> S ＋ have / has ＋過去分詞 (Vpp) ＋ since ＋ S ＋ V（用過去式）
> since ＋ N（表時間的名詞）
> for ＋一段時間（複數名詞）

- 與現在完成式連用，無論用 since 或 for 表達時間的長短皆可，但是，要注意後面接的是句子還是片語。
- since 當連接詞時，後面接句子，注意 since 子句中的動詞必須用過去式。

He has lived in Taipei since he graduated from university.
他從大學畢業後就一直住在台北。（since 當連接詞）

He has lived in Taipei since 2001.
他從 2001 年起就一直住在台北。（since 當介系詞）

He has lived in Taipei for seven years.
他在台北已經住了七年了。（for 當介系詞）

I have studied English since I was ten years old.
我從十歲開始學英語。（since 當連接詞）

I have studied English <u>since</u> last year.

我從去年開始學英文。（since 當介系詞）

I have studied English <u>for</u> ten months.

我英文已經學了十個月了。（for 當介系詞）

與現在完成式相關的問句

1. 以疑問句為起首的問句：

How long have / has ＋ S ＋ V?「做／在……有多久了？」

- 在完成式問句前面加上疑問詞 how long「多久」，是用來詢問他人「做某事的時間有多長」。
- 回答時，用現在完成式，通常會使用 since 或 for 來表達時間的長短。
- 遇到以疑問詞為起首的問句時，回答時不須用 yes / no。

問：<u>How long</u> have you known Erin?
　　你認識艾琳多久了？

答：I've known her <u>for many years</u>.
　　我認識她好幾年了。

問：<u>How long</u> has she lived in London?
　　她在倫敦住多久了？

答：She has lived there <u>since last year</u>.
　　她從去年開始住在那裡。

2. 以 Has / Have 為起首的問句：

Have ＋ I / you / we / they ＋過去分詞？
Has ＋ she / he / it ＋過去分詞？

簡答：Yes, 主詞＋ has. / have.
　　　No, 主詞＋ haven't. / hasn't.

- 這類問句的重點在於「經驗」，詢問他人「到目前為止是否做過某事」。

- 這類問句經常和副詞 ever, never 連用，放在主詞之後。
- 回答時，須用 yes / no 回答，動詞同樣要用現在完成式。簡答或完整回答皆可。

問：Have you ever read this novel?
　　你看過這本小說嗎

答：Yes, I've read it twice.
　　有的，我看過兩次。

問：Has Carol been to Italy?
　　凱蘿去過義大利嗎？

答：No, she hasn't.
　　不，她從沒去過。

No. she hasn't been to Italy.
不，她從沒去過義大利。

題 目

1. Have you _____ here for a long time?
   a. been living
   b. live
   c. living
   d. Either a or b

2. I've _____ on you. I'm sorry.
   a. giving up
   b. give up
   c. given up
   d. gave up

3. Doris _____ a letter to her sister, but hasn't _____ it.
   a. write ; mailed
   b. has written ; sent
   c. wrote ; send
   d. had written ; sent

4. They have _____ their son in London twice.
   a. visit
   b. visiting
   c. been visiting
   d. visited

5. I haven't _____ you _____ last year.
   a. seen ; since
   b. been seen ; since
   c. seen ; for
   d. been seeing ; in

6. I _____ UFOs _____ times.
   a. had see ; three
   b. have seen ; many
   c. see ; two
   d. did see ; few

7. I have _____ that band before, but I can't remember their style.
   a. heard
   b. been hearing
   c. heard of
   d. Either a or c

8. Randy _____ found the map, so we _____ start the adventure.
   a. has ; can
   b. hasn't ; can't
   c. have ; can
   d. Either a or b

9. _____ your homework? It's already 9:00.
   a. Have you finished
   b. Haven't you finished
   c. Did you finish
   d. All of the above

10. Frank has worked at the company _____ 10 months.
   a. for
   b. since
   c. before
   d. after

11. Twenty years ago, people _____ more.

    a. read

    b. have read

    c. have been reading

    d. haven't read

12. _____ they _____ the gym yet?

    a. Has ; entered

    b. Have ; entering

    c. Have ; entered

    d. Are ; enter

13. How long have you _____ here?

    a. been

    b. been waiting

    c. waiting

    d. Either a or b

14. How many times _____ you _____ Ireland?

    a. have ; been

    b. have ; been to

    c. did ; went to

    d. did ; be to

15. _____ three days, the sailors _____ hungry and thirsty.

    a. since ; been

    b. for ; are being

    c. since ; are

    d. for ; have been

16. Sarah _____ her dinner, so she can't have any dessert.
    a. hasn't finished
    b. wasn't eaten
    c. hadn't had
    d. hasn't ate

17. We've _____ a dog _____ about five years.
    a. own ; for
    b. having ; since
    c. gotten ; in
    d. had ; for

18. I _____ play golf last summer.
    a. haven't
    b. didn't
    c. have
    d. had

19. Jason _____ the password, so he can't log into his email account.
    a. has forgotten
    b. hasn't remember
    c. remembered
    d. has forgot

20. I've _____ my photography portfolio online, but I'm not finished yet.
    a. put
    b. putted
    c. been putting
    d. been put

解析

1.

英文 **Have you been living here for a long time?**

中譯 你在這裡住很久了嗎？

解說

　　本題測驗現在完成進行式。現在完成進行式的組成要素：S ＋ has / have ＋ been ＋ V-ing。答案應選 a。注意：been 是 be 動詞的過去分詞，而 V-ing 指的是一般動詞的現在分詞。

2.

英文 **I've given up on you. I'm sorry.**

中譯 我對你已經死心了。對不起。

解說

　　本題測驗現在完成式。動詞片語「give up on ＋某人／事」表示「對……不抱指望」。其中 I've 是 I have 的縮略語，空格應該填入過去分詞，與 I've 形成現在完成式，故 c 是正確答案。

3.

英文 **Doris has written a letter to her sister, but hasn't sent it.**

中譯 朵莉絲已經寫了一封信要給她妹妹，但還沒寄。

解說

　　本題測驗現在完成式。從第二空格前面有 hasn't，可知兩個空格應當填入現在完成式。故選 b。第一空格也可以填入選項 c 的過去式 wrote，表示「信寫完了」，寫信的動作結束了；但後面的 send 一定要改成過去分詞的 sent，現在完成式強調「過去與現在的關係」：表示信雖寫好了（過去式 wrote），但「到現在為止」還沒寄出（hasn't sent）。

4.　解答：d

英文 They have <u>visited</u> their son in London twice.

中譯 他們已經去了倫敦兩次看他們的兒子。

解說

　　本題測驗現在完成式。空格前面有 have，空格應填入過去分詞，現在完成式強調「一段時間的穩定狀態」，故答案選 d。選 c 會不合邏輯，因為 c 的時態是現在完成進行式（現在完成式＋進行式），強調「動作持續不斷進行中」、「一直都在……」。以 visit「探訪」這個動作本身的意思來看，人不可能一直處在這種狀態。適合用現在完成進行式表現的動詞，通常本身隱含「持續進行」的意味，例如：study（學習）／work（工作）／live（居住）／teach（教書）／stand（站著）／wait（等候）／rain（下雨）／play（遊戲）等等。例：He has been studying English for six years.「他已經學英語六年了。」

5.　解答：a

英文 I haven't <u>seen</u> you <u>since</u> last year.

中譯 我從去年起再也沒看過你了。

解說

　　本題測驗現在完成式與介系詞 since 的搭配。since 表示動作或事件進行的時間長短。第一空格前面是 haven't，由此可知空格應該填入 see 的過去分詞 seen。第二空格後面是 last year，前面要接表示時間起點的 since，不能用 for，因為 for 後面要接「一段時間」，時間用複數表示，例如：for ten years。

6.　解答：b

英文 I have <u>seen</u> UFOs many <u>times</u>.

中譯 我已經看到幽浮好幾次了。

解說

　　本題測驗現在完成式。第一空格要填入現在完成式，第二空格填入與次數相關的用字，故選 b：have seen 的 seen 是 see 的過去分詞。這裡的 time 指的不是「時間」，是「次數」，所以後面加 s。time 如果作「時間」解釋，是不可數名詞，不可加 s。

英文　I have <u>heard</u> that band before, but I can't remember their style.
　　　I have <u>heard of</u> that band before, but I can't remember their style.

中譯　那支樂團我曾聽說過，但已經不記得他們的風格了。

解說

　　本題測驗現在完成式與動詞 hear / hear of 的用法。空格內必須填入過去分詞，與前面的 have 形成現在完成式 have heard 或 have heard of。hear 作「聽聞；得知」解釋，也可以用 hear of 表示同樣意思，所以選項 a 或 c 皆是正確答案。

英文　Randy <u>has</u> found the map, so we <u>can</u> start the adventure.
　　　Randy <u>hasn't</u> found the map, so we <u>can't</u> start the adventure.

中譯　蘭迪已經找到地圖了，所以我們可以展開冒險之旅了。
　　　蘭迪還沒找到地圖，所以我們不能展開冒險之旅。

解說

　　本題測驗現在完成式與助動詞用法。第一空格後面是 find 的過去分詞，主詞 Randy 是第三人稱單數，所以空格要填入 has 或 hasn't。從文法和句意來看，選項 a 和 b 都可以選，只是一個是肯定語氣，另一個是否定語氣，中文的意思也因此不同。此外，助動詞 can 表「能力」。要注意句中使用連接詞 so 連結前後兩個句子。

　　　<u>Have you finished</u> your homework? It's already 9:00.
英文　**<u>Haven't you finished</u> your homework? It's already 9:00.**
　　　<u>Did you finish</u> your homework? It's already 9:00.

　　　你的作業寫完了沒？已經九點了。
中譯　你的作業還沒寫完嗎？已經九點了。
　　　你的作業寫完了沒？已經九點了。

解說

　　本題測驗「詢問動作完成與否」的幾種表達方式。選項 a、b、c 都是正確答案，只是意思有點不同。空格有待完成的是問句，本題用現在完成式（選項 a、b）或過去式（選項 c）皆可，主要差別在於：現在完成式強調「到目前為止」事件進行的狀態，過去式強調「與現在無關的過去事實」。選項 a 是現在完成式問句：「Have / Has ＋ S ＋過去分詞（V-pp）？」。選項 b 採現在完成式的「否定疑問句」：「Haven't / Hasn't ＋ S ＋過去分詞（V-pp）？」，否定疑問句的語氣帶有質疑的成分。

10.

英文 Frank has worked at the company <u>for</u> 10 months.

中譯 法蘭克已經在這家公司工作十個月了。

解說

　　本題測驗現在完成式與介系詞 for / since 的搭配。本題的時態採現在完成式 has worked，空格後面是 10 months，而 months 是複數名詞，表示一段期間，所以介系詞用 for，故選 a。

11.

英文 Twenty years ago, people <u>read</u> more.

中譯 人們在二十年前比較常看書。

解說

　　如何判斷動詞何時該用過去式，何時該用現在完成式？可以從句子的時間副詞找線索，本句的 twenty years ago「二十年前」表示過去的時間，動詞必須選擇過去式 read。

12.

英文 <u>Have</u> they <u>entered</u> the gym yet?

中譯 他們已經進入體育館了嗎？

解說

　　本題測驗現在完成式的問句：「Have / Has ＋ S ＋過去分詞（V-pp）？」。現在完成式的問句經常與副詞 yet「尚未；還沒」連用。本句主詞是複數的 they，所以選項 a 不用考慮，選項 b 與 d 無此用法，只有 c 是正確答案。

13.

英文
How long have you <u>been</u> here?
How long have you <u>been</u> waiting here?

中譯
你在這裡待多久了？
你在這裡等多久了？

解說

　　本題測驗現在完成式與詢問時間長短的疑問詞 how long。空格可填入 be 動詞的過去分詞 been 或 been waiting。選項 a 與 b 皆是正確答案，兩者意思近似，但時態不同。選項 a 採「現在完成式」，側重「一段時間的穩定狀態」。選項 b 採現在完成進行式，強調「動作還持續在進行」。

14.

英文 How many times <u>have</u> you <u>been to</u> Ireland?

中譯 你去過幾次愛爾蘭？

解說

　　本題測驗重點：用現在完成式詢問他人「到目前為止的經驗」，常用句型為：「How many times ＋ has / have ＋ S ＋ been to ＋地點？」；以 how many times 詢問次數的疑問詞引導出問句，經常用來詢問他人經驗。「S ＋ has / have ＋ been to ＋地點」表示「曾經去過（某地）」，故答案選 b。

15.

英文 <u>For</u> three days, the sailors <u>have been</u> hungry and thirsty.

中譯 這批船員已經連續三天沒有進食和飲水了。

解說

　　本題測驗現在完成式與介系詞 for / since 的搭配。表時間的介系詞 for / since 可說是辨識現在完成式的關鍵字，放在句首或句尾皆可，以句尾比較常見。本題一開始先點出時間長短。第一空格該填 since 還是 for？從空格後面的 three days 為複數的時間名詞可知，介系詞應當用表示「持續一段時間」的 for，而不是表達「某一時間起點」的 since。第二空格要填入現在完成式，答案選 d。選項 b 的問題出在動詞使用了現在進行式被動語態，不符文法。

16. 解答：**a**

英文 Sarah **hasn't finished** her dinner, so she can't have any dessert.

中譯 莎拉還沒吃完晚餐，所以她不可以吃甜點。

解說

　　選 b 不合邏輯，因為主詞是人 Sarah。選項 d 如果改成 hasn't eaten 就是正確答案。選項 c 的過去完成式（had ＋ V-pp）會造成語病。過去完成式很少單獨存在，經常與另一過去式子句連用：先發生的動作或事件→用過去完成式；後發生的動作或事件→用過去簡單式。區隔兩個過去事件的先後，是過去完成式的使用時機。例：The bank robber had run away when the police came.「當警察抵達時，銀行搶匪早已經跑了。」，故答案選 a。

17. 解答：**d**

英文 We've **had a dog for** about five years.

中譯 我們已經養狗五年了。

解說

　　本題測驗現在完成式與介系詞 for／since 的搭配。第一空格一定要填入過去分詞，才能與前面的 We've（We have）形成現在完成式。第二空格後面有 five years，這是表一段時間的複數名詞，介系詞要用 for，因此正確答案是 d。選項 a 的 own 如果改成 owned 就可以選。選項 c 的 in 如果改成 for，也可以選。

18. 解答：**b**

英文 I **didn't play** golf last summer.

中譯 我去年夏天沒有打高爾夫。

解說

　　如何判斷動詞何時該用現在完成式？何時該用過去式？這要從句子的時間副詞來判斷。last summer「去年夏天」很明顯的是過去的時間，動詞用過去式即可。注意 play ＋運動項目，中間不需要定冠詞 the，例：play tennis（打網球）／play basketball（打籃球）／play soccer（踢足球）。但是 play ＋ the ＋樂器名稱，要加定冠詞。例：play the piano（彈鋼琴）／play the flute（吹笛子）／play the guitar（彈吉他）。

解答：**a**

英文 **Jason has forgotten the password, so he can't log into his email account.**

中譯 傑森已經忘了密碼，所以無法登入自己的電子郵件信箱。

解說

　　空格應該填入現在完成式的動詞。答案選 a。選項 b 如果把 remember 改成過去分詞 remembered，就是正確答案。

解答：**c**

英文 **I've been putting my photography portfolio online, but I'm not finished yet.**

中譯 我正在把我的攝影作品放到網路上，但還沒放完。

解說

　　本題測驗重點：現在完成進行式。本題應該使用現在完成式？還是現在完成進行式？從後面的 but I'm not finished yet 可知攝影作品集正「持續上傳」到網路上，還沒結束，此時，用強調「還繼續在進行的」現在完成進行式，比用強調「穩地持續一段長時間」的現在完成式來得貼切，故選 c。

12 被動句

被動句的基本定義

» 句子的語態，可分成主動與被動兩種。

» 可以形成被動語態的動詞，一定是及物動詞──需要受詞的動詞。因為被動句中的主詞，是從主動句中的受詞而來。

主動語態變成被動句的方式

» 主動句： 主詞　　　　　動詞　　　　受詞

被動句： 主詞　　　be 動詞＋過去分詞　　by ＋動作的執行者

例：主動語態：The man in black stole my wallet.

　　　　　　　身穿黑衣的男子偷走了我的皮夾。

　　被動語態：My wallet was stolen by the man in black.

　　　　　　　我的皮夾被身穿黑衣的男子偷走了。

» 被動句的形成：把主動句中的受詞改成主詞，之後放置 be 動詞，再接過去分詞。

» 主動句轉被動句後的動詞時態不變，注意 be 動詞的單複數，要根據主詞的人稱來決定。

» 在被動句中，如果需要指出「動作的執行者」是誰時，可用介系詞 by 引導。

» 在被動句中，大多數不需要指出動作的執行者。之所以使用被動語態，通常是因為「執行動作的一方已為人所知、不確定或並非表達的重點」。

The museum <u>was built</u> two hundred years ago. (build)

這間博物館興建於兩百年前。

Stamps <u>are sold</u> in the post office. (sell)

郵票在郵局販售。

難以確定動作執行者是誰時，不用提出。如果動作者是 someone / somebody（某人），或者 people（人們），也不用提出。

The window <u>was broken</u> (by someone) yesterday. (break)

這扇窗戶昨天被打破了。

This word <u>is not used</u> (by people) very often. (use)

這個字很少使用。

如果需要指出動作的執行者時，用「介系詞 by ＋動作執行者」表示

- 注意介系詞後面接的是受格，原主動句中的主格到了被動句中，要轉換成受格。例如：I → me；he → him；they → them。

　　主動句：I borrowed the book.

　　　　　　我借了那本書。

　　被動句：The book was borrowed by me.

　　　　　　那本書被我借走了。

被動句的各種形式

簡單被動式：
S ＋ be 動詞＋過去分詞（＋ by ＋動作執行者）

- be 動詞的部分，注意時態與主詞人稱的搭配要一致。

- 一般名詞，例如：the room, the dog, the woman, the cup 等等，以單數視之。

	主詞	be 動詞		過去分詞	
		現在式	過去式		
單數	I	**am**	**was**	told	被告知
	you	**are**	**were**	loved	被愛
	he / she / it	**is**	**was**	beaten	被打
複數	we / you / they	**are**	**were**	bitten	被咬

The classroom is cleaned every day. (clean)
教室每天被打掃。

The door was locked and I could not open it. (lock)
門被鎖上了，我打不開。

Judy is never invited to parties. (invite)
茱蒂從未受邀參加派對。

使用助動詞的被動語態：S ＋助動詞＋ be 動詞＋過去分詞

- 助動詞有特定的意義與功能，例如：can 表示「能力」；should 表示「應該」；would 表示「意願」；could / may / might 表示「可能性」；must 表示「必須」等等。
- 助動詞後面必須接 be 動詞的原形動詞，即 be，之後再接過去分詞。

The novel can be borrowed from the library. (borrow)
這本小說可以在圖書館借到。

Julie's car will be sold next month. (sell)
茱莉的車子下個月會被賣掉。

The letter must be sent immediately. (send)
這封信必須立刻寄出去。

The work should be done before Friday. (do)
這項工作應該在星期五之前要完成。

完成式的被動語態：S ＋ has / have / had ＋ been ＋過去分詞

- 在完成式中，原本被動語態「be ＋過去分詞」當中的 be 動詞也要變成完成式 been。換言之，been 是 be 動詞的過去分詞，been 之後再接「一般動詞」變成的過去分詞。
- 完成式又可分為現在完成式（has / have ＋過去分詞）與過去完成式（had ＋過去分詞）。

主動句：Mark has built the house for one year. (build)
  這棟房子馬克已經蓋一年了。

被動句：The house has been built by Mark for one year. → 完成式被動句
  這棟房子已經被馬克蓋一年了。

比　較：The house was built by Mark. →簡單式被動句
  這棟房子是馬克蓋的。

主動句：Many singers have sung the song. (sing)
  許多歌手唱過這首歌。

被動句：The song has been sung by many singers. → 完成式被動句
  這首歌已經被許多歌手唱過了。

比　較：The song was sung by a pop singer last year. → 簡單式被動句
  這首歌去年被某位流行歌手唱過。

進行式的被動語態：S ＋ be 動詞＋ being ＋過去分詞

- 進行式強調動作當時正在進行中。

主動句：The workers are building the library.
  那些工人正在蓋圖書館。

被動句：The library is being built by the workers.
  那棟圖書館正由這群工人興建中。

主動句：My father is repairing my bicycle.
  我爸正在修理我的腳踏車。

被動句：My bicycle is being repaired by my father.
  我的腳踏車正由我爸修理中。

疑問句的被動語態

1. Yes / No 問句：回答會用 Yes / No 的問句。

Be 動詞（Was / Were / Is / Are...）＋主詞＋過去分詞？

A: Were the shoes made in France? (make)
這雙鞋是法國製的嗎？

B: Yes, they were.
是的，是法國製的。

A: Was the room cleaned yesterday?
這個房間昨天有沒有打掃？

B: No, it wasn't.
沒，沒有打掃。

2. 使用疑問詞的問句：指的是以 wh- 疑問詞起首的問句，例如：when / where / what / who / why / how ＋形容詞。

Wh- 疑問詞＋ be 動詞＋主詞＋過去分詞？

When was computer invented?
電腦是什麼時候發明的？

Why was window broken?
窗戶為什麼破了？

How often is the room cleaned?
這房間多久打掃一次？

否定句的被動語態

1. 主動語態中的助動詞 do / does / did，在句子改成被動語態後會消失，因為本身沒有涵義：

S ＋ be 動詞＋ not ＋過去分詞

主動句：The man did not steal the wallet.
　　　　那名男子沒有偷那只皮夾。

被動句：The wallet was not stolen by the man.
　　　　那只皮夾不是那名男子偷的。

主動句：The earthquake did not destroy his house.
　　　　那場地震並沒有摧毀他的房子。

被動句：His house was not destroyed by the earthquake.
　　　　他的房子並沒有被那場地震摧毀。

2. 被動語態中的助動詞 can / could / should / would / may / might / must 會保留，因為本身有涵義：

S ＋助動詞＋ not ＋ be 動詞＋過去分詞

The novel might not be published. (publish)
這本小說可能不會出版了。

Her name could not be found on the list. (find)
名單上看不到她的名字。

were / was born 表示「（人）出生」，沒有主動語態的用法，一定要用被動語態，時態一定用過去式。

I was born in Taipei in 1981.
我 1981 年在台北出生。

Where were you born?
你在哪裡出生的？

題 目

1. This book I found _____ in 1533!
   a. is written
   b. was written
   c. was writing
   d. was wrote

2. My wallet _____ stolen.
   a. is
   b. was
   c. has been
   d. Either b or c

3. _____ we _____ in euros or dollars?
   a. Do ; get paid
   b. Are ; paid
   c. Will ; be paid
   d. All of the above

4. To _____ was the letter addressed?
   a. who
   b. whom
   c. why
   d. how

5. When the police arrived at the accident scene, it was clear to them that she _____ instantly.
   a. had been killed
   b. was killed
   c. die
   d. had die

6. The president _____ an assassin.

    a. was killed by

    b. be killed by

    c. killed by

    d. None of the above

7. In whose name was this letter _____?

    a. writing

    b. written

    c. wrote

    d. been written

8. A: Did you break this window?

    B: No. It _____ before I got here.

    a. break

    b. did break

    c. was broken

    d. broken

9. A: Did Lionel pay for the meal?

    B: Yes. The meal _____ for by Lionel.

    a. has been paid

    b. was pay

    c. did be paid

    d. was paid

10. A: Did Fred take the car or the truck?

    B: He _____ the car.

    a. has taken by

    b. did taken

    c. took

    d. was taken by

11. You will _____ to the hotel by a member of our staff.
    a. be driven
    b. drive
    c. drove
    d. have driven

12. A: She _____ by her middle name.
    B: Is she?
    a. is known
    b. is knowing
    c. was known
    d. have known

13. This photo was taken _____ a friend of mine.
    a. of
    b. on
    c. than
    d. by

14. A: Open the safe and give me all the money!
    B: But the safe can't _____ until tomorrow morning.
    a. open
    b. opened
    c. be opened
    d. be opening

15. A: Who should sign the application?
    B: The person asking for the loan should _____ the application.
    a. sign
    b. signing
    c. be signing
    d. All of the above

16. Rain _____ for the next three days.

    a. is expecting

    b. is expected

    c. expects

    d. will expect

17. The election _____ held on November 4th of this year.

    a. will be

    b. is going to be

    c. is to be

    d. All of the above

18. The tower _____ being _____ by a Japanese construction company.

    a. is ; built

    b. have ; build

    c. will ; building

    d. None of the above

19. These wines _____ chosen for their fine quality and distinct flavor.

    a. have

    b. have been

    c. will have

    d. can

20. Scientists _____ new life forms in these deep ocean volcanoes.

    a. have been found

    b. were found

    c. found

    d. are found

解析

1.

解答：**b**

英文 This book I found <u>was written</u> in 1533!

中譯 我找到的那本書是 1533 年寫的！

解說

主詞是 this book，完成的時間是過去：1533 年，所以被動語態應該用過去式，答案選 b。注意本句結構可還原為：「This book (that) I found was written in 1533!」This book 後面省略關係代名詞 that，關係代名詞具有連接詞的功能，能夠連接兩個句子。

2.

解答：**d**

英文 My wallet <u>was</u> stolen.
My wallet <u>has been</u> stolen.

中譯 我的錢包被偷了。

解說

空格後面是動詞 steal 的過去分詞 stolen，但是 be 動詞的時態應該用哪一種？選項 a 的現在式不適合，因為按時間邏輯推斷，東西被偷是發生過的事情。選項 b 和 c 都是正確的，但意思不一樣。過去式的「My wallet was stolen.」表示錢包之前被偷了，現在已經找到了。現在完成式的「My wallet has been stolen.」表示錢包之前被偷了，現在還沒找到。過去式表示過去發生的事情，「現在已經不是事實」。現在完成式表示過去發生的事情，「到現在還是事實」。

3.

解答：**d**

英文 <u>Do</u> we <u>get paid</u> in euros or dollars?
<u>Are</u> we <u>paid</u> in euros or dollars?
<u>Will</u> we <u>be paid</u> in euros or dollars?

中譯 他們會付給我們歐元還是美元？

解說

選項 a、b、c 都是正確答案，皆是被動語態，但意思不太一樣。選項 a 的「get＋過去分詞」的被動語態比較強調動作。例：He got caught in a heavy rain.「他被一場大雨給困住了。」相較之下，「be 動詞＋過去分詞」的被動語態，既可以表示動作，又可以表示狀態。例：The widow was broken.「窗戶破了。／窗戶被弄破了。」雖然選項 b、c 都是被動語態，但是前者用現在式，後者用未來式。未來式後面必須用原形動詞 be，再接過去分詞。「用……（貨幣）付款」用介系詞 in。

4. 解答：**b**

英文 **To whom was the letter addressed?**

中譯 這封信要寄給誰？

解說

　　動詞 address 作「把……寄給某人」解釋時，要接介系詞 to，再接收件人：「address ＋物＋ to ＋人」。例：I addressed the letter to my sister.「我寄信給我妹。」若用被動語態：The letter was addressed to my sister.「那封信被寄給我妹。」本題收件人不明，所以使用 whom 疑問詞發問，且前面要加介系詞 to。因為 to 後面接的是受詞，所以疑問詞不能用主格 who，而要用受格 whom，故選 b。

5. 解答：**a**

英文 **When the police arrived at the accident scene, it was clear to them that she had been killed instantly.**

中譯 當警察抵達事故現場時，她顯然早已斷氣。

解說

　　本題測驗重點：被動語態的過去完成式。過去完成式很少單獨存在，經常與另一過去式子句連用：先發生的動作或事件，用過去完成式；後發生的動作或事件，用過去簡單式。過去完成式的使用時機，在於「區分兩個過去事件的先後」，答案應選 a。以本題而言，when 子句的發生時間比較晚，主要子句（it was clear to them that she had been killed instantly）發生時間比較早。注意這裡的 kill 不當「殺害」解釋，而是作「死於（意外或天災）」解釋，習慣上用被動語態。例：Thousands of people were killed in the earthquake.「數以千計的人死於地震。」

6. 解答：**a**

英文 **The president was killed by an assassin.**

中譯 總統遭刺客暗殺。

解說

　　本題的 kill 當「殺害」解釋，和第五題的不同。主詞是 the president，空格應該填入被動語態，表示「被殺害」，答案選 a。選項 b 的問題在 be 動詞用了原形動詞，這是不需要的，除非前面有助動詞（can / will / may 等等）。

7.

解答：**b**

英文 In whose name was this letter <u>written</u>?

中譯 這封信是以誰的名義寫的？

解說

　　whose 的意思是「誰的」，是 who 的所有格。「in one's name ＝ in the name of ＋某人／組織」表示「以……名義」。例：The letter was written in Brown's name.「這封信是以布朗的名義寫的。」如果不知道是以誰的名義寫的，就用疑問句「In whose name...」發問。空格內應填入過去分詞，和句中的was形成被動語態。

8.

解答：**c**

英文
A: Did you break this window?
B: No. It <u>was broken</u> before I got here.

中譯
A：窗戶是你弄破的嗎？
B：不是我，我到這裡之前，窗戶就已經破了。

解說

　　第二句的 It 代替前面的 the window，空格內要填入被動語態：be 動詞＋過去分詞。選項 a、b 都是主動語態，不符文法，故答案選 c。值得注意的是：「be 動詞＋過去分詞」的被動語態（The window was broken.），既可表示動作（「被弄破了」），又可表示狀態（「已經破掉了」）。

9.

解答：**d**

英文
A: Did Lionel pay for the meal?
B: Yes. The meal <u>was paid</u> for by Lionel.

中譯
A：這頓飯是羅內爾付的錢嗎？
B：是的。這頓飯是羅內爾付的。

解說

　　「pay for ＋ N」表示「付錢（買……）」。空格內應填入被動語態。問句的時態使用過去式，答句中動詞同樣使用過去式。答案選 d。

英文　A: Did Fred take the car or the truck?
　　　B: He <u>took</u> the car.

中譯　A：弗萊德買了汽車還是卡車？
　　　B：他買了汽車。

解說

　　動詞 take 作「買」解釋。空格前面的主詞是 He，後面的 the car 是受詞，故判斷本句用主動語態即可，答案選 c。

英文　You will <u>be driven</u> to the hotel by a member of our staff.

中譯　我們有位職員會開車送您到飯店。

解說

　　主詞是 you，動詞應該用主動還是被動，要從句子找線索。後面有 by a member of our staff，介系詞引導出「動作執行者」，由此可知空格應填入被動語態。動詞 drive 作「開車接送」解釋時，是需要受詞的：S ＋ drive ＋人（O）＋ to ＋地點。如果被接送的對象（受詞）當主詞，就要使用被動語態。空格前面有助動詞 will，所以要用原形動詞 be，故選 a。

英文　A: She is <u>known</u> by her middle name.
　　　B: Is she?

中譯　A：她的中間名廣為人知。
　　　B：是嗎？

解說

　　本句的過去分詞 known（原形動詞 know），經常當作形容詞使用，作「為……所知的」。空格後面的 by her middle name 引導的不是動作執行者，這裡的 by 表示「原因」。至於應該用 is known 還是 was known，從對方的回答 Is she 可知答案應選 a。

13.

英文 This photo was taken <u>by</u> a friend of mine.

中譯 這張照片是我的一個朋友拍的。

解說

　　「take a picture / photo of ＋ N」表示「幫（某人或某物）拍照」。本句主詞是無生命的 this photo，所以使用被動語態 was taken。空格須填入的介系詞不是 of，而是 by ＋動作執行者（a friend of mine）。take a photo（of ＋ N）其中 of 後面接的是「拍照的對象」，但 of ＋ N 不一定要提及，本題即為一例。

14.

英文 A: Open the safe and give me all the money!
B: But the safe can't <u>be opened</u> until tomorrow morning.

中譯 A：把保險櫃打開，把錢全拿給我！
B：但是保險櫃要到明天早上才打得開。

解說

　　主詞是無生命的 safe「保險櫃」，可知應該使用被動語態，空格前面有助動詞 can't，所以後面使用「原形 be 動詞＋過去分詞」，答案選 c。句中的 until 是「介系詞」，作「直到……為止」解釋。

15.

英文 A: Who should sign the application?
B: The person asking for the loan should <u>sign</u> the application.

中譯 A：誰應該在這份申請書上簽名？
B：申請貸款的人應該要在申請書上簽名。

解說

　　本句主詞是 the person，asking for the loan 是分詞片語的一種（現在分詞表主動），空格內應該填入動詞，用主動語態即可，答案選 a：助動詞 should ＋原形動詞。

16. 解答：**b**

英文 <u>Rain is expected</u> for the next three days.

中譯 預期接下來三天都會下雨。

解說

　　動詞 expect 作「預期；期待」解釋。本句主詞是無生命的 rain，所以空格應該填入被動語態，答案選 b。其他選項都是主動語態，不可選。被動語態的動作執行者（by + N），因為不是重點，所以往往不需要提出來，本題即是一例。

17. 解答：**d**

英文
The election <u>will be</u> held on November 4th of this year.
The election <u>is going to be</u> held on November 4th of this year.
The election <u>is to be</u> held on November 4th of this year.

中譯 選舉將於今年的 11 月 4 日舉行。

解說

　　選項 a、b、c 都是正確答案。選項 a 與 b 皆是未來式的被動語態：will + be +過去分詞＝ be（is / am / are / was / were）going to + be +過去分詞。未來式的主動語態：will +原形動詞＝ be going to +原形動詞。注意：未來式被動語態中「be +過去分詞」的位置，正是主動語態中的「原形動詞」。而 be going to 中的 be 動詞要根據主詞的單複數作變化，the election 是單數，所以用 is going to。held 是動詞 hold 的過去分詞，這個字習慣用被動語態。至於選項 c，「be 動詞+ to V」也是助動詞的一種，一般稱作「be + to + V」，可用來表示「預定」。例：Her next concert is to be held in Japan.「她的下一場演唱會預定在日本舉行。」

18. 解答：**a**

英文 The tower <u>is being built</u> by a Japanese construction company.

中譯 這座塔樓正由一家日本建築公司興建中。

解說

　　本題測驗重點：被動語態的現在進行式。主詞是 the tower，by 引導出的 a Japanese construction company 是動作執行者，可知空格應該填入動詞的被動語態。第一空格應填入第三人稱單數 is，之後的 being 表示「進行式」，強調動作正在進行當中；第二空格應填入 build 的過去分詞 built，故選 a。

19. 解答：**b**

英文　These wines have been chosen for their fine quality and distinct flavor.

中譯　這幾種酒會被挑選出來，是因為品質優良、風味獨特。

解說

　　本題測驗重點：現在完成式的被動語態。句型：S ＋ has / have ＋ been ＋過去分詞。注意：been 是 be 動詞的過去分詞；過去分詞指的是一般動詞的過去分詞。主詞是 these wines，空格後面有動詞 choose 的過去分詞 chosen，由此可知，空格應該填入被動語態，故選 b。

20. 解答：**c**

英文　Scientists found new life forms in these deep ocean volcanoes.

中譯　科學家在這些深海火山發現了新的生命體。

解說

　　空格前有主詞 scientists，空格後是受詞 new life forms，主詞是人，動詞用主動語態即可。其他選項都是被動句，故選 c。

13 附加問句

附加問句定義

» 附加問句是附在「直述句」之後的簡短問句，用來徵求對方的同意或確認，類似中文「對不對？」或「不是嗎？」等說法。

附加問句的類型

» 附加問句的基本句型：S + V,　助動詞／ be 動詞 + S？
　　　　　　　　　　　直述句　　　　　　附加問句

» 附加問句變化的基本原則：

　1. 如果前面的直述句是肯定句，附加問句便用否定句的縮略語。

　2. 如果前面的直述句是否定句，附加問句便用肯定句。

» 附加問句中的動詞型態與時態，必須和前面的直述句一致。

» 直述句與附加問句中間以逗點隔開。

» 附加問句中的主詞用代名詞來表示；代名詞的使用取決於直述句中的主詞。

直述句用 be 動詞的附加問句

Elaine is beautiful, **isn't she**?

伊蓮很漂亮，不是嗎？

Andrew is not your boss, **is he**?

安德魯不是你的老闆，對吧？

The novel is interesting, **isn't it**?

這本小說很有趣，不是嗎？（it 代替前句的 novel）

You are not angry, **are you**?

你沒生氣，對吧？

直述句用一般動詞的附加問句

All the children <u>like</u> candies, <u>**don't they**</u>?
所有的小朋友都喜歡吃糖果，不是嗎？（they 代替前句的 children）

She <u>walks</u> to school every morning, <u>**doesn't she**</u>?
她每天早上走路上學，不是嗎？

直述句用完成式的附加問句

Helena <u>has lived</u> in London for ten years, <u>**hasn't she**</u>?
海蓮娜已經在倫敦住了十年，對吧？

You <u>haven't told</u> me the truth, <u>**have you**</u>?
你沒對我說實話，對吧？

Tom <u>hasn't finished</u> his work yet, <u>**has he**</u>?
湯姆還沒完成工作，不是嗎？

The Smiths <u>have visited</u> Japan twice this year, <u>**haven't they**</u>?
史密斯一家人今年去了兩次日本，對吧？

直述句用助動詞的附加問句

You <u>didn't</u> lie to me, <u>**did you**</u>?
你沒有對我撒謊，對吧？

I <u>don't</u> have to do that, <u>**do I**</u>?
我不是一定得做這個，對吧？

He <u>can</u> run very fast, <u>**can't he**</u>?
他可以跑得很快，不是嗎？

Children under 18 <u>cannot</u> watch the movie, <u>**can they**</u>?
十八歲以下的孩子不能看這部電影，不是嗎？

We <u>should not</u> talk behind other people's back, <u>**should we**</u>?
我們不應該在背後說別人壞話，不是嗎？

You <u>won't</u> come to his party, <u>**will you**</u>?
你不會參加他的派對，對吧？

直述句中使用否定意義的字詞時

- 直述句如果出現 never / seldom / no / nothing / nobody / little / few 這類「本身帶有否定意義的字詞」時,形同否定句,附加問句用肯定句。
- nothing / nobody / someone / somebody / everyone 的人稱代名詞為 they。

Dale <u>seldom</u> goes to the movies, <u>does he</u>?
岱爾很少看電影,對吧?

Molly and Mary have <u>never</u> been to Greece, <u>have they</u>?
莫莉和瑪麗從未去過希臘,對吧?

<u>Nobody</u> called me this morning, <u>did they</u>?
今天早上沒人打電話給我,對吧?

直述句是 There is / There are... 的附加問句

- There is / There are... 作「有……」解釋,表達一種「存在的狀態」。
- There is(was / will be...)＋單數名詞／There are(were...)＋複數名詞。
- 在這類句子中,be 動詞後面的名詞是主詞,但是附加問句的主詞仍由 there is / there are 決定。

<u>There are</u> five people in your family, <u>aren't there</u>?
你家有五個人,對吧?

There is <u>no</u> one in the room, <u>is there</u>?
房內沒有人,不是嗎?(no 本身具有否定意味)

<u>There was</u> a fire accident in the downtown yesterday, <u>wasn't there</u>?
昨天市區發生了一場火災,不是嗎?

各種祈使句的附加問句

- 以原形動詞起首的句子稱作祈使句,用來向對方提出請求、下命令、邀約或建議,所以後面的附加問句也有所不同。
  1. 表示請求對方幫忙的祈使句,附加問句用 will you?
  2. 表示邀請對方做某事的祈使句,附加問句用 won't you?
  3. 「Let's ＋原形動詞」表示勸誘,附加問句用 shall we?

- 在祈使句中，受話的一方是「第二人稱 you（你；你們）」，you 是句中隱含的主詞，這就是為什麼附加問句的主詞都是 you。

1. 請求對方幫忙的祈使句：

Close the door, <u>will you</u>?
把門關上，好嗎？

Give me a hand, <u>will you?</u>
幫我個忙，好嗎？

2. 邀請對方做某事的祈使句：

Have a cup of tea, <u>won't you</u>?
喝杯茶，如何？

Please sit down, <u>won't you</u>?
請坐，好嗎？

3. 表示勸誘的「Let's ＋原形動詞」：

Let's take a break, <u>shall we</u>?
我們休息一下，好嗎？

Let's go home, <u>shall we</u>?
我們回家吧，好嗎？

附加問句的回答方式

- 附加問句的回答方式，和一般 yes / no 的問句一樣。
- 通常用簡答即可。

A: Elaine <u>is</u> your best friend, <u>isn't she</u>?
伊蓮是你最要好的朋友，不是嗎？

B: Yes, she is.
沒錯，她是。

A: Barry <u>doesn't</u> like tea, <u>does he</u>?
貝瑞不喜歡喝茶，對吧？

B: No, he doesn't.
沒錯，他不喜歡。

題 目

1. Yvonne _____ drive, _____ she?
   a. can ; can not
   b. can ; can't
   c. can ; cannot
   d. can't ; can't

2. Your mother-in-law _____ move in with you, _____ she?
   a. has ; hasn't
   b. won't ; will
   c. will not ; won't
   d. None of the above

3. The people who live in Sanchung _____ really angry about it, _____?
   a. are ; aren't they
   b. aren't ; are they not
   c. are not ; are them
   d. Either a or b

4. Your teacher is over 40, _____?
   a. isn't she
   b. is she not
   c. is she
   d. Either a or b

5. They _____ to New York, haven't they?
   a. went
   b. are gone
   c. have gone
   d. Either b or c

6. Hey, you over there. Try to be a little quieter, _____ you?
   a. won't
   b. will
   c. can
   d. could

7. She plays the violin in the orchestra, _____ she?
   a. can
   b. doesn't
   c. don't
   d. All of the above

8. There _____ left to do, _____ there?
   a. is nothing ; is
   b. isn't anything ; is
   c. are no tasks ; are
   d. All of the above

9. That is Mrs. Henderson's husband, isn't _____?
   a. he
   b. she
   c. it
   d. that

10. Those are the dogs' towels, aren't _____?
    a. those
    b. them
    c. they
    d. these

11. Let's dance, _____ we?
    a. will
    b. can
    c. could
    d. shall

12. A: Humans aren't the same species as gorillas, are they?
    B: _____, they _____.
    a. Yes ; aren't
    b. Yes ; not
    c. No ; aren't
    d. No ; are

13. A yard _____ ten inches, _____ it?
    a. is ; isn't
    b. isn't ; is
    c. isn't ; isn't
    d. Either a or b

14. Don't forget, _____ you?
    a. will
    b. won't
    c. would
    d. do

15. Please, come in and sit down, _____ you?
    a. will
    b. won't
    c. would
    d. wouldn't

16. You don't really mean that, _____?
    a. do you
    b. don't you
    c. do you not
    d. All of the above

17. You _____ give me a hand with this, could you?
    a. could
    b. couldn't
    c. would not
    d. can't

18. You _____ a few dollars you could lend me, _____ you?
    a. have ; haven't
    b. haven't got ; have
    c. don't have ; do
    d. Either b or c

19. Nobody saw the prisoner escape, _____?
    a. didn't they
    b. did they
    c. didn't he
    d. did he

20. Someone has taken the money, _____?
    a. has they
    b. hasn't they
    c. have they
    d. haven't they

解 析

　　　　　　　　　　　　　　　　　　　　　　　　　　　解答：**b**

英文 Yvonne <u>can</u> drive, <u>can't she</u>?

中譯 伊芳會開車，不是嗎？

解說

　　本題測驗重點：附加問句中有助動詞 can。在附加問句中，如果直述句是肯定，附加問句就用否定，故答案選 b。代名詞 she 代替前面的 Yvonne。選項 a 的問題出在第二個答案，如果附加問句改寫如下：can she not? 就是正確答案。

2.　　　　　　　　　　　　　　　　　　　　　　　　　　　解答：**b**

英文 Your mother-in-law <u>won't</u> move in with you, <u>will she</u>?

中譯 你婆婆不會和你們一起搬進去，對吧？

解說

　　本題測驗重點：附加問句與未來式助動詞 will。從空格後面的原形動詞 move 可知，直述句的時態與完成式無關，空格應該填入未來式助動詞 will，後面才會接原形動詞。選項 c 的兩個答案都是否定的，不可選，故答案選 b。代名詞 she 代替前面的 your mother-in-law。

3.　　　　　　　　　　　　　　　　　　　　　　　　　　　解答：**a**

英文 The people who live in Sanchung <u>are</u> really angry about it, <u>aren't they</u>?

中譯 那些住在三重的人對此真的很生氣，對吧？

解說

　　第一空格要填入 be 動詞，主詞是 the people，所以空格應填入 are。第二空格要填入附加問句，答案選 a：they 代替前面的 the people。選項 b 的問題出在兩個答案都是否定。此外，附加問句可縮寫（aren't they），也可不縮寫（are they not）。選項 c 的問題出在第二個答案：are 後面必須用主格 they，them 是受格。片語「be angry about ＋ N」表示「對……感到生氣」。

4. 解答：**d**

英文 **Your teacher is over 40, isn't she?**
Your teacher is over 40, is she not?

中譯 你的老師四十多歲了，不是嗎？

解說

　　本題測驗重點：附加問句的形式。附加問句一定要縮寫嗎？不一定。可縮寫
（isn't she），也可不縮寫（is she not）。這裡的 she 代替的是前面的 the teacher，
故答案選 d。

5. 解答：**c**

英文 **They have gone to New York, haven't they?**

中譯 他們已經去紐約了，不是嗎？

解說

　　本題測驗重點：附加問句的現在完成式。從附加問句的 haven't they 可知，直
述句的動詞也使用現在完成式，故選 c。「S ＋ has / have gone to ＋地點」表示
「人已經到了某地」，gone 是動詞 go 的過去分詞。選項 b 的 gone 不是過去分詞，
是形容詞，作「消失的；逝去的」解釋。

6. 解答：**b**

英文 **Hey, you over there. Try to be a little quieter, will you?**

中譯 喂，那邊的人安靜一點，可不可以？

解說

　　本題測驗重點：祈使句的附加問句。祈使句的形式有多種，遇到請求對方幫忙
或下令的祈使句，附加問句用 will you?，故答案選 b。

英文　She plays the violin in the orchestra, <u>doesn't she</u>?

中譯　她在管絃樂團拉小提琴，不是嗎？

解說

　　本題測驗重點：一般動詞的附加問句。直述句是肯定語氣，所以附加問句要用否定。因為 play 是一般動詞，所以否定句必須使用助動詞 doesn't / don't。主詞是she，所以助動詞用 doesn't，答案選 b。

　　　　There is <u>nothing</u> left to do, <u>is</u> there?

英文　There <u>isn't anything</u> left to do, <u>is</u> there?

　　　　There <u>are no tasks</u> left to do, <u>are</u> there?

中譯　接下來沒什麼要做的，對吧？

解說

　　本題測驗重點：there is / are... 的附加問句。句型：There is / are ＋ N 作「有……」解釋，表達一種「存在的狀態」。動詞的單複數由後面的名詞，也就是主詞來決定。選項 a、b、c 都是正確答案，而且有個共通點：第一個答案都讓直述句形成否定句。(1)選項 a 的不定代名詞 nothing 是單數，be 動詞用 is；因為 nothing 本身帶有否定意義，形同否定句；(2) 選項 b 的不定代名詞 anything 也是單數，be 動詞的否定用 isn't；(3)選項 c 中 no tasks 的 no 是否定用字。所以，這三個選項的附加問句全用肯定句。

英文　That is Mrs. Henderson's husband, isn't <u>it</u>?

中譯　那是安德森太太的先生，不是嗎？

解說

　　空格應該填入哪個代名詞？不要因為直述句提到 Mrs. Henderson's husband，就填入代名詞 he。本句主詞不是 Mrs. Henderson's husband，而是指示代名詞 that，所以附加問句的主詞用 it，不可用 that，答案選 c。只要直述句是「That / This is＋ N」，附加問句的主詞一律用 it。

英文　**Those are the dogs' towels, aren't <u>they</u>?**

中譯　那些是狗兒用的毛巾，不是嗎？

解說

　　本題也使用了指示代名詞當主詞，不同的是，這次是 that 的複數 those。只要直述句是「Those / These are ＋ N」，附加問句的主詞一律用複數的 they，所以答案選 c。

英文　**Let's dance, <u>shall we</u>?**

中譯　咱們來跳舞好嗎？

解說

　　本題測驗重點：祈使句的附加問句。遇到表示勸誘的「Let's ＋原形動詞」，附加問句沒有其他選擇，一律用 shall we。故選 d。

英文　**A: Humans aren't the same species as gorillas, are they?**
　　　B: <u>No, they aren't</u>.

中譯　A：人類和大猩猩不是同一物種，對吧？
　　　B：沒錯，他們不是。

解說

　　本題測驗重點：附加問句的回答方式。回應附加問句把握一個原則：(1) 肯定回答：如果用 Yes 回答，be 動詞後面一定不會有 not，因為這是肯定句。(2) 否定回答：如果用 No 回答，be 動詞後面一定有 not，因為這是否定句。所以答案選 c。

13.

英文　**A yard <u>is</u> ten inches, <u>isn't</u> it?**
A yard <u>isn't</u> ten inches, <u>is</u> it?

中譯　一碼等於十吋，不是嗎？

解說

　　直述句與附加問句，無論前面用否定、後面用肯定，還是前面用否定、後面用肯定，皆可，所以選項 a 或 b 皆是正確答案。

14.

英文　**Don't forget, <u>will</u> you.**

中譯　不要忘了，好嗎？

解說

　　本題測驗重點：祈使句的附加問句。本題的祈使句屬於「請求對方幫忙、下令」的一種，附加問句一律用 will you?，所以答案選 a。

15.

英文　**Please, come in and sit down, <u>won't</u> you?**

中譯　請進來坐，好嗎？

解說

　　本題測驗重點：祈使句的附加問句。本題的祈使句屬於「邀請對方做某事」的一種，附加問句一律用 won't you?，所以答案選 b。

英文　**You don't really mean that, <u>do you</u>?**

中譯　你不是當真的吧，對吧？

解說

　　直述句使用否定句 don't mean that，附加問句就用肯定，故答案選 a。動詞 mean 作「意指；意味」解釋。

英文　**You <u>couldn't</u> give me a hand with this, could you?**

中譯　你不能幫我處理這個，對吧？

解說

　　附加問句的 could you 是肯定句，所以直述句用否定。故答案選 b。動詞片語 give (someone) a hand 的意思是「幫忙」。如果附加問句為「can you?」，選項 d 的 can't 就是正確答案。

英文　**You <u>haven't got</u> a few dollars you could lend me, <u>have</u> you?**
　　　You <u>don't have</u> a few dollars you could lend me, <u>do</u> you?

中譯　你沒有一些錢可以借我，對吧？

解說

　　第一空格要填入意思與「擁有」相關的動詞。選項 b 或 c 都是正確答案。先看選項 b，have got 形式上是現在完成式（have＋get 的過去分詞），但實質意義上卻是現在式，在非正式的口語用法中，常常用來代替 have「有……」。例：We haven't got enough money＝We don't have enough money.「我們錢不夠多。」但，附加問句還是根據現在完成式的形式，用 have。再看選項 c，don't have 是動詞 have 的否定，因為 have 是一般動詞，所以附加問句要用助動詞 do。選項 a 的問題出在第二個答案：haven't 要改成 don't。此外，a few 的意思是「一些」。

19.

解答：**b**

英文 Nobody saw the prisoner escape, <u>did they</u>?

中譯 沒有人看到犯人脫逃，不是嗎？

解說

　　如果直述句的主詞是不定代名詞 nothing / nobody / someone / somebody / everyone 等等，附加問句的人稱代名詞一律用 they。本句主詞是 nobody，沒有其他選擇，答案選 b。

20.

解答：**d**

英文 Someone has taken the money, <u>haven't they</u>?

中譯 有人把錢拿走了，對吧？

解說

　　本句主詞 Someone 也是不定代名詞，所以附加問句的主詞必須用 they，答案選 d。直述句的動詞用現在完成式 has taken，附加問句也要用完成式的 have，不用 has 是因為 they 為複數人稱。

14 動名詞

動名詞的形式與定義

» 動名詞的形式是 V-ing，亦即，在動詞後面加上 ing。
» 動名詞是名詞，不是動詞，可以當句中的主詞、補語、受詞等等。
» 動名詞用來表示「習慣」或者「平常做的事」。

動名詞的功用

│當主詞：此時主詞當成「一件事」，故動詞必須用單數。│

Drinking too much coffee **is** bad for our health.
咖啡喝太多有礙我們的健康。

Writing letters **takes** too much time.
＝Writing a letter takes too much time.
寫信花太多時間。

【說明】主詞中的 letters 是複數，但是動詞不會因此用複數 take，因為 letters 只是主詞的一部分，本句的主詞是 writing letters「寫信」這件事，重點不在於寫了幾封信。所以如果用 writing a letter 表達，動詞也一樣要用 takes。

Losing his wallet **drove** him crazy.
遺失皮夾把他給急瘋了。

│當 be 動詞的補語│

My hobby is **taking** pictures.
我的嗜好是拍照。

My favorite leisure activity is **playing** tennis.
我最喜歡的休閒活動是打網球。

His favorite sport is **swimming**.

他最喜愛的運動是游泳。

> 當動詞的受詞：下列動詞後面不可接不定詞（to V），只能
> 接動名詞（V-ing）當受詞：enjoy「喜歡」；quit「戒除」；
> **practice**「練習」；**finish**「完成」；**mind**「在意」；**avoid**「避免」；
> **spend**「花費」。

My father enjoys **smoking** after dinner.

我爸喜歡飯後抽菸。

He quitted / stopped **gambling**.

他已經戒賭了。

Jessie practices **playing** piano every day.

潔希每天練習彈鋼琴。

Andy finished **writing** his homework and then went to bed.

安迪寫完作業便上床睡覺。

Do you mind **opening** the window?

你介意我開窗嗎？

You should always avoid **driving** after drinking.

你喝酒之後，一定不可以開車。

Joe spends two hours **playing** computer games every day.

喬每天花兩個小時玩電腦遊戲。

動名詞當介系詞的受詞

He is fond of **going** out at night.

他喜歡晚上出門。

【說明】be fond of + V-ing / N 作「喜歡……」解釋。

She is good at **making** a cake.

她很會做蛋糕。

【說明】be good at + V-ing / N 作「擅長……」解釋。

The book is <u>worth</u> **reading**.
這本書值得一讀。

【說明】be worth + V-ing / N 作「值得……」解釋。

He dreams <u>of</u> **traveling** around the world someday.
他夢想有一天可以環遊世界。

【說明】dream of + V-ing / N 作「夢想……」解釋。

She is interested <u>in</u> **reading** detective novels.
她對閱讀推理小說很感興趣。

【說明】be interested in + V-ing / N 作「對……感興趣」解釋。

Mr. Huang makes his living <u>by</u> **teaching**.
黃先生以教書維生。

【說明】介系詞 by 表示「方法；途徑」。

當 after / before 的受詞

- after 作「在……之後」解釋；before 作「在……之前」解釋。兩者有個共通點：兼具介系詞和連接詞兩種功能。
- after / before 當介系詞時，後面只能接名詞或動名詞。
- after / before 當連接詞時，後面必須接句子：主詞＋動詞。

1. after / before 當介系詞：

After <u>taking</u> out a key from her bag, Susan opened the door.
蘇珊從包包裡取出鑰匙之後，把門打開。

Don't forget to turn off the light **before** <u>going out</u>.
出門前，別忘了把燈關掉。

2. after / before 當連接詞時，前兩句可以改寫如下，意思不變：

After <u>she took out a key</u> from her bag, Susan opened the door.

Don't forget to turn off the light **before** <u>you go out</u>.

有些動詞後面可接動名詞（**V-ing**）或不定詞當受詞，意義皆同。

I <u>like / love</u> **swimming**.
＝I <u>like / love</u> **to swim**.
我喜歡游泳。

She <u>hates</u> **making** mistakes.
＝She <u>hates</u> **to make** mistakes.
她討厭犯錯。

He <u>continues</u> **telling** the story.
＝He <u>continues</u> **to tell** the story.
他繼續說故事。

The baby <u>began / started</u> **crying**.
＝The baby <u>began / started</u> **to cry**.
小嬰兒開始哭了起來。

題 目

1. Are you interested _____ a puppet show?
   a. to see
   b. in seeing
   c. of going to see
   d. to go see

2. _____ healthily is especially important for pregnant women.
   a. Eating
   b. Going to eat
   c. Eat
   d. By eating

3. It is fun _____ games, but sometimes _____ hard is necessary.
   a. playing ; to work
   b. playing ; working
   c. playing ; work
   d. to play ; to work

4. I don't mind _____ your stories, but don't expect me _____ them.
   a. listening ; believing
   b. hearing ; believe
   c. listening to ; to believe
   d. hearing ; to believing

5. You can get to Kimpo Airport _____ the subway from downtown Seoul.
   a. in taking
   b. by take
   c. to take
   d. by taking

6. All the kids _____ playing baseball at the summer camp.
   a. enjoying
   b. have enjoy
   c. enjoyed
   d. enjoyed to

7. If you don't _____ your English every day, then you are _____ your time.
   a. practicing ; wasting
   b. practicing ; a waste of
   c. practice ; wasting
   d. practice ; to waste

8. Excuse me. Could you _____ me how to find the _____ area?
   a. tell ; smoking
   b. telling ; smoker
   c. tell ; smoke
   d. be telling ; smoking

9. After _____ the paintings on the fourth floor, they went to the basement _____ the mummies.
   a. look at ; to see
   b. looking at ; seeing
   c. looking at ; to see
   d. looked at ; seeing

10. Like they always say, _____ is believing.
    a. to see
    b. seeing
    c. to have seen
    d. Either b or c

11. You could make some money _____ selling that car you never _____.

    a. by ; drive

    b. for ; driving

    c. by ; driving

    d. for ; drive

12. _____ drugs _____ a good way to land yourself in jail.

    a. Selling ; are

    b. You sell ; is

    c. To sell ; are

    d. Selling ; is

13. Thank you _____ us.

    a. for teach

    b. for teaching

    c. for taught

    d. Either b or c

14. It is important for our staff _____ the customers' needs.

    a. understand

    b. to understand

    c. understanding

    d. understands

15. My parents _____ about _____ Jordan a car for his sixteenth birthday.

    a. thought ; getting

    b. are thinking ; getting

    c. are thinking ; to get

    d. Either a or b

16. _____ is definitely not easy.

    a. Quitting smoking

    b. To quit smoke

    c. Quit smoking

    d. Either a or b

17. I'm not sure where they're going, but I think they're _____.

    a. go shopping

    b. going shopping

    c. going shop

    d. Either a or c

18. A: If you're free tonight, how about _____ a movie?

    a. seeing

    b. go see

    c. going to

    d. Either a or c

19. His worst habit, _____ his nails, totally drives me crazy!

    a. biting

    b. to bite

    c. bites

    d. Either a or c

20. Robert doesn't _____ well, but James is good at _____.

    a. singing ; it

    b. sing ; sing

    c. sing ; singing

    d. sings ; singing

解 析

1. 解答：**b**

英文 Are you interested <u>in seeing</u> a puppet show?

中譯 你對木偶戲感興趣嗎？

解說

　　本題測驗重點：介系詞後面接動名詞。片語「be interested in ＋ N／V-ing」表示「對……感興趣；喜歡……」。介系詞 in 後面只能接名詞或動名詞，故答案選 b。

2. 解答：**a**

英文 <u>Eating</u> healthily is especially important for pregnant women.

中譯 健康的飲食對孕婦特別重要。

解說

　　本題測驗重點：動名詞當主詞。答案選 a。動名詞當主詞視為一件事，用來陳述事實，動詞用單數 is。選 b 表未來，不合句意。選項 c 的 eat 是動詞，本句已經有 be 動詞 is，所以 c 不能選。選項 d 的介系詞 by 表示「藉由（方法）」，介系詞片語無法當主詞。

3. 解答：**b**

英文 It is fun <u>playing</u> games, but sometimes <u>working</u> hard is necessary.

中譯 玩遊戲是很有趣，但有時候努力工作也是必要的。

解說

　　句型「It is fun ＋ V-ing」表示「（做）……是很有趣的」。fun「樂趣」是名詞，第一空格必須填入動名詞 playing。第二空格要填入動名詞當主詞，後面的動詞是單數 is，故答案選 b。

4. 解答：**c**

英文 I don't mind <u>listening to</u> your stories, but don't expect me <u>to believe</u> them.

中譯 我不介意聽聽你的故事，但不要期待我會相信。

解說

　　動詞 mind 作「介意；在乎」解釋，這個字後面只能接動名詞。動詞 expect 作「期待；指望」解釋，後面必須接不定詞。所以答案選 c。注意「listen to ＋某人／某事」，一定要介系詞 to，才能接聆聽的對象（受詞）。

5. 解答：**d**

英文 You can get to Kimpo Airport <u>by taking</u> the subway from downtown Seoul.

中譯 你從首爾市中心搭地鐵可以到達金浦機場。

解說

　　「get to ＋地點」的意思是「到達……」。搭乘交通工具用 by 表示「方法；手段」。因為 by 是介系詞，後面只能接名詞（交通工具名稱）；如果要接動詞，動詞一定要變成動名詞，所以答案選 d：by taking the subway。如果用「by ＋交通工具」，交通工具前面不需要定冠詞 the。例：I go to work by subway every day.「我每天搭地鐵上班。」

6. 解答：**c**

英文 All the kids <u>enjoyed</u> playing baseball at the summer camp.

中譯 夏令營的小朋友都喜歡打棒球。

解說

　　本句缺少動詞，因此答案選 c。注意：動詞 enjoy 後面只能接動名詞。

7.

解答：**c**

英文 **If you don't practice your English every day, then you are wasting your time.**

中譯 你如果不每天練習英文，那你是在浪費自己的時間。

解說

第一空格要填入原形動詞，因為前面有否定助動詞 don't。第二空格要填現在分詞（V-ing），和前面的 are 形成現在進行式。waste 除了當動詞，也可以當名詞，經常以「a waste of + N」表現。例：Buying the brand-name goods is a waste of money.「花錢買名牌貨很浪費錢。」

8.

解答：**a**

英文 **Excuse me. Could you tell me how to find the smoking area?**

中譯 打擾一下。可以請你告訴我吸菸區在哪裡嗎？

解說

本句還缺少一般動詞。因為有助動詞 Could，所以第一空格應填入原形動詞 tell。第二空格需要動名詞當形容詞來修飾後面的名詞 area，故答案選 a。

9.

解答：**c**

英文 **After looking at the paintings on the fourth floor, they went to the basement to see the mummies.**

中譯 在欣賞完四樓的繪畫之後，他們走到地下室看木乃伊。

解說

句首的 after 在這裡當介系詞，介系詞後面只能接名詞或動名詞，所以第一空格答案是 looking at。第二空格因為前面有動詞 went，所以後面必須接不定詞 to see，所以答案選 c。

10.

英文 **Like they always say, <u>seeing</u> is believing.**

中譯 俗話說得好：眼見為憑。

解說

　　本題測驗重點：動名詞當主詞。空格後面有單數動詞 is，但還缺少主詞；動詞 is 後面是另一動名詞 believing，故答案應該選 b。如果要選 A 的不定詞 to see，那麼後面的也要改成不定詞 to believe：「To see is to believe.」和原句一樣意思。不定詞和動名詞一樣也可以當主詞，當一件事情看待，所以用單數動詞。句首的 like 是介系詞，作「和⋯⋯一樣」解釋。

11.

英文 **You could make some money <u>by</u> selling that car you never <u>drive</u>.**

中譯 你可以把你那輛從不開的車子賣了，賺一點錢。

解說

　　依照句意，第一空格要填入介系詞 by。by 表示「方法；途徑」，後面只能接名詞或動名詞，空格後面的 selling 是動名詞。第二空格還缺少一般動詞，因為「that car you never...」是關係子句，裡面有第二個句子，其中主詞是 you，但還缺動詞，故答案選 a。在「...that car (that) you never」當中，you 前面其實省略了關係代名詞 that。that 作為關代有兩大功能：一、代替前面的 car，成為下一句 you never drive 的受詞；二、扮演連接詞的角色，連接前後兩個句子。

12.

英文 **<u>Selling</u> drugs <u>is</u> a good way to land yourself in jail.**

中譯 販賣毒品只會讓你快一點進監牢。

解說

　　本句缺少主詞和動詞。第一空格要填入動名詞當主詞，因為是動名詞當主詞，當成一件事情看待，所以動詞一定用單數的 is。選項 c 的不定詞（To sell）也可以當主詞，但是和動名詞當主詞一樣，動詞用單數，are 改成 is 就可以選。

13.

解答：**b**

英文 Thank you <u>for teaching</u> us.

中譯 謝謝你教導我們。

解說

　　句型「Thank ＋人＋ for ＋ N / V-ing」表示「為了……謝謝某人」。介系詞 for 後面只能名詞或動名詞，所以答案選 b。

14.

解答：**b**

英文 It is important for our staff <u>to understand</u> the customers' needs.

中譯 我們的職員必須瞭解客戶的需求。

解說

　　句型「It is ＋形容詞＋（for 人）to V」表示「做……是必要的、重要的」，It 是虛主詞（形式上的主詞，本身沒有意義）。本句不缺少動詞（因為 It is），不定詞引導出的片語（to understand the customers' needs），才是真正的主詞，故答案選 b。另外，staff「職員」是集合名詞，本身已是複數，不可加 s。

15.

解答：**d**

英文 My parents <u>thought</u> about <u>getting</u> Jordan a car for his sixteenth birthday.
My parents <u>are thinking</u> about <u>getting</u> Jordan a car for his sixteenth birthday.

中譯 我的父母考慮買一輛汽車給喬丹當作他十六歲的生日禮物。

解說

　　本句缺少動詞。第一空格無論填入過去式（thought），還是現在進行式（are thinking），兩者皆可。第二空格前面是介系詞 about，所以後面要接動名詞 getting。故選項 a 或 b 皆是正確答案。「think about ＋ N / V-ing」作「考慮；打算」解釋。

英文　**Quitting smoking is definitely not easy.**

中譯　戒菸真的很不容易。

解說

　　本句缺少主詞。只有選項 a 的動名詞可以當主詞，動詞是單數的 is。quitting 是從動詞 quit 變化而來。quit 作「戒除、停止（某種習慣）」解釋，這個字後面只能接名詞或動名詞。例：He finally quit gambling and found a job in a factory.「他總算戒了賭，在一家工廠找到了工作。」（gambling 是 gamble 的動名詞）。

英文　**I'm not sure where they're going, but I think they're going shopping.**

中譯　我不太肯定他們去了什麼地方，但我知道他們去購物了。

解說

　　空格應該填入現在分詞，和前面的 be 動詞（they're）形成現在進行式，故答案選 b。

英文　**If you're free tonight, how about seeing a movie?**
　　　If you're free tonight, how about going to a movie?

中譯　如果你今天晚上有空，我們去看場電影好不好？

解說

　　「how about ＋ N／V-ing」表示「提議（做某事）」。因為 about 是介系詞，所以後面必須接名詞或動名詞，除了選項 a 的 seeing，選項 c 的 going to 也是正確答案。「go to ＋ V」表示「從事……」，例：We went to visit our grandmother in Hualien last month.「我們上個月去拜訪住在花蓮的外婆。」

英文　**His worst habit, biting his nails, totally drives me crazy!**

中譯　他有個習慣非常糟糕——咬指甲，真是讓我抓狂！

解說

　　本句主詞是 His worst habit，動詞是 drives，drive 作「逼使、迫使（人）……」解釋，後面需要人作受詞。形容詞 crazy 是受詞補語，用來說明受詞 me 處於什麼狀態。空格應該填入 bite 的現在分詞，現在分詞表主動，修飾前面的主詞。

英文　**Robert doesn't sing well, but James is good at singing.**

中譯　羅伯特歌唱得不是很好，但詹姆士很會歌唱。

解說

　　第一空格前面是 doesn't，所以後面空格必須填入原形動詞 sing。第二空格是介系詞 at 的受詞，介系詞後面要接動名詞 singing。「be good at ＋ N / V-ing」表示「對……很擅長」，例：Tina is good at playing chess.「蒂娜很會下棋。」

15 ｜ 不定詞

不定詞的用法和句型

» 定義：一個句子不可以有兩個動詞，第二個動詞須改為「不定詞」或「動名詞」形式，亦視為名詞，當作受詞。

» 形式：「不定詞」＝ to ＋動詞。否定＝ not to ＋動詞

» 用法：

1. 隨著主詞改變，主動詞會有單複數變化，「不定詞」不受影響。

2. 有些動詞後面一定要接不定詞，不可接動名詞。例如：

   want / need / ask / would like / expect / plan / decide / agree / ...

3. 有些動詞後面可以接動名詞或不定詞，而且意義相近。例如：

   begin / start / like / love / hate / ...

4. 有些動詞後面接動名詞或不定詞意義不同，要特別注意並瞭解。例如：

   remember / forget / try / regret / ...

5. 有些動詞後面必須先接人（sb.），再接不定詞，當作補語。例如：

   tell sb. to / ask sb. to / invite sb. to / allow sb. to / ...

主詞＋ V ＋不定詞 .

I want to buy this one.
我想買這一個。

We plan to rent a house.
我們計畫要租房子。

主詞＋ V ＋ not ＋不定詞 .

We decided not to go.
我們決定不去了。

I agree not to cook tonight.
我同意今晚不煮飯。

主詞＋Ｖ＋不定詞／動名詞．(意思相同)

I hate to do (= doing) housework.
我討厭做家事。

Let's start to work (= working).
我們開始來工作。

主詞＋Ｖ＋不定詞或動名詞．(意思不同)

Did you remember to lock the door?
你有記得鎖門嗎？

She still remembers taking the airplane for the first time.
她還記得第一次搭飛機的情形。

主詞＋Ｖ＋sb.＋不定詞．

He asked you to give him a call.
他要你給他打個電話。

I told you to stay here.
我叫你留在這裡。

主詞＋Ｖ＋sb.＋not＋不定詞．

She asked the child not to watch TV.
她要這個小孩別看電視。

I told her not to cook tonight.
我叫她今晚不要煮飯。

不定詞當名詞，也可以作「主詞」和「補語」

» 當主詞或補語用時，都可以改用動名詞，不過動名詞比較強調某個特定的動作，有 while 的意義存在；而不定詞則比較強調一般或未來的動作。

» 當主詞用時，視為第三人稱單數。

» 當主詞時，也可以用虛主詞形式：It... to ～ . 的句型。

» 當補語，可以作為主詞補語，或是受詞補語。It... to ～ . 的句型中，不定詞即為受詞補語。

不定詞＋第三人稱單數 be 動詞＋補語 .

To persuade her is impossible.
＝It is impossible to persuade her.

要說服她是不可能的。

To marry her has been my dream.
＝It has been my dream to marry her.

跟她結婚一直是我的夢想。

主詞＋第三人稱單數 be 動詞＋「不定詞」.

My wish is to see you once again.

我的願望是再見你一次。

To see is to believe.

眼見為憑。

主詞＋第三人稱單數 be 動詞＋形容詞＋「不定詞」.

We are glad to see you.

我們很高興見到你。

Are you ready to open the gifts?

你準備好要打開禮物了嗎？

too... （for sb.） to ～ / ... enough to ～ 的不定詞

This backpack is too heavy (for the boy) to carry.
這個背包（對男孩來說）太重了背不動。

You are now old enough to work.
你年紀夠大可以工作了。

in order to 的副詞用法

» 不定詞作副詞，表示目的，等於 in order to V 或 so as to V。
» 可置於句首，強調目的，與主要句子以逗號分開，用來修飾全句。這時的不定詞，等於 in order to，也可改為 in order that... 的子句型式。
» 注意，這時不可用「For ＋ Ving」，表示目的，必須用「For ＋名詞」。
» 其他修飾全句的獨立片語，還有：to be honest / to tell you the truth / needless to say...

The audience stood up to cheer.
＝The audience stood up in order (= so as) to cheer.
觀眾們起立歡呼。

To read newspaper, the old man put on his glasses.
＝In order to read newspaper, the old man put on his glasses.
＝In order that he could read newspaper, the old man put on his glasses.
為了看報紙，老人家戴上了眼鏡。

不含 to 的不定詞

» 作使役動詞 let, make, have 等的受詞補語。
» 作感官動詞 see, hear, feel 等的受詞補語，通常表示持續動作。感官動詞後面也可接動名詞，表示當下的動作。
» 慣用語 had better, would rather, can not but ～ , do nothing but ～等後面的不定詞，絕對不接 to。
» help 後面也可以省略 to，直接接動詞。

▌使役動詞＋主詞＋不定詞．▌

Just let him go.
就讓他去吧。

His words made her cry bitterly.
他的話讓她痛哭失聲。

▌主詞＋感官動詞＋不定詞．▌

I heard the baby cry all night.
我聽到寶寶哭了整夜。

He saw the thief sneaking into the house.
他看到小偷潛入屋裡。

▌主詞＋慣用語＋不定詞．▌

You had better say sorry to him.
你最好跟他說對不起。

They couldn't but do what their boss said.
他們不得不照老闆說的做。

▌主詞＋ help ＋不定詞．▌

Can you help me (to) buy something?
你可以幫我買點東西嗎？

I'll help Sara (to) move house.
我會幫莎拉搬家。

題 目

1. _____ NT$ 3,000,000 right now, you simply need to deposit NT$ 30,000 into this bank account.
   a. To win
   b. Winning
   c. To winning
   d. Win

2. The teacher asked _____ to draw three pictures about farming.
   a. she
   b. her
   c. we
   d. Either a or c

3. Harold _____ move to Hawaii.
   a. plans to
   b. plans
   c. has plans
   d. is planning

4. Lois wants us _____ ourselves.
   a. enjoy
   b. enjoyment
   c. to enjoy
   d. for enjoy

5. Do you want _____ cook dinner tonight?
   a. me to
   b. to
   c. I
   d. Either a or b

6. _____ a _____ must be very confident about the subject.
   a. To write ; book, you
   b. If write ; book, you
   c. Writing ; book
   d. Either a or c

7. _____ yourself is the highest achievement in life.
   a. Know
   b. To know
   c. Knowledge
   d. All of the above

8. You have the power _____ the world!
   a. change
   b. changing
   c. to change
   d. Either b or c

9. I especially love _____.
   a. to swim
   b. swimming
   c. to do swim
   d. Either a or b

10. The purpose of the mask is _____ the eyes and face.
    a. protect
    b. for protect
    c. to protect
    d. All of the above

11. Do you want _____ it or not?

    a. do

    b. to do

    c. doing

    d. Either b or c

12. I told you _____ do that!

    a. don't

    b. not

    c. not to

    d. All of the above

13. I think it is quite difficult _____ French.

    a. learns

    b. to learn

    c. learning

    d. for learning

14. The post is too _____ into that hole.

    a. big to fit

    b. big a fit

    c. big to fitting

    d. Either a or c

15. I'm sorry; I didn't _____ insult you.

    a. trying to

    b. mean to

    c. want for

    d. plan on

16. I am so _____ to see you here.
    a. surprised
    b. pleased
    c. happy
    d. All of the above

17. It is better _____ anything than _____ stupid.
    a. not to say ; to sound
    b. to not say ; sounding
    c. not saying ; sounding
    d. Either a or c

18. Elaine agreed _____ it.
    a. to do
    b. doing
    c. to have done
    d. Either a or b

19. Roger finished _____ it before the time was up.
    a. to do
    b. doing
    c. to have done
    d. Either a or b

20. I love _____ baseball.
    a. to play
    b. playing
    c. play the
    d. Either a or b

解 析

1.

英文 <u>To win</u> NT$ 3,000,000 right now, you simply need to deposit NT$ 30,000 into this bank account.

中譯 只需要存三萬台幣到這家銀行戶頭即可立刻贏得三百萬元台幣。

解說

　本句已經有主詞（you）＋主動詞（need），故選項 d（win）可以刪除。而選項 a（To win ＝ In order to win），表示目的，是修飾整個句子的副詞。注意，選項 b 必須在前面加上介系詞 For 才是正確答案。

2.

解答：**b**

英文 The teacher asked <u>her</u> to draw three pictures about farming.

中譯 老師要她畫三幅有關農作的畫。

解說

　動詞 ask 的用法為「ask ＋ sb. ＋ to ＋ V」，sb. 如果是代名詞，必須用受格，故答案選受詞 b（her）。

3.

解答：**a**

英文 Harold <u>plans</u> to move to Hawaii.

中譯 哈洛德打算搬去夏威夷。

解說

　句子已經有一個動詞（move），前面空格要填的動詞 plan 用法必須為「plan ＋ to ＋ V」，故答案選 a。

4. 解答：**c**

英文 **Lois wants us to enjoy ourselves.**

中譯 洛依絲要我們開心地玩。

解說

　　動詞 want 後面接人（us），再接動詞的用法為「want ＋ sb. ＋ to ＋ V」，故答案選 c。

5. 解答：**d**

英文 **Do you want me to cook dinner tonight?**
Do you want to cook dinner tonight?

中譯 你要我今晚煮晚餐嗎？
你今晚想煮晚餐嗎？

解說

　　動詞 want 的用法有二：「want ＋ to ＋ V」，或「want ＋ sb. ＋ to ＋ V」，故答案選 d。

6. 解答：**a**

英文 **To write a book, you must be very confident about the subject.**

中譯 要寫一本書，你必須對那個主題很有信心。

解說

　　因為 confident 必須用來形容人，不可形容事物，所以雖然不定詞 to write 和動名詞 Writing 都可以當名詞，不過，這裡不可用動名詞 Writing 作主詞，因此不可以選 c，必須選 a，以 you 作主詞，To write a book 則成為副詞（＝ In order to write a book...），表示目的，修飾整個主要句子。

7.

英文　**To know yourself is the highest achievement in life.**

中譯　了解自己是生命中最大的成就。

解說

　　本句動詞為 is，yourself 不可作為主詞，故需要選項 b 的不定詞 To know 形成不定詞片語，作為主詞。

8.

英文　**You have the power to change the world!**

中譯　你有改變世界的力量！

解說

　　have 作動詞的用法為 sb. have sth. to V，故答案選 c。

9.

英文　**I especially love to swim.**
　　　I especially love swimming.

中譯　我特別喜歡游泳。

解說

　　動詞 love 後面出現另一個動詞的用法為：「love + Ving」或「love + to + V」，句意相同，故答案選 d。

10.
解答： **c**

英文　**The purpose of the mask is to protect the eyes and face.**

中譯　面罩的目的是要保護眼睛和臉。

解說

　　本句的主詞為 the purpose of the mask，動詞為 is，而 protect 也是動詞，所以必須以不定詞呈現，作為補語之用，故答案為 c。

11.
解答： **b**

英文　**Do you want to do it or not?**

中譯　你要做還是不做？

解說

　　動詞 want 後面出現另一個動詞時，用法為：「want ＋ to ＋ V」，故答案選 b。

12.
解答： **c**

英文　**I told you not to do that!**

中譯　我告訴過你不要那麼做的！

解說

　　不定詞的否定形式為「not ＋不定詞」，故答案選 c。

13. 解答：**b**

英文 I think it is quite difficult <u>to learn</u> French.

中譯 我覺得學法文滿難的。

解說

形容詞 difficult 後面接補語，必須使用不定詞形式，故答案選 b。

14. 解答：**a**

英文 The post is too <u>big to fit</u> into that hole.

中譯 這竿子太大放不進那個洞。

解說

too... to ～用法為「too ＋ adj. / adv. ＋ to ＋ V」，故答案選 a。

15. 解答：**b**

英文 I'm sorry; I didn't <u>mean to</u> insult you.

中譯 對不起，我不是有意要侮辱你的。

解說

分號後的句子中有動詞（insult），前面還要有動詞，所以兩個動詞之間需要不定詞 to，故選項 c 和 d 可先刪除。另外，空格前還有助動詞，故必須選擇原形動詞 mean to（有意做……）。

英文　I am so <u>surprised</u> to see you here.
　　　I am so <u>pleased</u> to see you here.
　　　I am so <u>happy</u> to see you here.

中譯　我太驚喜可以在這裡見到你了。
　　　我太高興可以在這裡見到你了。
　　　我太開心可以在這裡見到你了。

解說

　形容詞 surprised（驚喜的）、pleased（高興的）、happy（開心的），語意接近，用法也一樣，都是以人為主詞、不定詞作為補語，故答案為 d。

英文　It is better <u>not to say</u> anything than <u>to sound</u> stupid.

中譯　與其說出蠢話，不如什麼都不說。

解說

　這題考的是特殊句型「It is better ＋ to V」，以句子的語意來判斷，不定詞必須加上否定詞，而否定詞的用法為「not ＋ to V」。另外，遇到連接詞 than 作比較的時候，後面的動詞（sound ～）也一定要用不定詞 to sound。故答案選 a。

英文　Elaine agreed <u>to do</u> it.

中譯　依蓮同意去做。

解說

　動詞 agree（同意）後面出現另一個動詞時，用法為：「agree ＋ to ＋ V」，故答案選 a。

英文　**Roger finished <u>doing</u> it before the time was up.**

中譯　羅傑在時間結束之前做完。

解說

　　動詞 finish 這個字後面出現另一個動詞時，可以用不定詞和動名詞，但句意不同。「finish + to V」表示完成手邊的工作去做另外的事，「finish + Ving」表示完成手邊在做的事，以這個句子的意思，答案選 b 比較適合。另外，time be up 是「時間到」的意思。

英文　**I love <u>to play</u> baseball.**
　　　I love <u>playing</u> baseball.

中譯　我喜歡打棒球。

解說

　　動詞 love 後面出現另一個動詞時，用法為：「love + Ving」或「love + to + V」，句意相同，故答案選 d。

16 現在分詞片語、過去分詞片語與介系詞片語

分詞片語和介系詞片語的用法和句型

» 定義：片語是不足以構成句子的字群，即不含主詞和動詞。形容詞關係子句可以簡化為介系詞片語或分詞片語。

» 句型簡化有三：

1. 關係子句為「關係代名詞＋ be 動詞＋介系詞」時，，省略關係代名詞和 be 動詞，形成介系詞片語。

2. 關係子句若為「關係代名詞＋ be 動詞＋分詞」時，也是直接省略關係代名詞和 be 動詞，形成分詞片語。

3. 關係子句若為「關係代名詞＋一般動詞」時，則省略關係代名詞，將一般動詞改成分詞，形成分詞片語。

» 用法：

1. 形容詞子句或片語都必須放在主詞之後，作後位修飾。

2. 現在分詞表示主動；過去分詞片語表示被動。

3. 特別注意，形容詞子句含有主格關係代名詞 who / which / that，才可簡化為形容詞片語。

4. 分詞片語 wearing ～＝介系詞片語「in ＋服裝、服裝顏色」或「with ＋首飾、配件」；「with ＋身體特徵」＝分詞片語 having ～。

現在分詞片語＝「關係代名詞＋ be 動詞＋現在分詞」或「關係代名詞＋一般動詞」

The woman talking to John is our new manager.
＝The woman who is talking to John is our new manager.
和約翰說話的那個女人是我們新任經理。

Students studying hard will pass the test.
＝Students who study hard will pass the test.
用功的學生將會通過考試。

過去分詞片語＝「關係代名詞＋ be 動詞＋過去分詞」

The shark caught in the net escaped.

＝The shark which was caught in the net escaped.

被網抓住的那隻鯊魚逃脫了。

The main language spoken in America is English.

＝The main language which is spoken in America is English.

在美國主要說的語言是英語。

介系詞片語＝「關係代名詞＋ be 動詞＋介系詞」

The girl in a red dress is our class leader.

＝The girl who is in a red dress is our class leader.

＝The girl who is wearing a red dress is our class leader.

＝The girl wearing a red dress is our class leader.

穿紅洋裝的那個女生是我們班長。

The man, with only one leg, feels pity for himself.

＝The man, who is with only one leg, feels pity for himself.

＝The man, who has only one leg, feels pity for himself.

＝The man, having only one leg, feels pity for himself.

這個只有一隻腳的男人覺得自己很可憐。

題 目

1. The girl _____ under the tree looks happy.
    a. sitting
    b. sits
    c. is sitting
    d. None of the above

2. Would all students _____ please stand up.
    a. in the fourth grade
    b. wearing yellow
    c. in gym clothes
    d. All of the above

3. Curious George looked everywhere for the man _____.
    a. in the yellow hat
    b. wearing yellow hat
    c. has the yellow hat
    d. with yellow hat

4. The woman _____ red is my wife.
    a. wearing
    b. who is wearing
    c. in
    d. All of the above

5. The team _____ gets to take home the trophy.
    a. with the most wins
    b. that most wins
    c. wins the most
    d. All of the above

6. The report _____ by Stacy is much better than the one _____ by Clara.

   a. wrote ; written

   b. wrote ; wrote

   c. written ; written

   d. written ; wrote

7. The UFO _____ by my mother didn't look like this picture.

   a. seeing

   b. seen

   c. saw

   d. was seen

8. The girl _____ short, blond hair and blue eyes is my sister.

   a. with

   b. who has

   c. having

   d. Either a or b

9. That man _____ the line _____ red hair is the guy I was telling you about.

   a. in ; who has

   b. who is in ; with

   c. standing in ; has

   d. in ; of

10. The _____ looks _____ the one you are looking for.

   a. student, who ; nervous, is

   b. student who ; nervous is

   c. student, who ; nervous is

   d. student who ; nervous, is

11. I'm trying to find a man _____ Michael. Is he in here?

   a. who named

   b. named

   c. whose name

   d. Either a or b

12. That dog _____ the window is so cute!

   a. is in

   b. sitting in

   c. in

   d. Either b or c

13. Children _____ thirteen cannot watch this film without a parent.

   a. under

   b. who are under

   c. are under

   d. Either a or b

14. Kids _____ at home can call this help line number.

   a. having problems

   b. have problems

   c. with problem

   d. All of the above

15. I hope that all students _____ the test before will pass this time.

   a. who have taken

   b. who taken

   c. taken

   d. have taken

16. A boy _____ by a dog becomes a man _____ of dogs.

    a. was bitten ; is scared

    b. being bitten ; who is scared

    c. bitten ; scared

    d. Either b or c

17. The horse _____ broken leg still runs fast.

    a. having

    b. with

    c. with the

    d. which is having a

18. I heard a song _____ by her on the radio yesterday.

    a. sing

    b. singing

    c. sang

    d. sung

19. Houses _____ the highway have to put up with noise pollution.

    a. along

    b. next to

    c. beside

    d. All of the above

20. A lot of skyscrapers _____ before 1930 are still standing today.

    a. built

    b. were built

    c. that are built

    d. All of the above

解析

1.

英文 **The girl <u>sitting</u> under the tree looks happy.**

中譯 坐在樹下的那個女孩看起來很快樂。

解說

　　此句的主詞為 the girl，動詞為 looks，故不可選 b 或 c，正確答案應為 a，現在分詞用法，還原成形容詞子句後為 who is sitting...，補充說明主詞。

2.

英文
Would all students <u>in the fourth grade</u> please stand up.
Would all students <u>wearing yellow</u> please stand up.
Would all students <u>in gym clothes</u> please stand up.

中譯
請所有四年級的學生站起來。
請所有穿黃色的學生站起來。
請所有穿運動服的學生站起來。

解說

　　此句的主詞為 all students，動詞為 stand up，選項 a 和 c 為介系詞片語，選項 b 為分詞片語，都可以補充說明主詞（省略了 who are），全部正確，故答案為 d。

3.

英文 **Curious George looked everywhere for the man <u>in the yellow hat</u>.**

中譯 好奇的喬治四處尋找戴黃色帽子的男子。

解說

　　此句已經有主詞 George、動詞 looked，和受詞 the man，故刪除選項 c。空格處需要有補充說明受詞 the man 的形容詞片語或子句，子句 who is wearing the yellow hat 修飾受詞不可省略 who is；形容詞片語用法為「in ＋服裝」，故答案為選項 a。

4. 解答：**d**

英文
The woman <u>wearing</u> red is my wife.
The woman <u>who is</u> wearing red is my wife.
The woman <u>in</u> red is my wife.

中譯　穿紅衣服的那個女人是我太太。

解說

　　此句主詞為 the woman、動詞為 is，補充說明主詞可以用子句 who is wearing / in red、或省略 who is，改用分詞 wearing red，或用片語 in red，故答案 d。

5. 解答：**a**

英文　The team <u>with the most wins</u> gets to take home the trophy.

中譯　贏最多分的隊伍就可以把獎品帶回家。

解說

　　本句主詞為 the team、動詞為 gets，故不可選 c。選項 b 為子句，錯在子句中的動詞 win 需要接受詞。故選項 a 為正確答案，這裡的 wins 為名詞，「with ＋名詞」為介系詞片語，表示「擁有……」。

6. 解答：**c**

英文　The report <u>written</u> by Stacy is much better than the one <u>written</u> by Clara.

中譯　史黛西寫的報告比克拉拉寫的好太多了。

解說

　　主要子句主詞為 the report、動詞為 is。than 之後的 the one ＝ the report。由於報告是由人撰寫，故需要過去分詞 written 來修飾主詞，可還原為 which is written...。

7.

英文　The UFO <u>seen</u> by my mother didn't look like this picture.

中譯　我媽媽看到的那個幽浮看起來不像這張照片。

解說

　　此句主詞為 the UFO、動詞為 didn't look like，由於 UFO 是被人看見，故需要過去分詞 seen，可還原為 which was seen。注意，修飾主詞的子句，必須同時有 which was，故選項 d 不可選。

8.

英文　The girl <u>with</u> short, blond hair and blue eyes is my sister.
　　　The girl <u>who has</u> short, blond hair and blue eyes is my sister.

中譯　那個有金短髮和藍眼睛的女生是我姊姊。

解說

　　本句主詞 the girl、動詞 is，兩者之間的字全都是用來修飾主詞。形容人的外在特徵，可用介系詞片語 with～，選項 a 正確，也可以用子句 who has，選項 b 也對，故答案為 d。注意，形容詞子句中如果有一般動詞，可以簡化主詞、將動詞改為動名詞（主動），但是 have 作一般動詞時，不可以有動名詞形式，故選項 c 錯誤。

9.

英文　That man <u>in</u> the line <u>who has</u> red hair is the guy I was telling you about.

中譯　在排隊的那個紅髮男子就是我跟你說的那傢伙。

解說

　　本句的主詞為 That man，動詞為 is，之間的所有字都是補充說明主詞。選項 c 出現了另一個動詞原形 has，故錯誤。說明人的外觀特徵，用介系詞 with～或形容詞子句 who has～，故選項 d 錯誤。注意，選項 b 不可選，沒有這種用法。正確答案為選項 a。

英文　The <u>student</u> <u>who</u> looks <u>nervous</u> is the one you are looking for.

中譯　那個看起來很緊張的學生就是你在尋找的人。

解說

　　本句主詞為 you，動詞為片語 are looking for，在主詞 you 前面的所有字都是受詞。這是有關形容詞子句的限定或不限定用法，若是限定，則與前面的名詞之間沒有逗號，若為不限定，則需要逗號。從語意上瞭解，由於在尋找的是某個特定對象，所以必須用限定用法，答案為選項 b。

英文　I'm trying to find a man <u>named</u> Michael. Is he in here?

中譯　我在找一位叫做麥可的男子，他在這裡嗎？

解說

　　空格以後的文字需要關係代名詞引導的形容詞子句來說明 a man，選項 a 和 c 都少了 be 動詞（who is named；whose name is）。正確答案為選項 b，此乃形容詞子句省略的關係代名詞和 be 動詞之後的結果。

英文　That dog <u>sitting</u> <u>in</u> the window is so cute!
　　　That dog <u>in</u> the window is so cute!

中譯　（坐）在櫥窗裡的那隻狗好可愛！

解說

　　本句已經有主要動詞 is，故選項 a 錯誤，少了關係代名詞 who。選項 b 和 c 都是省略了主詞和 be 動詞的用法，而動名詞和介系詞都可作為後位形容詞。

英文　**Children <u>under</u> thirteen cannot watch this film without a parent.**
　　　Children <u>who are under</u> thirteen cannot watch this film without a parent.

中譯　十三歲以下的兒童沒有父母陪伴不准觀看這部電影。

解說

　　本句已經有動詞 cannot watch，主詞 children 則需要關係代名詞 who 引導的形容詞子句，故 b 正確。另外，還可以「同時」省略主詞和 be 動詞，故選項 a 也正確，正確答案為 d。

英文　**Kids <u>having problems</u> at home can call this help line number.**

中譯　在家遇上麻煩的孩子可以打這支求救電話號碼。

解說

　　本句已有動詞 can call，主詞 kids 需要 who 引導的關係子句。原來的關係子句應該是 who is having problem，這題考的是省略主詞和 be 動詞的用法，故答案為 a。此外，選項 c 當中的 problem 若改為複數，則是介系詞片語作為後位形容詞的用法，也會是正確答案。

英文　**I hope that all students <u>who have taken</u> the test before will pass this time.**

中譯　我希望以前參加過測驗的所有學生這次都會通過。

解說

　　這題本身有 that 引導的名詞子句，在子句中的主詞為 all students，動詞為 will pass，兩者之間的文字需要 who 引導的形容詞子句，故答案為 a。其他選項的都是錯誤的省略。

16.

英文　**A boy bitten by a dog becomes a man scared of dogs.**

中譯　小時被狗咬，長大會怕狗。

解說

　　本句的動詞為 becomes，主詞 a boy 和補語 a man 都需要形容詞子句。本題考的是「同時」省略關係代名詞和被動式（was bitten）、形容詞（is scared）當中的 be 的用法，答案為 c。

17.

英文　**The horse with the broken leg still runs fast.**

中譯　那隻斷了條腿的馬仍然跑得很快。

解說

　　這題不可選 a 或 d，如果要用 have 的一般動詞用法，必須改為 that / which has a broken leg。答案為 c，因為 broken leg 為單數，需要冠詞 a / the。

18.

英文　**I heard a song sung by her on the radio yesterday.**

中譯　我昨天在收音機裡聽到一首她唱的歌。

解說

　　本句受詞 a song 需要形容詞子句 which is sung by her 來修飾，此為被動句，省略 which 和 is，故答案為 d。

19. 解答：d

英文
Houses <u>along</u> the highway have to put up with noise pollution.
Houses <u>next to</u> the highway have to put up with noise pollution.
Houses <u>beside</u> the highway have to put up with noise pollution.

中譯
沿著高速公路旁邊的房子必須忍受噪音污染。
緊鄰高速公路旁邊的房子必須忍受噪音污染。
在高速公路旁邊的房子必須忍受噪音污染。

解說

本句主詞 houses 需要介系詞片語作後位修飾，a、b、c 三個選項的語意都符合，故答案為 d。其中，put up with ～為動詞片語，是「忍受……」之意。

20. 解答：a

英文 A lot of skyscrapers <u>built</u> before 1930 are still standing today.

中譯 許多 1930 年以前蓋的摩天大樓現今依然矗立。

解說

本句主詞 skyscrapers 前面有 a lof of 作前位修飾，後面還需要形容詞子句修飾。但是特別注意，由於時間是在 1930 年以前，選項 c 的 be 動詞必須改為過去式 were 才正確。形容詞子句 that / which were built... 可「同時」省略關係代名詞和 be 動詞，故答案為 a。

17 情緒動詞改變而成的現在分詞和過去分詞以及非情緒性形容詞

由情緒動詞衍生為情緒形容詞的用法和句型

» 定義：用來修飾人或物的喜怒哀樂等的動詞，稱之為情緒動詞。分詞，是一種作為形容詞用的動詞型態。

» 情緒形容詞有兩類：

1.「過去分詞」屬於被動，用來修飾被引起情緒者，通常是有生命的「人」。

2.「現在分詞」屬於主動，通常用來修飾引起情緒者，通常是無生命的「物」。

» 用法：

物＋情緒動詞＋人.

＝物＋ be 動詞＋情緒現在分詞＋ to ＋人.（介系詞固定用 to）

＝人＋ be 動詞＋情緒過去分詞＋介系詞＋物.（介系詞因分詞而異）

» 此外，be 動詞也改用 feel / become / get / look / seem / ... 等動詞。不過，上面三個句型要互換只能在使用 be 動詞的情況下。

情緒動詞衍生的現在分詞和過去分詞

» 分詞形態的情緒形容詞與一般形容詞一樣，可修飾名詞或作為補語。修飾名詞時，通常置於名詞前面。

» 介系詞的使用：

1.「現在分詞」＋ to ～.（介系詞 to 的意思是「對～而言」）

2.「過去分詞」＋介系詞～.，每個音單字不同，必須個別記憶。

» 動詞（使……感到～）vs. 現在分詞（令人感到～）vs. 過去分詞（感到～）：

1. bore 使……感到無趣：boring / bored (with)

2. excite 使……感到興奮：exciting / excited (about)

3. interest 使……感到興趣：interesting / interested (in)

4. surprise 使……感到驚訝：surprising / surprised (at)

5. tire 使……感到厭倦：tiring / tired (of / with)

6. touch 使……感動：touching / touched (by)

7. scare 使……感到驚嚇：scaring / scared (of)

8. confuse 使……感到困惑：confusing / confused (by / with / about)

9. trouble 使……感到麻煩：troubling / troubled (with)

10. embarrass 使……感到尷尬：embarrassing / embarrassed (in)

» 有些情緒動詞，與名詞同形，如：interest, surprise 等。用法：

1. 人＋ have ＋ an interest in ＋物

2. 物＋ be 動詞＋ a surprise to ＋人。

修飾名詞

This is a boring book.

這是一本無趣的書。

The excited dog started to bark.

那隻興奮的狗開始吠叫。

主詞＋ be 動詞（feel, become, ...）＋現在分詞的情緒形容詞 ＋ to ～.

This news is surprising to us.

（＝We're surprised at this news.）

（＝This news surprises us.）

（＝This news is a surprise to us.）

這個消息對我們而言很意外。

That movie is too scaring to little kids.

那部電影對小孩子而言太恐怖了。

主詞＋ be 動詞（feel, become, ...）＋過去分詞的情緒形容詞 ＋ prep. ～.

His mother feels touched by the card he made.

他母親被他做的卡片感動了。

They have got tired of / with eating frozen food.

他們已經對冷凍食物感到厭倦了。

非情緒性形容詞

» 情緒性形容詞除了上述的分詞型態，也有一般型態，如：glad, mad, kind, nice, foolish, cruel... 等。

» 情緒性形容詞 vs. 非情緒性形容詞的相似句型比較：

1. 人＋ be 動詞（feel, become, ...）＋情緒性 adj. ＋ to V.

　＝人＋ be 動詞（feel, become, ...）＋情緒性 adj. ＋子句.

2. It ＋ be 動詞＋情緒性 adj. ＋ of 人＋ to V.

　＝句型 1.

3. 物＋ be 動詞＋非情緒性 adj.（＋ for 人）＋ to V.

　＝ To V ＋物＋ be 動詞＋非情緒性 adj.（＋ for 人）.

　＝句型 4.

　（＊但 to V 的動詞後面必須沒有其他受詞，上面兩個等式方可成立。）

4. It ＋ be 動詞＋非情緒性 adj.（＋ for 人）＋ to V.

人＋ be 動詞（feel, become, ...）＋情緒性 adj. ＋ to V.

His old friends were glad to see him.

（＝His old friends were glad when they saw him.）

他的老朋友很高興見到他。

My parents will get mad to see you.

（＝My parents will get made if they see you.）

我父母見到你會生氣的。

It ＋ be 動詞＋情緒性 adj. ＋ of 人＋ to V.

It's so kind of you to help us.

（＝You are so kind to help us.）

你真好心願意幫助我們。

It was foolish of me to believe you.

（＝I was so foolish to believe you.）

我真是愚蠢，竟然相信你。

物＋ be 動詞＋非情緒性 adj.（＋ for 人）＋ to V.

The Internet is very convenient to look for information.

網路很方便找資料。

This game is very easy for anyone to play.

（＝To play this game is very easy for anyone.）

（＝It's very easy for anyone to play this game.）

這個遊戲對任何人來說都很容易玩。

It ＋ be 動詞＋非情緒性 adj.（＋ for 人）＋ to V.

It is always wrong to tell a lie.

（＝To tell a lie is always wrong.）

說謊就是不對的。

It's very natural for everyone to love this lovely animal.

（＝To love this lovely animal is very natural for everyone.）

對每個人來說，很自然就會愛上這隻可愛的動物。

題目

1. The players were all very _____ because it was their first time playing in a foreign country.
   a. excite
   b. exciting
   c. excited
   d. excitement

2. Tell me what you are _____.
   a. interesting
   b. interested in
   c. interested
   d. interesting in

3. Nobody likes me. I think I must be too _____.
   a. bored
   b. boring
   c. bore
   d. boredom

4. Laurence of Arabia _____ everyone by marching his army across the Arabian Desert.
   a. surprised
   b. was surprising to
   c. was a surprise on
   d. was surprised by

5. This grammar is too _____ to me. I keep getting things _____.
   a. confused ; confusing
   b. confused ; confused
   c. confusing ; confusing
   d. confusing ; confused

6. Mary _____ by the news of her father's illness.
   a. was troubling
   b. is trouble
   c. was troubled
   d. troubled

7. A: Doctor, will I be OK?
   B: Well, these test results do look _____.
   a. trouble
   b. troubled
   c. troubling
   d. as trouble

8. Were you _____ with your meal, sir?
   a. satisfaction
   b. satisfy
   c. satisfied
   d. satisfying

9. Don't you ever get _____ that stupid video game?
   a. tired of
   b. tire with
   c. tiring of
   d. tire

10. Aren't you _____ going to the dance without a date?
    a. embarrassed to
    b. embarrassed about
    c. embarrassing to
    d. embarrassing

11. Army life is very _____.
    a. tiring
    b. tired
    c. tire
    d. tired of

12. I am very _____ ancient Chinese history.
    a. interesting in
    b. interested in
    c. interest in
    d. interesting

13. It was so nice _____ you to let us stay in your home.
    a. of
    b. for
    c. with
    d. Either a or b

14. The woman wore a very _____ dress.
    a. reveal
    b. revealed
    c. revealing
    d. reveals

15. You look _____ about something. What's up?
    a. trouble
    b. troubled
    c. troubling
    d. troubles

16. The driver said the accident occurred because he _____ the brake
    and the gas pedals.
    a. confuses
    b. confused
    c. confusing
    d. confuse

17. What a _____ it is to see you! Really, this is so _____ because
    I'm only here for a day.
    a. surprising ; surprised
    b. surprised ; surprising
    c. surprise ; surprising
    d. surprise ; surprise

18. The teacher is _____ by the slow progress of his students.
    a. frustrating
    b. frustrate
    c. frustrated
    d. None of the above

19. I'm very _____ about the exam next week.
    a. worried
    b. worry
    c. worrying
    d. Either a or c

20. It's really _____ Kevin to concentrate in class.
    a. hard to
    b. hard for
    c. hard of
    d. hard in

解析

1.　　　　　　　　　　　　　　　　　　　　　　　　解答：**c**

英文　**The players were all very <u>excited</u> because it was their first time playing in a foreign country.**

中譯　選手們全都非常興奮，因為那視他們第一次在外國比賽。

解說

　　本題考情緒動詞 excite 的「人＋ be 動詞＋的過去分詞」用法，故答案選 c。

2.　　　　　　　　　　　　　　　　　　　　　　　　解答：**b**

英文　**Tell me what you are <u>interested in</u>.**

中譯　告訴我你對什麼有興趣。

解說

　　本題考情緒動詞 interest 的「人＋ be 動詞＋的過去分詞」用法，另外，特別要注意，名詞子句的 what 為受詞，故必須使用介系詞 in，答案為 b。

3.　　　　　　　　　　　　　　　　　　　　　　　　解答：**b**

英文　**Nobody likes me. I think I must be too <u>boring</u>.**

中譯　沒有人喜歡我，我想我一定是太無趣了。

解說

　　這題要特別注意，雖然主詞為人（I），但這個人是引起別人覺得無趣者，故需要現在分詞 boring，答案為 b。

4.

解答：**a**

英文　Laurence of Arabia <u>surprised</u> everyone by marching his army across the Arabian Desert.

中譯　阿拉伯的勞倫斯行軍橫跨阿拉伯沙漠，震驚了每個人。

解說

　　本句缺少動詞，從語意上瞭解，勞倫斯是做出壯舉之人，而且句中又有介系詞 by + marching... 作為副詞，故只能用動詞 surprise（過去式 surprised），答案為選項 a。

5.

解答：**d**

英文　This grammar is too <u>confusing</u> to me. I keep getting things <u>confused</u>.

中譯　這個文法對我來說太令人混淆了，我一直把事情搞混了。

解說

　　第一句情緒動詞的用法為「物＋ be 動詞＋現在分詞＋ to ＋人」；第二句用法為「人＋ get ＋物＋過去分詞」，這裡的 get 是「使……（成某種狀態）」之意。

6.

解答：**c**

英文　Mary <u>was troubled</u> by the news of her father's illness.

中譯　瑪莉為她父親生病的消息而心神不寧。

解說

　　本句考的是情緒動詞 trouble 的被動用法「人＋ be 動詞＋情緒過去分詞（troubled）＋ by ＋物」。

7. 解答：**c**

英文
A: Doctor, will I be OK?
B: Well, these test results do look **troubling**.

中譯
A：醫生，我會沒事嗎？
B：嗯，這些檢查結果看起來確實令人心煩。

解說

　　題目的動詞為感官動詞 look「看起來……」，前面的 do 為副詞，意思是「確實」。本題考的是情緒動詞 trouble「物＋ look ＋現在分詞」的用法。

8. 解答：**c**

英文　Were you **satisfied** with your meal, sir?

中譯　您滿意您的餐點嗎，先生？

解說

　　這題考情緒動詞 satisfy「人＋ be 動詞＋過去分詞＋ with ＋物」的用法，故答案為選項 c。

9. 解答：**a**

英文　Don't you ever get **tired of** that stupid video game?

中譯　你難道從來不會對那個蠢透了的電動玩具感到厭倦嗎？

解說

　　這題考情緒動詞 tire「人＋ get ＋過去分詞＋ of ＋物」的用法，故答案為選項 a。

10.　　　　　　　　　　　　　　　　　　　　　　　解答：**b**

英文　**Aren't you embarrassed about going to the dance without a date?**

中譯　沒有攜伴參加舞會你不會難為情嗎？

解說

　　這題考情緒動詞 embarrass「人＋ be 動詞＋過去分詞＋ about / at ＋物」的用法，故答案為選項 b。

11.　　　　　　　　　　　　　　　　　　　　　　　解答：**a**

英文　**Army life is very tiring.**

中譯　從軍生涯非常累人。

解說

　　這題考 tire 的「物＋ be 動詞＋現在分詞」用法，故答案為選項 a。

12.　　　　　　　　　　　　　　　　　　　　　　　解答：**b**

英文　**I am very interested in ancient Chinese history.**

中譯　我對古代中國歷史非常感興趣。

解說

　　這題考情緒動詞 interest「人＋ be 動詞＋過去分詞＋ in ＋物」的用法，故答案為選項 b。

13.

英文 **It was so nice _of_ you to let us stay in your home.**

中譯 你真是太好心了，竟讓我們待在你家。

解說

　　這題考「It ＋ be 動詞＋情緒性形容詞＋ of ＋人」的用法，故答案為選項 a。

14.

英文 **The woman wore a very revealing dress.**

中譯 這個女人穿著一件非常暴露的洋裝。

解說

　　這題考一般動詞 reveal 的現在分詞，用來形容物品（dress）的用法。

15.

英文 **You look troubled about something. What's up?**

中譯 你看起來為某事所苦，怎麼了？

解說

　　這題考情緒動詞 trouble「人＋ look ＋過去分詞＋ about ＋物」的用法。

16. 解答：b

英文 The driver said the accident occurred because he <u>confused</u> the brake and the gas pedals.

中譯 該名駕駛說意外之所以發生是因為他把煞車和加油踏板搞混了。

解說

because 引導子句，需要主詞（he）和動詞，故空格需要填入動詞（過去式），答案為 b。

17. 解答：c

英文 What a <u>surprise</u> it is to see you! Really, this is so <u>surprising</u> because I'm only here for a day.

中譯 見到你真是個驚喜！真的，這真是一個驚喜啊，因為我只來這裡一天而已。

解說

第一個句子考驚嘆句的用法「What a ＋名詞＋ it is ～」，第二句考「物＋ be 動詞＋現在分詞（surprising）」的用法，答案為選項 c。

18. 解答：c

英文 The teacher is <u>frustrated</u> by the slow progress of his students.

中譯 這位老師對他的學生進步緩慢感到挫折。

解說

這題考情緒動詞 frustrate「人＋ be 動詞＋過去分詞＋ by ＋物」的用法，答案為選項 c。

19.

英文 I'm very <u>worried</u> about the exam next week.

中譯 我非常擔心下週的考試。

解說

　　這題考情緒動詞 worry「人＋ be 動詞＋過去分詞＋ about ＋物」的用法，答案為選項 a。

20.

英文 It's really <u>hard for</u> Kevin to concentrate in class.

中譯 要凱文專心上課實在很難。

解說

　　這題考「It is ＋情緒性形容詞＋ for ＋人＋ to V」的用法，答案為選項 b。

18 關係代名詞引導的形容詞子句

關係代名詞引導的形容詞子句

» 定義：關係代名詞引導的子句，作主要子句中（代）名詞的後位修飾，稱為形容詞子句。而關係代名詞兼有連接詞和代名詞的作用，修飾的（代）名詞稱為「先行詞」。

» 句型：先行詞＋關係代名詞（＋名詞）＋動詞……

» 用法：

1. 先行詞為「人」，關係代名詞為 who / that（主格）、whose（所有格）、whom / who / that（受格）

2. 先行詞為「物」，關係代名詞為 which / that（主格）、whose / of which（所有格）、which / that（受格）

3. 先行詞為「人」或「物」，關係代名詞的 who / whom / which（主格、受格）皆可改為 that。甚至在某些情況下（例如：先行詞前面有強烈限定的最高級形容詞、或序數 the first,... the last、先行詞包括人和物、先行詞已經是疑問詞），關係代名詞反而只能使用 that。要特別注意的是，that 前面不可以有介系詞。

» 關係代名詞的「格」，須根據它在子句中的關係而定。

» 關係代名詞本身沒有人稱和單複數之別，但如果是「主格」時，其後的動詞必須和先行詞的人稱和單複數一致。

» 關係代名詞如果是「受格」時，可以省略。但特別注意，如果是緊接在「介系詞」之後，則不可省略。而且，一定只能用 whom 和 which，不可以用 who 或 that。

» 先行詞為「物」，關係代名詞所有格可以用 whose 或 of which，但是 whose 後面的名詞不需要定冠詞 that，of which 卻需要，而且 of which 也可置於修飾的名詞之後。

關係代名詞為「主格」

The child who is waving to us is my son.
＝The child that is waving to us is my son.
（＝The child waving to us is my son.）
在跟我們揮手的那個孩子是我兒子。

I like stories which have happy endings.
I like stories that have happy endings.
（＝I like stories with happy endings.）
我喜歡有快樂結局的故事。

關係代名詞為「所有格」

I have a friend whose name is Jerry too.
我有一個朋友的名字也叫傑瑞。

They found a house whose door is open.
＝They found a house of which the door is open.
＝They found a house the door of which is open.
他們發現了一棟門打開著的房子。

關係代名詞為「受格」

Mr. Patrick is the man whom you're going to meet.
Mr. Patrick is the man who you're going to meet.
Mr. Patrick is the man that you're going to meet.
（＝Mr. Patrick is the man you're going to meet.）
派翠克先生就是你要見的人。

This is the car which we lost.
This is the car that we lost.
（＝This is the car we lost.）
這是我們遺失的那輛車。

介系詞後面的關係代名詞受格

The man to whom I talked is right there.
≠ The man to who I talked is right here.
≠ The man to that I talked is right here.
≠ The man to I talked is right here.
= The man I talked to is right there.
= The man whom I talked to is right there.
= The man who I talked to is right there.
= The man that I talked to is right there.
我說過話的那名男子就在那裡。

The cottage in which we stayed was by the lake.
≠ The cottage in that we stayed was by the lake.
≠ The cottage in we stayed was by the lake.
= The cottage we stayed in was by the lake.
= The cottage which we stayed in was by the lake.
= The cottage that we stayed in was by the lake.
我們住的那間小木屋位在湖邊。

關係代名詞只能用 that

Gary was the first person that showed up.
≠ Gary was the first person who showed up.
蓋瑞是第一個現身的人。

She's the most beautiful girl that I know.
≠ She's the most beautiful girl whom I know.
（= She's the most beautiful girl I know.）
她是我認識的最美的女生。

They're searching for the boy and his dog that got lost in the woods.
≠ They're searching for the boy and his dog which got lost in the woods.
≠ They're searching for the boy and his dog who got lost in the woods.
（＝They're searching for the boy and his dog got lost in the woods.）
他們正在搜尋在森林迷路的那個男孩和他的狗。

Who that has common sense will believe this?
≠ Who who has common sense will believe this?
有常識的人哪會相信這件事？

關係代名詞的限定用法與補述用法

» 限定用法通常是：在先行詞與關係代名詞之間沒有逗號。

» 補述用法則必須在先行詞與關係代名詞之間加上逗號。

» 注意，只有主格和受格 who、whom 和 which 有補述用法。

» 補述用法中的關係代名詞不可替換成 that，也不可省略。但是，若前面有插入
語（如 as far as I know），則可替換，但仍不可省略。

限定用法 vs. 補述用法：主格 who

We have two sons who are studying abroad.
我們有兩個兒子在國外讀書。（也許還有其他孩子）

We have two sons, who are studying abroad.
＝ We have two sons, and they are studying abroad.
我們有兩個兒子，他們在國外讀書。（只有兩個兒子）

限定用法 vs. 補述用法：主格 which

He runs two stores which are in downtown.
他有兩家位於市中心的店。（也許還有其他店）

He runs two stores, which are in downtown.
他開了兩家店，店面位於市中心。（只有兩家店）

受格 whom / which 的補述用法

I will never leave her, whom I love so much.
我永遠不會離開她，她是我這麼鍾愛的人。

We plan to build a house, which is designed by ourselves.
我們打算蓋一棟房子，一棟我們自己設計的房子。

what 的用法

» what 是本身兼作先行詞的關係代名詞，故前面不需要先行詞。

» what = that which / those which / the thing which / the things which / all that的簡化，
在句子中比較建議使用。

在形容詞子句中作主格

What makes me angry is not your failure on the test.
（＝That which makes me angry is not your failure on the test.）
讓我生氣的不是你沒通過考試。

We must do what is to be done.
（＝We must do all that is to be done.）
我們必須做該做的事。

在形容詞子句中作受格

These are what she bought.
（＝These are the things which she bought.）
這些就是她買的東西。

Do you believe what he said?
（＝Do you believe those which he said?）
你相信他說的事嗎？

題 目

1. I really like the gift _____ you bought for me.
   a. that
   b. which
   c. what
   d. Either a or b

2. The new DVD, _____ is sitting on the table over there, won't play in your DVD player.
   a. that
   b. which
   c. where
   d. whose

3. The place _____ she lives is located in a beautiful river valley with pine trees all around.
   a. that
   b. which
   c. what
   d. where

4. _____ shoes are these green ones?
   a. Who's
   b. Whom's
   c. Whose
   d. None of the above

5. To _____ photo are you pointing?
   a. whom
   b. whom's
   c. whose
   d. that

6. Is this the desk _____ found on the street?

   a. you

   b. that you

   c. which you

   d. All of the above

7. All _____ need to do is make a small deposit.

   a. you can

   b. that you

   c. which you

   d. All of the above

8. Is this the best wine _____ you have?

   a. which

   b. what

   c. that

   d. if

9. The president didn't like _____ Jack said about company's main product.

   a. who

   b. what

   c. that

   d. which

10. I think it was John _____ was late yesterday.

   a. who

   b. whom

   c. that

   d. Either a or c

11. The man _____ you met on the subway was my sailing coach.
   a. who
   b. whom
   c. which
   d. Either a or b

12. Is that the man _____ you met on the subway?
   a. who
   b. whom
   c. that
   d. All of the above

13. I'm not sure of _____ you are speaking.
   a. who
   b. whom
   c. that
   d. Either a or b

14. Who is the lady _____ an umbrella?
   a. holding
   b. that is holding
   c. which is holding
   d. Either a or b

15. My _____ lives in New York _____ a teacher. My other son
   is a dentist.
   a. son who ; City is
   b. son, who ; City, is
   c. Either a or b
   d. Neither a nor b

16. The books _____ pages are torn must be repaired or replaced.
    a. with
    b. that
    c. whose
    d. which have

17. The English newspaper, _____ is available online for free, costs NT$ 15 at the newsstand.
    a. that
    b. which
    c. what
    d. when

18. About _____ is this book you are currently writing?
    a. who
    b. whom
    c. what
    d. Either b or c

19. She is the most beautiful woman _____ I have ever seen.
    a. whom
    b. that
    c. which
    d. All of the above.

20. _____ is the letter addressed to?
    a. Who
    b. Whom
    c. To whom
    d. Either a or b

解析

1.

解答：d

英文　I really like the gift <u>that</u> you bought for me.
　　　I really like the gift <u>which</u> you bought for me.

中譯　我真的很喜歡你買給我的禮物。

解說

　　形容詞子句的先行詞為物（the gift），關係代名詞必須使用 which 或 that，答案為選項 d。

2.

解答：b

英文　The new DVD, <u>which</u> is sitting on the table over there, won't play in your DVD player.

中譯　放在那邊桌子上的新 DVD 用你的放影機不能播放。

解說

　　先行詞為物（DVD），關係子句需要主詞，故應選 which 作引導，答案為選項 b。注意，關係代名詞引導的子句若用逗號與主要子句隔開，則不可使用 that，不可選 a。

3.

解答：d

英文　The place <u>where</u> she lives is located in a beautiful river valley with pine trees all around.

中譯　她住的地方坐落於美麗的河谷，四周松樹環繞。

解說

　　關係子句的動詞 live 表示（居住），後面需要介系詞，本句沒有，所以需要 where（＝ in which）來引導，答案為選項 d。

英文　**Whose shoes are these green ones?**

中譯　這雙綠色的鞋子是誰的？

解說

　　這是疑問句，主詞為 these green ones，動詞為 are，空格需要所有格代名詞 whose 加上一般名詞 shoes 作為受詞，意思是「誰的鞋子？」，答案為選項 c。

英文　**To whose photo are you pointing?**

中譯　你在指誰的照片？

解說

　　這也是一句疑問句，動詞 point to ～當中的介系詞移到句首的變化形，一般名詞 photo 前面需要所有格 whose，這個句子還原後應該是 Whose photo are you pointing to?，答案為選項 c。

英文　**Is this the desk <u>you</u> found on the street?**
　　　Is this the desk <u>that you</u> found on the street?
　　　Is this the desk <u>which you</u> found on the street?

中譯　這是你在街上找到的那張桌子嗎？

解說

　　空格後所有的字形成關係子句，這個子句需要 which / that 和主詞 you 引導，而且因為關係代名詞的功能為子句的受詞，所以可以省略，只留下 you，因此 a、b、c 選項皆對，答案為 d。

7.

英文　**All that you need to do is make a small deposit.**

中譯　你必須做的就只是存一小筆錢。

解說

　　本句需要名詞子句作為主要子句的主詞，名詞子句需要以 that 引導，故答案為選項 b，其中子句裡的 make a deposit 是「存款」的意思。

8.

英文　**Is this the best wine that you have?**

中譯　這是你們最好的葡萄酒嗎？

解說

　　這題的關係子句中前面有先行詞 the best wine，故不可選 b. what。先行詞為物，關係代名詞原本可用 which 或 that，但是這個先行詞中有最高級 the best，因此只能用 that，答案為 c。

9.

英文　**The president didn't like what Jack said about company's main product.**

中譯　董事長不喜歡傑克對公司主要產品所說的事情。

解說

　　主要子句的動詞 like「喜歡」需要受詞（the things）、形容詞子句則缺少了關係代名詞 which / that，所以空格內需要填入 the things which，也就等於 what，答案選 b。

英文　**I think it was John <u>who</u> was late yesterday.**
　　　I think it was John <u>that</u> was late yesterday.

中譯　我想昨天遲到的那個人是約翰。

解說

　　本句的關係子句用來修飾名詞子句（that）it was John 的 John，先行詞為人，在關係子句中作為主詞用，因此關係代名詞可用 who 或 that，答案為選項 d。

英文　**The man <u>who</u> you met on the subway was my sailing coach.**
　　　The man <u>whom</u> you met on the subway was my sailing coach.

中譯　你在地鐵遇到的那個男人就是我的航海教練。

解說

　　先行詞 the man 為人，不可用 which 引導關係子句，故選項 c 錯。由於關係代名詞在子句中是作為受格，故可用 whom 或 who，因此答案選 d。

　　　Is that the man <u>who</u> you met on the subway?
英文　**Is that the man <u>whom</u> you met on the subway?**
　　　Is that the man <u>that</u> you met on the subway?

中譯　那是你在地鐵遇到的那名男子嗎？

解說

　　先行詞 the man 為人，需要的關係代名名詞在子句中是作為受格，a、b、c 三個選項的 whom / who / that 皆可用，因此答案為選項 d。

13.

英文　I'm not sure of <u>whom</u> you are speaking.

中譯　我不確定你說的是誰。

解說

　　形容詞子句的部分是從 of... speaking，乃是將 speak of 的 of 移到句首的用法，這裡的關係代名詞是作為受格用，而且在介系詞之後，故只可以用 whom，答案為選項 b。

14.

英文　Who is the lady <u>holding</u> an umbrella?
　　　Who is the lady <u>that is holding</u> an umbrella?

中譯　拿著雨傘的那位小姐是誰？

解說

　　先行詞是 the lady，關係代名詞不可用 which，選項 c 錯。這裡的關係代名詞需要 who 或 that，以及動詞 is holding，所以選項 b 正確。此外，選項 a 乃是關係代名詞作為主格，同時省略 that is 的用法，也正確。因此答案為選項 d。

15.

英文　My <u>son who</u> lives in New York <u>City</u> is a teacher. My other son is a dentist.

中譯　我那個住在紐約市的兒子是老師。我另一個兒子是牙醫。

解說

　　這題考限定或非限定用法，由於後面句子出現 my other son，可知不只一個兒子，不可用非限定用法，因此答案必須選 a 的限定用法。

16. 解答：**c**

英文 The books <u>whose</u> pages are torn must be repaired or replaced.

中譯 書籍頁面破損者必須修補或更換。

解說

　　此句出現兩個動詞 are 和 be repaired（or replaced），需要關係代名詞，不可選 a. with。關係子句中主詞有一般名詞 pages，故需要所有格 whose 引導，答案為選項 c。

17. 解答：**b**

英文 The English newspaper, <u>which</u> is available online for free, costs NT$ 15 at the newsstand.

中譯 這份英文報提供線上免費閱讀，在報攤上買要台幣十五元。

解說

　　選項 d. when 不可以在形容詞子句中作主詞，故不可選。關係子句前有先行詞（the English newspaper），故不可選 c. what。由於子句與先行詞以逗號分隔，不可使用 that 作引導，故正確答案為選項 b（which）。

18. 解答：**d**

英文 About <u>whom</u> is this book you are currently writing?
About <u>what</u> is this book you are currently writing?

中譯 你目前正在寫的這本書是在講誰？
你目前正在寫的這本書是在講什麼？

解說

　　這題的後半部（which / that）you are currently writing 是形容詞子句，修飾主要主詞 this book，省略不看，只看主要子句，並將介系詞 about 放在句尾，則選項 b 和 c 形成的疑問句分別是 Whom is this book about? 和 What is this book about?，皆為正確句子，故答案為選項 d。

英文　She is the most beautiful woman <u>that</u> I have ever seen.
中譯　她是我見過最美麗的女人。

解說

　　本題的關係子句先行詞為人（woman），而且使用最高級形容詞 the most beautiful 修飾，因此只可以用 that 引導，答案為選項 b。

英文　<u>Who</u> is the letter addressed to?
　　　<u>Whom</u> is the letter addressed to?
中譯　這封信是寄給誰的？

解說

　　這個問句在句尾已經有介系詞 to，故不可選 c。要填入的疑問代名詞是受格，故 who 和 whom 皆可，答案為選項 d。

19 that 所引導的名詞子句

名詞子句的用法和句型

» 定義：名詞子句就是作用等同名詞的子句。子句自己本身需要主詞和動詞，不可獨立存在。

» 如果名詞子句為直述句，通常以 that 引導。

» 名詞子句除了作為主詞，置於句首之外，其他時候的 that 皆可省略，特別是口語時。

» 名詞子句當主詞、動詞為連綴動詞（is, seem, look,...）時，可以用虛主詞 It 代替，將子句改放在句尾。

» 動詞後面接 that 子句，常見的有：

think / believe / know / understand / realize / learn / hear / find out / notice / hope / dream / forget / remember / decide / feel / ...

» 形容詞後面接 that 子句，常見的有：

sure / sorry / aware / ... 和 surprised / afraid / glad / ... 等情緒形容詞。

» 後面常接 that 子句的常見慣用語，如：

1. It is true / obvious / ...

2. It is a fact / pity / ...

» 否定形式：not ＋動詞／形容詞＋ that 子句

▌that 子句作主詞▐

That I won the lottery is true.

＝It is true that I won the lottery.

我中樂透是真的。

That he hit a homerun helped his team win the game.

≠It helped his team win the game that he hit a homerun.

他擊出一支全壘打幫他的球隊贏了比賽。

that 子句作補語

The fact is (that) I don't trust you.
事實是我不信任你。

The most important thing is (that) you're alive.
最重要的事情是你還活著。

動詞＋ that 子句

I think (that) she has regretted.
我想她已經後悔了。

Don't you believe (that) he is ninety years old?
你不相信他已經九十歲了嗎？

形容詞＋ that 子句

I'm not sure (that) they'll like you.
我不確定他們會喜歡你。

The teacher was surprised (that) David was early this morning.
老師很驚訝大衛今天早上竟然早到了。

It is ... ＋ that 子句

It is true (that) they were married yesterday.
確實，他們昨天結婚了。

It's a fact (that) everything he said was a lie.
事實是，他說的每件事都是謊言。

題 目

1. I didn't know _____ were a skydiver.
   a. you
   b. that you
   c. Either a or b
   d. Neither a nor b

2. _____ were a brave soldier is not being questioned.
   a. That you
   b. You
   c. If you
   d. Either a or c

3. Tom said that _____ could drive a car.
   a. he
   b. him
   c. himself
   d. Either a or c

4. If we get lost, the most important thing _____ we stay together.
   a. is
   b. is that
   c. will be
   d. Either a or b

5. I couldn't believe _____ won the lottery.
   a. I
   b. myself
   c. that I
   d. Either a or c

6. The teacher asked the student _____ movie they most wanted to see.
   a. what
   b. which
   c. that
   d. Either a or b

7. I know that _____.
   a. you have ever seen
   b. she lives in
   c. you have more money
   d. he was saying

8. What was she doing _____ the teacher didn't approve of?
   a. who
   b. what
   c. that
   d. where

9. That pen on the table is _____.
   a. mine
   b. true
   c. whose
   d. None of the above

10. That the dog is sleeping is _____.
    a. my dog
    b. true
    c. whose
    d. None of the above

11. Please tell _____ you didn't lock the keys _____ the house!
    a. me that ; in
    b. me ; that in
    c. me ; in
    d. Either a or c

12. I saw _____ girl _____ short hair.
    a. that ; with
    b. the ; that has
    c. that the ; had
    d. All of the above

13. _____ you did well on the test makes me feel proud.
    a. When
    b. If
    c. That
    d. Either a or c

14. Look at _____ dog with pink fur! Who would ever do _____
    to a dog?
    a. that ; that
    b. which ; that
    c. that ; what
    d. whose ; which

15. If you know _____ junk food is bad for you, then why do you eat
    it?
    a. if
    b. what
    c. that
    d. None of the above

16. Is she the girl _____ were telling me about?

    a. that you

    b. that

    c. you

    d. Either a or c

17. I heard that _____.

    a. you two are getting married

    b. you said yesterday

    c. the couple who got married

    d. they are going with

18. I hear _____ you want to attend university overseas.

    a. that

    b. where

    c. which

    d. when

19. Did you _____ that all the trees are dying in this area?

    a. know

    b. see

    c. notice

    d. All of the above

20. Ralph _____ that his parents wouldn't discover _____ he had broken the ornament.

    a. knows ; why

    b. hoped ; that

    c. thought ; which

    d. saw ; what

解析

1.

英文 I didn't know <u>you</u> were a skydiver.
　　 I didn't know <u>that you</u> were a skydiver.

中譯 我不知道你是一位跳傘選手。

解說

　主要子句的動詞 know 為及物動詞，需要受詞，因此需要 that 所引導的名詞子句，而且 that 經常省略，故答案為選項 c。其中 either... or 表示「不是……就是……」，而 neither... nor 則表示「既不是……也不是……」。

2.

解答：**a**

英文 <u>That you</u> were a brave soldier is not being questioned.

中譯 你是一位勇敢的軍人這件事是不容懷疑的。

解說

　本句出現兩個動詞 were 和 is，需要子句，從語意上來判斷，That you... 是比較適當，答案為選項 a。注意，that 子句作主詞用時，that 絕對不可省略，故選項 b 錯誤。

3.

解答：**a**

英文 Tom said that <u>he could drive a car.</u>

中譯 湯姆說他會開車。

解說

　主要動詞 said 後面接 that 引導的名詞子句，子句一定要有主詞和動詞，因此空格內須填入主格人稱代名詞，答案為 a。

4.

解答：**d**

英文 If we get lost, the most important thing <u>is</u> we stay together.
If we get lost, the most important thing <u>is that</u> we stay together.

中譯 如果我們迷路了，最重要的事情是我們在一起。

解說

　　主要句子有主詞 the most important thing，有主詞補語 we stay together，需要動詞 is 和從屬連接詞 that，故答案為選項 d。注意，that 子句作主詞、主詞補語、同位語時，絕對不可省略 that。

5.

解答：**d**

英文 I couldn't believe <u>I</u> won the lottery.
I couldn't believe <u>that I</u> won the lottery.

中譯 我不敢相信我中了樂透。

解說

　　主要動詞 believe 後面要接受詞，需要名詞子句 that ～，而且 that 可以省略，另外子句還缺少主詞，故選項 a 和 c 都正確，答案為選項 d。

6.

解答：**d**

英文 The teacher asked the student <u>what</u> movie they most wanted to see.
The teacher asked the student <u>which</u> movie they most wanted to see.

中譯 老師問學生他們最想看的電影是哪一部。

解說

　　這題主要動詞 ask 的用法為「ask sb. sth.」，空格以後的全部文字為名詞子句，what / which 在語意上皆對，因此答案為選項 d。

英文 I know that you have more money.

中譯 我知道你有更多錢。

解說

　　這裡的 that 引導子句，作主要動詞 know 的受詞。子句必須是完整句子，因此選擇 c。

英文 What was she doing that the teacher didn't approve of?

中譯 她在做什麼老師不允許的事情？

解說

　　What ～疑問句為倒裝句，空格以後的文字形成子句，修飾 what，因此只有以 that 引導的子句才正確，答案為選項 c。

英文 That pen on the table is mine.

中譯 在桌上的那枝筆是我的。

解說

　　這裡的 that pen 為主詞，that 為指示形容詞。be 動詞後面需要主詞補語，只有選項 a（mine）符合語意，因此為正確答案。另外，疑問詞不會放在句尾，所以選項 c（whose）在文法上錯誤。

10. 解答：b

英文 That the dog is sleeping is <u>true</u>.

中譯 那隻狗在睡覺是事實。

解說

That... 引導的子句在此為主詞，be 動詞 is 後面需要主詞補語，選項 b（true）為正確答案。可改寫為 It is true (that) the dog is sleeping.。

11. 解答：d

英文 Please tell <u>me</u> that you didn't lock the keys <u>in</u> the house!
Please tell <u>me</u> you didn't lock the keys <u>in</u> the house!

中譯 請告訴我你沒有把鑰匙鎖在房子裡！

解說

主要句子為祈使句「Please tell me ～」，後面接 that 子句，而且可以省略 that，所以選項 a 或 c 皆對，答案為 d。至於選項 b 在 the keys 後面如果要使用 that 子句，則缺少了動詞 is，所以錯誤。

12. 解答：d

英文 I saw <u>that girl with</u> short hair.
I saw <u>the girl that has</u> short hair.
I saw <u>that the girl had</u> short hair.

中譯 我看到那個短髮的女孩子。
我看到那個短髮的女孩子。
我看到那個女孩有短頭髮。

解說

選項 a 構成的句子為 I saw that girl with short hair.，that girl 為受詞，with short hair 為介系詞片語修飾 that girl，所以是正確句子。選項 b 構成的句子為 I saw the girl that has short hair.，the girl 為受詞，that has short hair 為形容詞子句，修飾 the girl，也正確。這兩個句子意思相近。選項 c 構成的句子為 I saw that the girl had short hair. 意思稍有不同，表示「我看到那個女孩有短頭髮。」that the girl had short hair 為名詞子句，作 saw 的受詞。

13.

英文　That you did well on the test makes me feel proud.

中譯　你考試考得很好，讓我覺得很驕傲。

解說

在主要動詞 make(s) 之前需要主詞，只有選項 c（that）可以引導名詞子句作主詞，故答案為 c。

14.

英文　Look at <u>that</u> dog with pink fur! Who would ever do <u>that</u> to a dog?

中譯　看看那隻毛是粉紅色的狗！誰會對一隻狗做那種事啊？

解說

兩個空格後面都沒有完整句子，所以不是子句，答案為選項 a，這裡的 that 一個為指示形容詞，修飾 dog，另一個為指示代名詞，作 do 的受詞。

15.

英文　If you know <u>that</u> junk food is bad for you, then why do you eat it?

中譯　如果你知道垃圾食物對你不好，那你為什麼還吃？

解說

主要動詞 know 後面需要子句作受詞，只有選項 a 可以引導名詞子句，故為正確答案。

16.

英文　**Is she the girl that you were telling me about?**
　　　Is she the girl you were telling me about?

中譯　她就是你跟我說的那個女孩子嗎？

解說

　　本句的 the girl 為子句的先行詞，關係代名詞 that 可以省略，但是主詞 you 與先行詞不是同一人，不能省略，因此選項 b 錯誤。答案為選項 d。

17.

英文　**I heard that you two are getting married.**

中譯　我聽說你們兩個人要結婚了。

解說

　　主要動詞 heard 後面需要受詞，that 引導名詞子句作受詞，而子句必須是完整句子，只有選項 a 正確。

18.

英文　**I hear that you want to attend university overseas.**

中譯　我聽說你想要就讀國外的大學。

解說

　　主要動詞 hear 後面要接名詞子句作為受詞，空格後為完整句子，只有選項 a（that）合乎語意，為正確答案。

19.　　　　　　　　　　　　　　　　　　　　　　　　　　　解答：**d**

英文　Did you <u>know</u> that all the trees are dying in this area?
　　　Did you <u>see</u> that all the trees are dying in this area?
　　　Did you <u>notice</u> that all the trees are dying in this area?

中譯　你知道這地區所有的樹都快死了嗎？
　　　你看到這地區所有的樹都快死了嗎？
　　　你注意到這地區所有的樹都快死了嗎？

解說

　　這個句子有主詞 you、受詞 that all the trees... area，但缺少及物動詞，a、b、c 三個選項都是及物動詞，後面可接名詞子句。

20.　　　　　　　　　　　　　　　　　　　　　　　　　　　解答：**b**

英文　Ralph <u>hoped</u> that his parents wouldn't discover <u>that</u> he had broken the ornament.

中譯　賴夫希望他的父母不會發現他打破了這件裝飾品。

解說

　　第一個空格後為 that 所引導的名詞子句，子句為過去式 wouldn't discover，所以第一個空格的主要動詞必須是為過去式，因此選項 a 錯誤。第二個空格後面為完整句子，因此需要 that 所引導的名詞子句作受詞，正確答案為選項 b。

20 連接詞

連接詞的用法和句型

» 定義：用來連接單字、片語或句子的字詞，稱為連接詞。
» 連接詞分為兩種：對等連接詞（and, or, but, ...）、從屬連接詞（when, although, because, unless, ...）。
» 對等連接詞：用來連接文法功能相同（作名詞、形容詞、副詞等）的單字、片語或子句。
» 從屬連接詞：用來連接從屬子句和主要子句。
» 從屬連接詞可以引導三種子句：名詞子句（that, whether）、形容詞子句（that, who, which, ...）、副詞子句（because, although, when, ...）。

對等連接詞

» 特別注意：對等連接詞前後的單字或片語，詞性和功能必須一致。尤其是遇到不定詞片語，在兩個連接詞後面都必須有不定詞 to。
» 相關連接詞：一組固定使用的連接詞，如 both... and, neither... nor，具有對等連接詞的相同功能。
» 除了連接詞的意思之外，更須特別注意後面動詞的使用：

主　　　　　　　　　　　詞	動　　詞
A and B（A 和 B）→	複數
A or B（A 或 B）	和 B 一致
both A and B（A 和 B 兩者都是）	複數
A as well as B（A 和 B 一樣）	和 A 一致
not only A but (also) B（不但 A，而且 B）	和 B 一致
either A or B（不是 A 就是 B）	和 B 一致
neither A nor B（既非 A，也非 B）	和 B 一致

and

My sister and I are twins.
我和我姐姐是雙胞胎。

This alley is narrow, dark, and dangerous.
這條巷子很窄、很暗,而且很危險。

or

Do you like the red dress or the blue one?
你喜歡紅色的洋裝還是藍色的?

I don't think you or Charlie has the time.
我不認為你或查理有時間。

both A and B / not only A but (also) B / A as well as B

Both he and his wife love dogs.
他和他太太都喜歡狗。

Not only the actors but (also) the director is invited.
不只演員們,連導演也受到邀請。

The girls as well as their mother are beautiful.
這些女孩們和她們的母親一樣都很美麗。

either A or B / neither A nor B

Either he or you are likely to be in charge of the project.
不是他就是你可能要負責這個案子。

We decide neither to drive a car nor to take a taxi. We'll take the MRT.
我們決定不開車,也不搭計程車。我們要搭捷運。

對等連接詞，連接獨立句子

» and「而且」、but「但是」、or（= or else）「或者」連接兩個獨立句子時，前面通常會以逗點隔開。

» and 和 but 後面所接的句子可進行省略，省略原則如下：

1. 如果動詞相同，則以助動詞代替。助動詞的時態須與前句一致，人稱則必須與連接句的主詞一致。

2. but 連接兩個句子，一個肯定，一個否定。

3. and 必須連接兩個都是肯定或都是否定的句子。若都是肯定，句尾加上 too；都是否定，句尾加上 either。

and, but, or

He plays the piano, and she sings.
他彈鋼琴，她唱歌。

I like the car, but it's too expensive.
我喜歡這部車，可是太貴了。

They must leave, or they can stay?
他們必須離開，或者他們可以留下？

but 後面的助動詞使用

I want to keep a pet, but my wife doesn't.
（= I want to keep a pet, but my wife doesn't want to keep a pet.）
我想養隻寵物，可是我太太不想。

My father doesn't want to move, but my mother and I do.
（= My father doesn't want to move, but my mother and I want to move.）
我父親不想搬家，可是我母親和我想。

and 後面的助動詞使用

Jane has taken a shower, and I have too.
珍已經沖完澡了，我也是。

They're not here, and Peter isn't either.
他們不在這裡，彼德也不在。

從屬連接詞，連接副詞子句

» 特別要注意的是：so（所以）和 because（因為）、although（雖然）和 but
（但是）都是連接詞，不可同時出現兩個。

» 位置：but / so 一定放在兩個句子之間，although（＝ though）/ because 還可以
置於句首，且與後面的句子一定要用逗號隔開。

» 表時間：when（＝ as）「在……時候」、before「在……之前」、after「在……
之後」、as soon as「一……就……」

» 表讓步：although（＝ though）「雖然」、even though（＝ even if, if）「即使」

» 表理由、原因：because（＝ since, as）「因為」，because 子句有時可改寫為：
because of ＋（動）名詞

» 表結果：so that...「因此」，特別句型：so ＋ adj. / adv. ＋ that...、such ＋ N ＋
that...

» 表條件：if「如果」、unless（＝ if... not）「除非」、as long as（＝ so long as）
「只要」

表時間：when, before, after, as soon as

When he saw Sophie, he waved to her.
當他看到蘇菲時，他向她揮手。

Before you go to bed, brush your teeth first.
在你上床睡覺之前，先刷牙。

We can watch a movie together after I finish my homework.
在我寫完作業之後，我們可以一起看部電影。

Tell him to see me as soon as he comes back.
他一回來就叫他來見我。

表讓步：although, even though

Although we like the house, we can't afford it.
＝We can't afford it although we like the house.
＝We like the house, but we can't afford it.
雖然我們喜歡這間房子，可是我們買不起。

Even though Sean studies hard, he can't catch up with his classmates.
即使尚恩很用功，他還是跟不上同班同學們。

表理由、原因：because

Because he had a cold, he went to the doctor.
＝He had a cold, so he went to the doctor.
（＝Because of his cold, he went to the doctor.）
因為他感冒了，所以去看醫生。

Because of the accident, I stuck in the jam for two hours.
因為這個意外，我在路上塞了兩個小時。

表結果：so ～ that... / such ～ that...

The puppy is so lovely that Nancy asked her mother to keep it.
這隻小狗太可愛了，所以南西請求媽媽把它留下來養。

That was such a big surprise that she couldn't say a word.
那實在是太大的一個驚喜了，所以她說不出半句話。

表條件：if, unless, as long as

If you give up, you'll regret.
你如果放棄，你會後悔。

Unless he apologizes, she won't forgive him.
（＝If he doesn't apologize, she won't forgive him.）
除非他道歉，否則她不會原諒他。

As long as it doesn't rain, we will go.
＝So long as it doesn't rain, we will go.
＝If it doesn't rain, we will go.
只要不下雨，我們就會去。

從屬連接詞，連接名詞子句

» that 子句請參考 Unit 19。

» whether.. or not 引導名詞子句，表示「是否」之意，可以用 if 代替，這時的 if 並非「如果」之意。

» whether 子句中出現第二個動詞時，通常以 or 連接。

» whether 引導名詞子句當主詞，和 that 子句相同，可以用 It... 句型替換。

» 另外，疑問詞 who, when, where, how,... 也可以引導名詞子句。特別要注意的是，寫疑問句時，動詞在前、主詞在後，但是寫名詞子句時，與一般句子相同，是主詞在前、動詞在後。

whether... （or not）

We don't care whether you can make a lot of money (or not).
＝We don't care if you can make a lot of money (or not).
我們並不在乎你是否可以賺很多錢。

Whether you succeed or fail won't matter. At least you try.
＝It won't matter whether you succeed or fail. At least you try.
無論你成功或失敗都沒有關係，至少你試了。

疑問詞＋名詞子句

The boss wants to know who is to blame.
老闆想知道該歸咎誰。

Women don't like to be asked about how old they are.
女人不喜歡被問到她們幾歲。

題 目

1. Isabel _____ Doris are going to drive there together.
   a. or
   b. and
   c. with
   d. All of the above

2. _____ my brother, _____ my three sisters, caught the flu last winter.
   a. Me ; and
   b. I ; and
   c. Not only ; but also
   d. Not only ; and

3. The armchairs are _____ heavy _____ awkward to carry.
   a. not only ; but also
   b. both ; and
   c. very ; and
   d. All of the above

4. Are you telling me that _____ you _____ boyfriend can remember what you did that night?
   a. neither ; nor
   b. not only ; nor
   c. not ; or
   d. Either a or c

5. The coach said _____ Carl _____ Justin would start in tomorrow's game.
   a. either ; or
   b. neither ; nor
   c. both ; and
   d. All of the above

6. _____ Ella _____ Josie will sing the lead, but not both.

    a. either ; or

    b. neither ; nor

    c. both ; and

    d. Either a or b

7. I don't know _____ Louis has finished _____ not.

    a. if ; and

    b. when ; or

    c. whether ; or

    d. that ; but

8. _____ taking a shower, he dried himself off with a towel.

    a. Before

    b. After

    c. When

    d. While

9. I would love to go to the party, _____ I have other plans that night.

    a. and

    b. or

    c. but

    d. if

10. Call me _____ you get to the airport. I'll be waiting for your call!

    a. as soon as

    b. whenever

    c. if

    d. All of the above

11. _____ she walked into the room, she saw a mouse.
    a. When
    b. As soon as
    c. After
    d. All of the above

12. _____ I eat breakfast, I quickly brush my teeth and run out the door.
    a. After
    b. When
    c. Before
    d. As soon as

13. I was feeling tired, _____ I didn't want to drive. _____ I took the bus, I was late for work.
    a. because ; Because
    b. because ; So
    c. so ; Because
    d. so ; So

14. The test was _____ difficult _____ only a few students passed it.
    a. very ; because
    b. so ; that
    c. so ; because
    d. very ; but

15. _____ the storm, the ship couldn't sail for two days.
    a. Because of
    b. In spite of
    c. So long
    d. Unless

16. _____ his wife died last week, he refuses to take time off work.
   a. Though
   b. Because
   c. Unless
   d. So

17. As _____ as I get my computer set up, I'll send you an e-mail.
   a. often
   b. quickly
   c. fast
   d. soon

18. Check it carefully _____ you hand it in.
   a. unless
   b. before
   c. but
   d. and

19. You can't have any dessert _____ you finish all your vegetables
   and rice.
   a. though
   b. because
   c. unless
   d. if

20. This car goes fast _____ to outrun the fastest police car!
   a. so
   b. enough
   c. because
   d. that

解析

1. 解答：b

英文 Isabel <u>and</u> Doris are going to drive there together.

中譯 伊莎貝爾和朵莉絲要開車一起去那裡。

解說

　　兩個人名之後的 be 動詞為複數形（are），所以需要的連接詞是 and，答案為選項 b。

2. 解答：c

英文 <u>Not only</u> my brother, <u>but also</u> my three sisters, caught the flu last winter.

中譯 不只我的弟弟，還有我的三個妹妹去年冬天都感冒了。

解說

　　選項 a. Me 為受格人稱代名詞，不可作為主詞，所以錯誤。選項 b. I 雖然可以作為主詞，但是當三個名詞用連接詞相連，第一和第二個名詞之間需要逗號，所以選項 b 也錯。Not only... but also 為相關連接詞，此為固定用法，故答案為 c。

3. 解答：d

英文 The armchairs are <u>not only</u> heavy <u>but also</u> awkward to carry.
The armchairs are <u>both</u> heavy <u>and</u> awkward to carry.
The armchairs are <u>very</u> heavy <u>and</u> awkward to carry.

中譯 這些扶手椅子重又難搬。

解說

　　動詞 are 後面的兩個形容詞 heavy、awkward 之間需要連接詞，a、b、c 三個選項在語意上都符合，所以正確答案為選項 d。

4.

英文 **Are you telling me that <u>neither</u> you <u>nor</u> boyfriend can remember what you did that night?**

中譯 你是在跟我說，妳和妳男朋友都記不得你們那天晚上做了什麼事嗎？

解說

　　that 後面引導名詞子句，主詞 you 和 boyfriend 之間需要連接詞，a、b、c 選項中的連接詞用法，只有 neither... nor... 正確，故答案為 a。

5.

英文 **The coach said <u>either</u> Carl <u>or</u> Justin would start in tomorrow's game.**
The coach said <u>neither</u> Carl <u>nor</u> Justin would start in tomorrow's game.
The coach said <u>both</u> Carl <u>and</u> Justin would start in tomorrow's game.

中譯 教練說卡爾和賈斯汀其中一人會在明天的比賽先發。
教練說卡爾和賈斯汀兩人都不會在明天的比賽先發。
教練說卡爾和賈斯汀兩人都會在明天的比賽先發。

解說

　　主要動詞 said 後面是省略了 that 的名詞子句，子句中的主詞 Carl 和 Justin 之間需要連接詞，a、b、c 三個選項的連接詞都是正確用法，故正確答案為選項 d。

6.

英文 **Either Ella or Josie will sing the lead, but not both.**
中譯 艾拉或是裘西其中一人會擔任主唱，但不是兩個人都行。

解說

　　由於句尾的 but not both 限制，所以只有選項 a（either... or）符合語意，為正確答案。

7.

英文 I don't know <u>whether</u> Louis has finished <u>or not</u>.

中譯 我不知道路易斯完成了沒有。

解說

　　主要動詞 know 後面需要有名詞子句，只有選項 c. whether... or（not）是正確的用法，也符合語意，為正確答案。這裡的 or not 也可以省略。

8.

英文 <u>After</u> taking a shower, he dried himself off with a towel.

中譯 洗完澡後，他用毛巾把自己擦乾。

解說

　　四個選項都可以引導副詞子句，修飾主要子句，但從語意上判斷，以 b（After）最正確。

9.

英文 I would love to go to the party, <u>but</u> I have other plans that night.

中譯 我很想參加宴會，但是我那天晚上有別的計畫。

解說

　　四個選項都可以引導副詞子句，修飾主要句子，但從語意上判斷，只有 c（but）最正確。

10.

英文 Call me <u>as soon as</u> you get to the airport. I'll be waiting for your call!

中譯 你一到機場就打電話給我。我會等你的電話！

解說

　　由於後面的句子 I'll be waiting... 表示未來一定會發生的事情，所以空格只有填入 as soon as 最符合語意。

11.

英文 <u>When</u> she walked into the room, she saw a mouse.
　　 <u>As soon as</u> she walked into the room, she saw a mouse.
　　 <u>After</u> she walked into the room, she saw a mouse.

中譯 當她走進房間的時候，她看到一隻老鼠。
　　 她一走進房間就看到一隻老鼠。
　　 她走進房間之後，看到一隻老鼠。

解說

　　a、b、c 三個選項都可以引導副詞子句，表示時間，在此都符合語意，因此正確答案為選項 d。

12.

英文 <u>After</u> I eat breakfast, I quickly brush my teeth and run out the door.

中譯 我吃了早餐以後，很快刷了牙就跑出門了。

解說

　　這題的四個選項都可以引導副詞子句，表時間，但只有 a 符合語意，因此為正確答案。

13. 解答：**c**

英文　**I was feeling tired, <u>so</u> I didn't want to drive. <u>Because</u> I took the bus, I was late for work.**

中譯　我覺得很累，所以不想開車。因為我搭了公車，上班才遲到。

解說

　　這題有兩個主要子句，第一個句子中，I was feeling tired 表原因，後面需要表結果的連接詞 so。第二個句子的 I was late for work 表結果，前面需要表原因的連接詞 Because，所以正確答案為選項 c。

14. 解答：**b**

英文　**The test was <u>so</u> difficult <u>that</u> only a few students passed it.**

中譯　考試很難，所以只有一些學生通過。

解說

　　這題考「so + adj. / adv. + that + 子句」的固定用法，答案為選項 b。

15. 解答：**a**

英文　**Because of the storm, the ship couldn't sail for two days.**

中譯　因為暴風雨的緣故，這艘船兩天無法航行。

解說

　　選項 c 和 d 為連接詞，須連接子句，不可選。選項 a 的 Because of「因為」和選項 b 的 In spite of「儘管」皆為介系詞，後面可以接名詞（the storm），從語意上判斷，選項 a 最為正確。

解答：**a**

英文　**Though his wife died last week, he refuses to take time off work.**

中譯　雖然他太太上星期過世了，他還是拒絕上班請假。

解說

　　四個選項都可以用來連接副詞子句，因此從語意上判斷，選項 a（Though）最正確。

17.

解答：**d**

英文　**As soon as I get my computer set up, I'll send you an e-mail.**

中譯　我的電腦一組裝好，就寄電子郵件給你。

解說

　　這題考連接詞 as soon as「一……就……」的固定用法，答案為選項 d。

18.

解答：**b**

英文　**Check it carefully before you hand it in.**

中譯　交件前要仔細檢查一遍。

解說

　　本題四個選項都可當連接詞，但符合題意的只有選項 b。

19. 解答：**c**

英文　You can't have any dessert <u>unless</u> you finish all your vegetables and rice.

中譯　除非你把所有飯菜都吃完，否則你不可以吃任何甜點。

解說

　　四個選項都可以連接副詞子句，從語意上判斷，選項 c 中的 unless「除非……」最正確。

20. 解答：**b**

英文　This car goes fast <u>enough</u> to outrun the fastest police car!

中譯　這輛車跑得很快，足以跑贏最快的警車！

解說

　　空格後為不定詞片語，並非完整句，不可選 c 或 d。選項 a 可以作為連接詞或副詞，若為副詞則必須放在 fast 前面。正確答案為選項 b，用法為「主詞＋動詞＋副詞＋ enough ＋ to ～」。

21 倒裝句

倒裝句的用法和句型

» 敘述句的字序，原則上是「主詞＋動詞＋（補語或受詞）」。所謂的倒裝句，就是字序對調，以達到強調作用。

» 倒裝原則，大部分和 yes - no 疑問句的形成方法一樣：

1. 有 be 動詞時 → 將 be 動詞移至主詞前。

2. 有助動詞（have, had, will, would...）時 → 將助動詞移到主詞之前。

3. 有動詞、無助動詞時 → 加 do, does 或 did。

» 特別注意：當主詞為代名詞，則代名詞在前、動詞在後。

» 倒裝句型，最常見的是疑問句，在此不多談。其他還有：

1. there / here 的倒裝，例：Here it is.

2. 連接詞 and 後面句子的倒裝，例：and neither / nor ～（否定）/ and so ～（肯定）

3. 否定詞的倒裝，例：Never do I hear of such a thing.

4. only ＋副詞的倒裝，例：Only at my home do I feel comfortable.

5. If 假設句的倒裝，例：Were I you, I would say yes.（→ 請參考 Unit 22）

there / here 的倒裝

» 當主詞為「一般名詞」時，倒裝句型為：

Here / There ＋動詞＋主詞（名詞）.

» 當主詞為「代名詞」時，倒裝句型為：

Here / There ＋主詞（代名詞）＋動詞.

» 對於主詞為代名詞的句子，有許多無法一目了然，須特別了解其意義。

當主詞為「一般名詞」時

Here comes the bus.

公車來了。

There goes the last train.
末班火車走了。

Here I am.
我在這裡。

There they are.
他們在那裡。

連接詞 and 後面句子的倒裝

» too, either（前面可以有逗號，也可以沒有逗號）

　1. 肯定句：..., and ＋主詞＋助動詞 , too

　2. 否定句：..., and ＋主詞＋助動詞 , either

» so, neither, nor（倒裝句）

　1. 肯定句：..., and so ＋助動詞＋主詞

　2. 否定句：..., and neither ＋助動詞＋主詞 / ..., nor ＋助動詞＋主詞

» 注意，助動詞必須隨著人稱而變化。

肯定句

He is a teacher, and I am too.
＝He is a teacher, and so am I.
他是老師，我也是。

I like traveling, and my husband does too.
＝I like traveling, and so does my husband.
我喜歡旅行，我先生也是。

否定句

He can't watch TV, and you can't either.
＝He can't watch TV, and neither can you.
＝He can't watch TV, nor can you.
他不可以看電視，你也不行。

My mother has never left Taiwan, and I have never either.
＝My mother has never left Taiwan, and neither have I.
＝My mother has never left Taiwan, nor have I.
我媽媽從沒離開過台灣，我也沒有。

否定詞、only 置於句首的倒裝

» 否定詞：never, little, hardly / scarcely / barely, seldom / rarely, not only... but also
» 句型：
    1. 否定詞＋倒裝句
    2. only ＋副詞片語、子句＋倒裝句

否定詞＋倒裝句

Never have I heard of such a thing.
我從來沒聽過這種事。

Seldom does he doubt the truth of his mother's words.
他很少懷疑母親所言的真實性。

only ＋副詞片語、子句＋倒裝句

Only in country can you see the starry sky.
只有在鄉下才看得到滿天星斗。

Only at home is he comfortable.
只有在家裡，他才會自在。

題 目

1. A: What time does the bus come?

   B: _____ it comes now.

   a. Here

   b. There

   c. When

   d. Either a or b

2. What a great parade, Mommy! Look! _____ some elephants!

   a. There come

   b. Here come

   c. Here are coming

   d. There is

3. A: Pass the salt, please.

   B: Certainly. _____ it is.

   a. Here

   b. There

   c. Where

   d. None of the above

4. Lily is a good girl, and so _____ .

   a. you are

   b. you too

   c. are you

   d. Either a or c

5. You haven't got any money, _____ have I.

   a. and neither

   b. nor

   c. and either

   d. Either a or b

6. You play the flute, and _____.
   a. I do too
   b. I do, too
   c. so do I
   d. All of the above

7. My sister _____ like pears, and I _____ either.
   a. does ; do
   b. doesn't ; don't
   c. doesn't ; do
   d. does ; don't

8. Seldom _____ I go to a movie theater these days.
   a. do
   b. does
   c. don't
   d. Either a or c

9. Hardly _____ she believe her eyes.
   a. can
   b. could
   c. is
   d. Either a or b

10. _____ before had they seen such a large grasshopper.
   a. Never
   b. Usually
   c. Not
   d. Until

11. Rachael has done her homework, and _____ Heather.
    a. so had
    b. so does
    c. so has
    d. so did

12. My father doesn't care, and my mother _____.
    a. doesn't too
    b. neither does
    c. doesn't either
    d. too

13. You aren't an expert, _____.
    a. nor am I
    b. and neither am I
    c. and I'm not either
    d. All of the above

14. Oh, no! _____ the bus. Now, we'll be really late.
    a. Here comes
    b. There goes
    c. Here goes
    d. There comes

15. A: Can you see the whale just off that small island?
    B: Yes, _____ it _____.
    a. there ; is
    b. I see ; there
    c. there ; be
    d. Either a or b

16. Here comes _____.

    a. John

    b. he

    c. him

    d. All of the above

17. I don't like broccoli, _____ my mother _____.

    a. and so does ; too

    b. nor ; does

    c. but ; does

    d. Either a or b

18. Dad _____, nor was my mother.

    a. was angry

    b. wasn't angry

    c. didn't feel angry

    d. Either b or c

19. Fanny will _____ do her fair share of the work, so I _____ either.

    a. not ; won't

    b. always ; will

    c. never ; seldom do

    d. either ; will

20. Randall has _____ to New Zealand, _____ I haven't.

    a. gone ; and

    b. driven ; so

    c. been ; but

    d. neither been ; nor

解 析

1.
解答：**a**

英文
A: What time does the bus come?
B: <u>Here it comes now.</u>

中譯
A：公車什麼時候來？
B：現在來了。

解說

　這題考地方副詞倒裝用法，因此選項 c 錯誤，也由於 comes 這個動詞，因此選 a（Here）。

2.
解答：**b**

英文　What a great parade, Mommy! Look! <u>Here come</u> some elephants!

中譯　好棒的遊行喔，媽咪！你看！有一些大象過來了！

解說

　選項 d 的 There is 為單數，句子裡的 elephants 為複數，故不可選。選項 c 和 a 是錯誤的用法。答案為選項 b。

3.
解答：**a**

英文
A: Pass the salt, please.
B: Certainly. <u>Here it is.</u>

中譯
A：請把鹽遞給我。
B：沒問題。拿去。

解說

　這題考地方副詞倒裝 Here it is. 表「拿去」的用法，在拿東西給別人時使用。如果用 there，可以說 There you go.。

4.

英文　**Lily is a good girl, and so are you.**

中譯　莉莉是個好女孩，妳也是。

解說

　　and so ～的用法，必須將主詞和 be 動詞倒裝，故答案選 c。注意，and so are you ＝ and you are(,) too，因此 and so... 在後面又加上 too 就等於重複了，不可以選 b。

5.

英文　**You haven't got any money, and neither have I.**
　　　You haven't got any money, nor have I.

中譯　你沒有任何錢，我也沒有。

解說

　　前面句子使用否定（haven't got），連接的句子要用表示否定的「也」，用法有三：and neither ～、nor ～、and ～ either，所以選項 c 是錯誤用法，故答案為選項 d。

6.

英文　**You play the flute, and I do too.**
　　　You play the flute, and I do, too.
　　　You play the flute, and so do I.

中譯　你吹笛子，我也是。

解說

　　前面的主要句子為一般動詞（play），後面連接的句子要用表示肯定的「也」，用法有二：and so ～、and ～ too，第二個用法前面可加逗號、也可以不加，故答案為選項 d。

7.

英文　**My sister doesn't like pears, and I don't either.**

中譯　我妹妹不喜歡梨子，我也不喜歡。

解答：**b**

解說

　　前面主要句子為一般動詞（like），後面連接的句子中有 and... either，即表示否定的「也」，所以前、後句子都要有否定詞，答案為選項 b。

8.

英文　**Seldom do I go to a movie theater these days.**

中譯　我最近很少上電影院。

解答：**a**

解說

　　句首出現副詞 seldom，是否定詞倒裝句，主詞為第一人稱 I、一般動詞 go (to)，前面空格需要用肯定助動詞 do，答案為選項 a。

9.

英文　**Hardly can she believe her eyes.**
　　　Hardly could she believe her eyes.

中譯　她簡直不敢相信她的眼睛。

解答：**d**

解說

　　句首出現副詞 hardly，是否定詞倒裝句，主詞為第三人稱 she、動詞為 believe，前面空格需要用助動詞，現在式 can、過去式 could 皆正確，故答案為選項 d。

10.

解答：**a**

英文 <u>Never</u> before had they seen such a large grasshopper.

中譯 他們以前從來沒見過這麼大隻的蚱蜢。

解說

句子中 had they seen... 的字序為「助動詞＋主詞＋動詞」，判斷這是倒裝句，而且句首須用否定詞，因此答案選 a. Never。注意，在倒裝句中，Not 不可單獨存在，必須搭配其他字 Not only, Not until 等，選項 c 錯誤。

11.

解答：**c**

英文 Rachael has done her homework, and <u>so has</u> Heather.

中譯 瑞秋已經做完作業，海若也是。

解說

連接詞前的主要子句動詞 has done 為現在完成式，has 為助動詞，連接詞後的主詞為第三人稱單數，因此要表示「也」，必須選 c。

12.

解答：**c**

英文 My father doesn't care, and my mother <u>doesn't either</u>.

中譯 我父親不在乎，我母親也是。

解說

連接詞前 doesn't care 為否定，連接詞後要表示「也」，同樣也必須用否定，因此選 c. doesn't either。注意，neither does ～亦可表示否定的「也」，但是必須放在主詞前面。

英文　You aren't an expert, <u>nor am I</u>.
　　　You aren't an expert, <u>and neither am I</u>.
　　　You aren't an expert, <u>and I'm not either</u>.

中譯　你不是專家，我也不是。

解說

　　連接詞前的 aren't 為否定，連接詞後要表示「也」，同樣也必須用否定，選項 a、b、c 三種用法皆正確，故答案為選項 d。

英文　Oh, no! <u>There goes the bus</u>. Now, we'll be really late.

中譯　喔，不！公車走了。現在，我們真的會遲到了。

解說

　　選項 c. Here goes 和 d. There comes 都是錯誤的搭配用法。而從句子的語意判斷，選項 b. There goes 是最正確的答案。

　　　A: Can you see the whale just off that small island?
英文　B: Yes, <u>there it is</u>.
　　　B: Yes, <u>I see it there</u>.

中譯　A：你可以看到那座小島那裡的那隻鯨魚嗎？
　　　B：可以啊，就在那裡。

解說

　　從第一個句子的「off」that small island 可以知道 whale「鯨魚」是在遠處，而要表達看到遠處的東西，可以用倒裝句 "There it is." 或 "I see it there."，故答案為選項 d。

16.

解答：**a**

英文 **Here comes John.**

中譯 John 過來了。

解說

　　此句為倒裝句，主詞在動詞（comes）後面時，不可用代名詞，因此答案為選項 a。

17.

解答：**c**

英文 **I don't like broccoli, but my mother does.**

中譯 我不喜歡花椰菜，可是我媽媽喜歡。

解說

　　第一個句子為否定句，連接詞後不可使用表示肯定的「也」，而且 and so ～ 與 ～ too 不可同時使用，選項 a 錯誤。如果要表示否定「也不」的倒裝句，nor does 必須一起放在主詞之前，所以選項 b 錯誤。選項 c 的連接詞 but 即有表示「但是」，前面句子為否定，則後面句子用肯定，因此正確。

18.

解答：**b**

英文 **Dad wasn't angry, nor was my mother.**

中譯 我爸爸沒生氣，我媽媽也是。

解說

　　連接詞 nor 表示否定，動詞為 be 動詞 was，因此連接詞前面的句子也用「be 動詞＋否定」，答案為選項 b。

19. 解答：**a**

英文　Fanny will <u>not</u> do her fair share of the work, so I <u>won't</u> either.

中譯　芬妮不做她份內該做的工作，所以我也不做。

解說

　　句尾的 either 表示前面句子的助動詞 will 後面需要否定詞 not，選項 b 和 d 可先行刪除。選項 c 第二個空格填 seldom do，表示一般狀況，與前面句子的 will 表示未來不一致，所以錯誤，故答案選 a。

20. 解答：**c**

英文　Randall has <u>been</u> to New Zealand, <u>but</u> I haven't.

中譯　藍道去過紐西蘭，但我沒去過。

解說

　　句首 Randall has～為肯定、句尾 I haven't 為否定，連接詞須使用 but 或 nor，所以刪除選項 a 和 b。選項 d（neither been）用法錯誤，neither 不可接動詞或 be 動詞，故答案為選項 c。

22 假設語氣

假設語氣的用法和句型

» 假設事情的結局與事實不符，或與事實相反，在英文裡就稱為假設句。

» 口訣：時態往前推一格。

» 人們許願時，動詞 wish 後面常接名詞子句，與事實相反的情形有二：

　　1. 對現況的願望 → 動詞用「過去式」，be 動詞一律用 were

　　　 ... wish（＋ that）＋ S ＋ were / V（過去式）

　　2. 對過去的願望 → 動詞用「過去完成式」

　　　 ... wish（＋ that）＋ S ＋ V（過去完成式）

» 注意，對現況的願望如果是否定，就要加過去式助動詞，再加上否定詞。如果是對過去的願望，則否定詞直接加在原來的助動詞後面。

» 連接詞 if 後面的子句，與事實相反時，子句的用法與 wish 相同，另外要注意的是主要句子的動詞也會有變化。

　　1. 連接對「未來」事情可能發生的假設子句時，須用「現在式」：

　　　 If ＋ S ＋ V（現在式），S ＋ will / can / may ＋ V（原形）

　　2.「與現在事實相反」的子句：

　　　 If ＋ S ＋ were / V（過去式），S ＋ should / would / could / might ＋ V（原形）

　　3.「與過去事實相反」的子句：

　　　 If ＋ S ＋ V（過去完成式），S ＋ should / would / could / might ＋ have ＋ V-pp（現在完成式）

» if 子句在句首時，與主要子句之間須以逗號隔開；如果在句尾，則不需要。

▌wish 對現況的願望

The poor man said, "I wish (that) I had a lot of money."

（The truth is: He doesn't have a lot of money.）

這個窮人說：「我希望有很多的錢。」

（事實：他沒有很多錢）

The student said, "I wish (that) I didn't have to study all day."

（The truth is: He has to study all day.）

這個學生說：「我希望我可以不用整天讀書。」

（事實：他必須整天讀書。）

wish 對過去的願望

Monica wishes she had been with her parents when the accident happened.

（The truth is: She was not with her parents.）

莫妮卡真希望意外發生時，她和父母在一起。

（事實：她當時沒跟父母在一起。）

How I wish they hadn't taken the deadly flight!

（The truth is: They took the deadly flight!）

我多希望她們沒搭上那班死亡飛機！

（事實：他們搭上了那班死亡飛機。）

if 接「未來」假設子句

If it rains tomorrow, we'll cancel the field trip.

如果明天下雨，我們就取消校外教學。

We'll catch up the train if the traffic is not busy.

如果交通順暢，我們就可以趕上火車。

if 接「與現在事實相反」的子句

If I were you, I would take this job.

（The truth is: I am not you.）

如果我是你，我就會接受這份工作。

（事實：我不是你。）

If I had enough money, I would buy the car.

（The truth is: I do not have enough money.）

如果我有足夠的錢，我會買那部車。

（事實：我沒有足夠的錢。）

if 接「與過去事實相反」的子句

If we had had more time, we could have visited more places.

（The truth is: We did not have more time, and we did not visit more places.）

如果我們有更多時間，我們就已經參觀更多地方了。

（事實：我們當時沒有更多時間，所以沒有參觀更多地方。）

If he had not broken his leg, he would have come along.

（The truth is: He broke his leg, and he did not come along.）

如果他的腿沒斷，他就已經來了。

（事實：他的腿斷了，所以沒有一起來。）

題 目

1. A: We will go to the park if it is fine.

   B: And if it _____ will we do?

   a. isn't, what

   b. rains what

   c. doesn't rain, how

   d. None of the above

2. If you _____ right now, you could catch the last train.

   a. leave

   b. left

   c. had left

   d. Either a or b

3. You could have become a queen if you _____ married the elder prince.

   a. would

   b. should

   c. have

   d. had

4. _____ I _____ known you would be here, I would have brought you your book.

   a. Whether or not ; had

   b. If ; had

   c. Had ; not

   d. All of the above

5. If you had worn the pink tie, you _____ looked like an idiot!

   a. will have

   b. would have

   c. should have

   d. may have

6. _____ Sherry _____ enough money, she would have bought the dress.
   a. Had ; had
   b. Had ; not
   c. Has ; got
   d. If ; had

7. If I _____ you, I wouldn't go in there.
   a. were
   b. was
   c. am
   d. All of the above

8. I wish I _____ in New York City right now.
   a. were
   b. was
   c. could be
   d. Either a or c

9. Do you ever wish _____ be someone else?
   a. you should
   b. them could
   c. you could
   d. you can

10. Alicia _____ she _____ gone on the trip with her friends.
    a. wishes ; could have
    b. wished ; could have
    c. wished ; should have
    d. Either a or b

11. I wish I _____ there when you graduated.

    a. have been

    b. had been

    c. were

    d. All of the above

12. I think we _____ stayed together. It would have been safer.

    a. should

    b. should have

    c. had

    d. had better

13. I wish you _____ have _____ on time, but you are always late, aren't you?

    a. better ; come

    b. can ; arrived

    c. could ; been

    d. Either b or c

14. If you _____ ask me now, I _____ say no.

    a. will ; would

    b. were ; should

    c. were to ; would

    d. are ; am

15. If you _____ the cheaper compact car, you _____ a lot of money.

    a. buy ; could have saved

    b. had bought ; would have saved

    c. buy ; will save

    d. Either b or c

16. _____ I _____ the other car, I wouldn't have run into it.
    a. Had ; seen
    b. If ; had seen
    c. Did ; see
    d. Either a or b

17. If she _____ a little older, she would understand things better.
    a. were
    b. was
    c. had been
    d. has been

18. I wish that I had _____ more money so that I could have bought the better model.
    a. have
    b. been
    c. had
    d. to have

19. We will go hiking _____ the weather is good tomorrow.
    a. if
    b. when
    c. for
    d. whether

20. _____ I you, I _____ it.
    a. Were ; will buy
    b. Were ; would buy
    c. Was ; would have bought
    d. None of the above

解析

英文　A: We will go to the park if it is fine.
　　　B: And if it **isn't, what** will we do?

中譯　A：如果天氣好，我們就去公園。
　　　B：那如果不好，我們要做什麼呢？

解說

　　第一句的 it is fine 表示「天氣好」，空格若填選項 c，it doesn't rain 也表示「天氣好」，語意矛盾，不可選。選項 a 和 b 都表示「天氣不好」，但是因為 if 子句在句首必須用逗號與主要句子隔開，所以選項 b 錯誤，故答案為選項 a。

英文　If you **left** right now, you could catch the last train.

中譯　如果你現在離開，你還可以趕上末班火車。

解說

　　主要子句用助動詞 could 來和 if 子句搭配，表示與現在事實相反，所以 if 子句動詞用過去式，答案為 b。這句話的言外之意表示：現在並沒有要離開。如果選 a 的現在式，則主要句子的助動詞須改為 will。

英文　You could have become a queen if you **had** married the elder prince.

中譯　如果妳當初嫁給了較年長的那個王子，妳現在可能已經是皇后了。

解說

　　主要子句用「could have ＋過去分詞」來搭配 if 子句，表示與過去事實相反，所以 if 子句必須用過去完成式，因此選項 d（had）才是正確的助動詞。

4.

英文 If I had known you would be here, I would have brought you your book.

中譯 如果我知道你會在這裡，我就把你的書帶過來了。

解說

　　主要子句的「would have ＋過去分詞」搭配 if 子句，表示與過去事實相反，if 子句必須用過去完成式，助動詞使用 had，選項 b 是正確的。若選 a，主要子句須改為過去式。若選 c 的倒裝句用法，須去掉 if 這個字。

5.

英文 If you had worn the pink tie, you would have looked like an idiot!

中譯 如果你當時戴了粉紅色領帶，你就會看起來像個傻瓜了！

解說

　　If 子句中 had worn 為過去完成式，主要子句必須選 b →「would have ＋過去分詞」，表示與過去事實相反。這句話的言外之意是沒有戴粉紅色領帶，也就沒有看起來像傻瓜的問題了。

6.

英文 Had Sherry had enough money, she would have bought the dress.

中譯 如果 Sherry 有足夠的錢，當時她就會買下洋裝了。

解說

　　主要子句的「would have ＋過去分詞」搭配 if 子句，表示與過去事實相反，if 子句必須用過去完成式，選項 d 的 had 表示一般動詞的過去式，所以錯誤。選項 a 是省略 if 的倒裝句用法：「Had ＋主詞＋過去分詞」。

7.

英文　**If I were you, I wouldn't go in there.**

中譯　如果我是你，我就不會進去那裡。

解說

　　主要子句用「would＋動詞現在式」來搭配 if 子句，代表與現在事實相反，而 be 動詞無論人稱，都必須用 were，所以選項 a 正確。

8.

英文　**I wish I were in New York City right now.**

中譯　我希望我現在在紐約。

解說

　　wish 後面接子句，句尾有 right now，代表與現在事實相反的希望，所以 be 動詞一律用 were，選項 a 為正確答案。

9.

英文　**Do you ever wish you could be someone else?**

中譯　你曾經希望你可以成為其他人嗎？

解說

　　wish 後面接子句，表達與現在事實相反的希望，助動詞及動詞一律要用「過去式」，所以選項 d 不對。再從語意上判斷，選項 c 為最適當的答案。

10.

英文　Alicia wishes she could have gone on the trip with her friends.
　　　Alicia wished she could have gone on the trip with her friends.

中譯　艾莉西亞希望她跟朋友一起去旅行了。

解說

　　wish 接的子句要表達與現在事實相反，應該用過去式；要表達與過去事實相反，應該用過去完成式。選項 b 用 should 不合語法，故正確答案為選項 d。

11.

英文　I wish I had been there when you graduated.

中譯　我希望你畢業時我有出席。

解說

　　從 when you graduated 中知道是過去的事情，wish 後面的假設句必須用過去完成式，所以選 b. had been。

12.

英文　I think we should have stayed together. It would have been safer.

中譯　我想我們那時應該待在一起的。那就會安全一點了。

解說

　　從第二句子 would have been 知道是希望發生但沒有發生的事情，所以選 b. should have (stayed)。選項 a 和 d 後面都必須皆動詞原形。選項 c 的 had (stayed) 表示過去確實發生，語意不符。

13.

英文 I wish you <u>could</u> have <u>been</u> on time, but you are always late, aren't you?

中譯 我希望你可以準時，不過你老是遲到，對吧？

解說

從 you are always late 知道要對方準時是不可能的，因此 wish 後面的子句必須用過去式，表示與現在事實相反的願望，必須選 c。

14.

英文 If you <u>were</u> to ask me now, I <u>would</u> say no.

中譯 如果你現在問我，我會說不。

解說

這題考 If 子句表達與現在事實不符的用法：「If ＋主詞＋過去式，主詞＋would／should／... ＋動詞原形」，所以刪除選項 a 和 d。至於選項 b 的錯誤，在於出現兩個動詞 were 和 ask，如果 ask 改成 asking 就可以，故答案為選項 c。

15.

英文 If you <u>had bought</u> the cheaper compact car, you <u>would have saved</u> a lot of money.

If you <u>buy</u> the cheaper compact car, you <u>will save</u> a lot of money.

中譯 如果你當初買便宜的小車，你就會省下許多錢。

如果你買較便宜的小車，你將會省許多錢。

解說

與現在事實不符，if 子句要用過去式，選項 a 錯誤。與過去事實不符，if 子句用過去完成式，選項 b 正確。選項 c 則是對未來的假設，if 子句用現在式，主要子句用未來式，所以正確。

英文　Had I seen the other car, I wouldn't have run into it.
　　　If I had seen the other car, I wouldn't have run into it.

中譯　如果我有看到另一輛車，我就不會撞到它了。

解說

　　從主要子句 wouldn't have run 知道是陳述與過去事實相反的事情，假設句必須用過去完成式：If I had seen ～＝ Had I seen ～，所以選項 a 和 b 皆正確，答案為選項 d。

英文　If she were a little older, she would understand things better.

中譯　如果她年紀稍長一點，她就會更懂事了。

解說

　　從主要子句 would understand 知道是陳述與現在事實相反的事情，假設句須用過去式，be 動詞恆用 were，不可用 was，因此答案為選項 a。

英文　Wish that I had had more money so that I could have bought the better model.

中譯　我希望我有更多錢，那麼我就可以買較好的車款。

解說

　　從子句中 could have bought 知道是已經買了，陳述的是過去的事情，所以 wish 接的子句必須用過去完成式，刪除選項 a 和 d。從語意上判斷，正確答案為 c. had（動詞 have「有」的過去分詞）。

英文　We will go hiking <u>if</u> the weather is good tomorrow.

中譯　如果明天天氣好，我們就去健走。

解說

　　句子出現兩個動詞 will go (hiking) 和 is，所以需要連接詞。四個選項中只有 if 子句的用法是以現在式（is）表示對於未來事情的假設，因此答案為選項 a。

英文　<u>Were I you, I would buy it.</u>

中譯　如果我是你，我就買了。

解說

　　這題是省略 if、將 be 動詞置於句首的倒裝用法。表示與現在事實相反，be 動詞恆用 were，所以選項 c 錯誤；主要句子用法為「would / could / ... ＋動詞原形」，所以答案為選項 b。

23 直接問句、間接問句與名詞片語

間接問句的用法和句型

» 一個問句併入另一個主要句子中，稱為間接問句。間接問句也就是附屬子句，屬於名詞子句。

» 問句又分為兩類：有疑問詞的疑問句，和 yes / no 問句：

1. 疑問詞問句：疑問詞＋ be 動詞＋主詞（＋～）？
   間接問句 → 主要子句＋疑問詞＋主詞＋ be 動詞（＋～）．

2. 疑問詞問句：疑問詞＋ do / does / did ＋主詞＋ V（原形）～？
   間接問句 → 主要子句＋疑問詞＋主詞＋ V（適當形式）～．

3. 疑問詞問句：疑問詞＋ can / will / should ＋主詞＋ V（原形）～？
   間接問句 → 主要子句＋疑問詞＋主詞＋ can / will / should ＋ V（原形）～．

4. 疑問詞問句：疑問詞（Who 當主詞）＋ V（各種形式）～？
   間接問句 → 主要子句＋疑問詞（who）＋ V（各種形式）～．

5. yes / no 問句：在主要子句和子句之間，加上 if / whether，其他子句的主詞和動詞位置規則相同。

» 間接問句在句尾時，句尾的標點符號須視主要子句而定，不一定是問號。

» 間接問句如果含有一般動詞，子句可以改成「疑問詞＋ to 片語」，例如：how to ～。

主要子句＋疑問詞＋主詞＋ be 動詞（＋～）．

I know where she is.

（＝I know... ＋Where is she?）

我知道她在哪裡。

I wonder who that girl in red is.

（＝I wonder... ＋Who is that girl in red?）

我不知道那個穿紅衣服的女孩是誰。

Did she tell you where she was going?

（＝Did she tell you...＋Where was she going?）

她有告訴你她要去哪裡嗎？

主要子句＋疑問詞＋主詞＋ V（適當形式）～.

Can you show us how you do it?

＝Can you show us how to do it?

（＝Can you show us...＋How do you do it?）

你可以讓我們看你是怎麼做的嗎？

I wonder how many hours the man works a day.

（＝I wonder...＋How many hours does the man work a day?）

不知道那個男人一天工作幾個小時。

Who noticed when he left?

（＝Who noticed...＋When did he leave?）

誰有注意到他什麼時候離開的？

主要子句＋疑問詞＋主詞＋ can / will / should ＋ V（原形）～.

Who knows how fast he can run?

（＝Who knows...＋How fast can he run?）

誰知道他能跑多快？

Everyone has to know clearly what he should do.

（＝Everyone has to know clearly...＋What should he do?）

每個人都必須清楚知道自己應該做什麼。

主要子句＋疑問詞（who 當主詞）＋ V（適當形式）～.

The policeman is asking who saw the rubber.

（＝The policeman is asking...＋Who saw the rubber?）

警察在問有誰看到搶匪？

Ask the workers who wants to attend the seminar.

（＝Ask the workers...＋Who wants to attend the seminar?）

問問員工們誰想要參加研習會。

主要子句＋ if / whether ～．

The teacher asks if Joe is in the 3rd grade.

＝The teacher asks whether Joe is in the 3rd grade.

（＝The teacher asks...＋Is Joe in the 3rd grade?）

老師問喬是不是三年級。

The doctor asked if he had a fever.

The doctor asked whether he had a fever.

（＝The doctor asked...＋Did he have a fever?）

醫生問他是否有發燒。

How can we know if the hen will lay eggs?

＝How can we know whether the hen will lay eggs?

（How can we know...＋Will the hen lay eggs?）

我們怎麼知道這隻母雞會不會生蛋？

題 目

1. Do you know _____ time _____?
   a. what the ; is
   b. what ; it is
   c. what ; is it
   d. Either a or b

2. So, tell me what _____ for a living.
   a. you do
   b. do you
   c. do you do
   d. you doing

3. I have no idea _____ every night.
   a. where do you go
   b. where you go
   c. where are you going
   d. None of the above

4. No one understands why he _____ his job.
   a. leaves
   b. left
   c. did leave
   d. had left

5. I don't know what _____.
   a. should I do
   b. should do I
   c. I should do
   d. should to do

6. Do you know when _____ off work?

   a. he'll get

   b. he gets

   c. when will he

   d. Either a or b

7. A: What _____ about this problem?

   B: I don't know what _____.

   a. can we do ; can we do

   b. we can do ; we can do

   c. can we do ; we can do

   d. None of the above

8. A: What _____ him?

   B: I don't know what _____.

   a. happened to ; to him happened

   b. happened to ; happened to him

   c. to him happened ; happened to him

   d. has happened to ; did happen to him

9. A: Do you want me to show you how to write it?

   B: Yes, please show me _____ write it.

   a. how to

   b. how I should

   c. how

   d. Either a or b

10. I'd like to know _____ read Chinese. Could you ask him?

    a. if Alex can

    b. can Alex

    c. Alex can

    d. if can Alex

11. I need to know _____ .
    a. where is Joe

    b. where Joe is

    c. Joe is where

    d. is Joe where

12. Would you like to know _____ ?
    a. how much is it

    b. it is how much

    c. how much it is

    d. is it how much

13. The tourists asked the Boy Scout how _____ the ferry terminal.
    a. they got to

    b. should get to

    c. to get to

    d. get to

14. I want to know _____ .
    a. when to start

    b. when I should start

    c. when should I start

    d. Either a or b

15. I can easily see _____ here last night.
    a. what happened

    b. what happens

    c. had happened

    d. None of the above

16. I want to know why _____ at home.

    a. isn't he

    b. he isn't

    c. is he

    d. Either a or b

17. What do you think _____ with the TV?

    a. is wrong

    b. could be wrong

    c. might be wrong

    d. All of the above

18. Can you guess what _____.

    a. does he want

    b. he wants

    c. is he wanting

    d. Either a or b

19. Guess _____ I am.

    a. where

    b. who

    c. how come

    d. Either a or b

20. _____ you remember what you _____ last week?

    a. Do ; did

    b. Can ; had done

    c. Would ; done

    d. Did ; have done

解 析

1.　　　　　　　　　　　　　　　　　　　　　　　　　解答：**d**

英文 **Do you know <u>what the time is</u>?**
Do you know <u>what time it is</u>?

中譯 你知道現在幾點嗎？

解說

　　動詞後面接疑問詞引導的名詞子句（即間接問句），原來的直接問句：What is the time? / What time is it?，主詞分別是 the time / it。改為間接問句句型：「疑問詞＋主詞＋ be 動詞（＋～）」，即 what the time is / what time it is，選項 a 或 b 皆正確。故答案為選項 d。

2.　　　　　　　　　　　　　　　　　　　　　　　　　解答：**a**

英文 **So, tell me what <u>you do</u> for a living.**

中譯 所以，告訴我你是如何維持生計的。

解說

　　本題考疑問詞直接問句：「疑問詞＋ do / does / did ＋主詞＋ V（原形）～？」如何改成間接問句→「主要子句＋疑問詞＋主詞＋ V（適當形式）～ .」。原問句：What do you do for a living?，改寫第一步是刪除助動詞 do，第二步要判斷動詞 do 的形式應為現在式、原形→ what you do for a living，答案為選項 a。

3.　　　　　　　　　　　　　　　　　　　　　　　　　解答：**b**

英文 **I have no idea <u>where you go</u> every night.**

中譯 我不知道你每天晚上到哪裡去了。

解說

　　本題與上一題同樣考間接問句「主要子句＋疑問詞＋主詞＋ V（適當形式）～ .」的用法。從句尾的時間副詞 every night 知道是一般情況，不可用現在進行式，而是現在式，所以原問句為：Where do you go every night?，改寫第一步是刪除助動詞 do，第二步為判斷動詞 go 的形式→ where you go every night，答案為選項 b。

4.

英文　**No one understands why he left his job.**

中譯　沒有人了解為什麼他會離開他的工作。

解說

　　本題同樣考間接問句「主要子句＋疑問詞＋主詞＋ V（適當形式）～ .」的用法。從主要動詞 understands（現在式）和語意上得知，動詞必須用過去式 left 的形式，答案為選項 b。

5.

英文　**I don't know what I should do.**

中譯　我不知道我該怎麼做。

解說

　　本題與上一題同樣考間接問句「主要子句＋疑問詞＋主詞＋ should ＋ V（原形）～ .」的用法。答案選 c。注意，間接問句 what I should do 可以改為不定詞：what to do，選項 d 用法錯誤。

6.

英文　**Do you know when he'll get off work?**
　　　Do you know when he gets off work?

中譯　你知道他什麼時候下班嗎？

解說

　　從語意上了解，疑問句可以用現在式表一般情況、用未來式表未來動作，選項 a 和 b 的間接問句問法皆正確、也符合語意，答案為選項 d。

英文　A: What <u>can we do</u> about this problem?
　　　B: I don't know what <u>we can do</u>.

中譯　A：關於這個問題我們可以怎麼做呢？
　　　B：我不知道我們可以怎麼做。

解說

　　第一個句子為直接問句，第二句為間接問句，所以助動詞 can 分別在主詞 we 的前面和後面，所以答案為選項 c。

英文　A: What <u>happened to him</u>?
　　　B: I don't know what <u>happened to him</u>.

中譯　A：他發生什麼事了？
　　　B：我不知道他發生什麼事。

解說

　　第一個句子為直接問句，選項 c 用法錯誤，刪除。第二個句子為間接問句，原問句為：What (has) happened to him?，主詞為 What，改為間接問句字序不變，選項 b 正確。

英文　A: Do you want me to show you how to write it?
　　　B: Yes, please show me <u>how to write it</u>.
　　　B: Yes, please show me <u>how I should</u> write it.

中譯　A：你要我示範給你看怎麼寫嗎？
　　　B：好，請示範給我看怎麼寫。

解說

　　第一個句子中 how to write it 為不定詞形式，可改寫為 how you should write it，同樣的，第二句，主詞改為 I，也可以用不定詞和間接問句用法，所以選項 a 與 b 皆正確，答案為選項 d。

10.

英文　**I'd like to know if Alex can read Chinese. Could you ask him?**

中譯　我想知道艾力克斯可不可以讀中文，你可以問他嗎？

解說

　　第一個句子出現了兩個動詞 know 和 read，而且 know 為及物動詞，需要受詞，所以空格處需要的字必須包括可以形成名詞子句的 if（＝ whether），刪除選項 b 和 c。名詞子句為間接問句，主詞在助動詞之前，所以答案為選項 a。

11.

英文　**I need to know where Joe is.**

中譯　我必須知道喬在哪裡。

解說

　　這題考包含疑問詞的間接問句。原問句應為 Where is Joe? 所以間接問句即為 Where Joe is，故選項 b 正確。

12.

英文　**Would you like to know how much it is?**

中譯　你想知道這個多少錢嗎？

解說

　　這題考包含疑問詞 how much、be 動詞、代名詞作主詞的間接問句用法，選項 c 為正確字序。

13.

解答：**c**

英文 The tourists asked the Boy Scout how <u>to get to</u> the ferry terminal.

中譯 旅客們問男童子軍要怎麼到渡輪站。

解說

疑問詞 how 可引導間接問句，用法為：how they should get to ～，選項 b 缺少主詞、選項 a 不合語意，所以錯誤。不定詞用法為 how to get to ～，選項 c 正確。

14.

解答：**d**

英文 I want to know <u>when to start</u>.
I want to know <u>when I should start</u>.

中譯 我想知道（我應該）什麼時候開始。

解說

這題考主要句子與 wh- 間接問句的主詞相同時，間接問句可以省略主詞，改成「疑問詞＋ to 片語」，選項 a 和 b 為正確用法，答案為選項 d。

15.

解答：**a**

英文 I can easily see <u>what happened</u> here last night.

中譯 我很容易就明白昨晚這裡發生了什麼事。

解說

本句已經有主要動詞 see，不可選另一個動詞 c. had happened。這裡需要間接問句作 see 的受詞，從時間副詞 last night 判斷子句需要過去式的動詞，答案為選項 a。

16.

解答：**b**

英文 **I want to know why <u>he isn't</u> at home.**

中譯　我想知道他為什麼不在家。

解說

　　這題考有代名詞為主詞、be 動詞的 wh- 間接問句用法，選項 b 為正確字序。

17.

解答：**d**

What do you think <u>is wrong</u> with the TV?

英文 **What do you think <u>would be wrong</u> with the TV?**

What do you think <u>might be wrong</u> with the TV?

中譯　你認為電視（可能）出了什麼問題？

解說

　　原來的主要動詞 think 後面所接的名詞子句中，疑問詞 what 為主詞，現在挪到了句首，因此間接問句還缺少動詞，選項 a、b、c 用法皆對，且符合語意，故答案為選項 d。

18.

解答：**b**

英文 **Can you guess what <u>he wants</u>.**

中譯　你猜得到他想要什麼嗎？

解說

　　間接問句不可有助動詞 does，選項 a 錯誤。間接問句有 be 動詞時，要放在主詞之後，選項 c 錯誤。答案為選項 b。

19.

英文　Guess <u>where</u> I am.
　　　　Guess <u>who</u> I am.

中譯　猜猜我在哪裡。
　　　　猜猜我是誰。

解說

選項 a 和 b 形成的間接問句皆符合語意，答案為選項 d。選項 c 不可選，否則子句會出現兩個動詞 come 和 am，造成文法錯誤。

20.

英文　<u>Do</u> you remember what you <u>did</u> last week?

中譯　你記得你上星期做了什麼事嗎？

解說

從句尾的時間副詞判斷，第二個空格須用過去式，只有選項 a 正確。